NINE MINUTES

A Novel By
Beth Flynn

This book is a work of fiction. Names, characters, places and incidents are either products of the author's imagination or used fictitiously. Any similarity to actual people and/or events is purely coincidental.

All trademarked names are honored by capitalization and no infringement is intended.

For Jim, my soul mate and forever best friend. He always believed, even when I didn't.

Prologue
Summer 2000

I'd never attended an execution before. Well, at least not a legal one. My husband sat to my left. A reporter for *Rolling Stone* was on my right.

The reporter, Leslie Cowan, fidgeted nervously, and I looked over at her. I'm pretty sure this was her first execution of any kind. *Rolling Stone* had an upcoming issue dedicated to celebrity bikers. They thought it would be interesting to include a real biker story in that issue. The story of a girl who'd been abducted by a motorcycle gang in 1975.

That girl was me.

The remnants of Leslie's accident three weeks before were still visible. The stitches had been removed from her forehead, but there was a thin red line where the cut had been. Her eyes weren't quite as raccoonish as before, but it was apparent she'd recently suffered two severe black eyes. The swelling of her nose had almost gone down completely, and she'd been to a dental surgeon to replace her broken teeth.

When we'd first started the interview, she'd told me she wanted me to be completely honest about my experience with the man who was about to be executed. I'd spent the last three months with her and held almost nothing back about my relationship with him. Today was supposed to be the culmination of the interview, a chance for her to truly understand the real side of that experience. To see the unpleasant alongside the rest.

Of course, a man's death should be more than just unpleasant.

I knew as well as he did that he deserved what he was getting. It was strange. I thought knowing it and believing it would make it a little easier, but it didn't. I thought I would get through his execution unscathed emotionally. But I was only fooling myself.

Just because I hadn't been with him for almost fifteen years did not mean I didn't have feelings for him. He was my first love. He was a true love. In fact, he was the biological father of my firstborn, though she would never meet him. He wanted it that way. And deep down, so did I.

The curtain opened. I was no longer aware of anyone else in the small viewing room around me. I stared through a large glass window at an empty gurney. I'd read up on what to expect at an execution. He was supposed to be strapped to the gurney when the curtain opened, wasn't he? I'm sure that was procedure. But he was never one for following rules. I wondered how he'd managed to convince law enforcement to forego this important detail.

With a jolt, I realized someone had entered the sterile-looking room. It was him, along with two officers, the warden and a physician. No priest or pastor. He didn't want one.

Him.

His name was Jason William Talbot. Such a normal-sounding name. It's funny. I'd known him almost twenty-five years and it wasn't until his arrest fifteen years earlier that I learned his real middle and last name. That is, if it was his real name. I'm still not certain.

He was always Grizz to me. Short for Grizzly, a nickname he'd earned due to his massive size and brutal behavior. Grizz was a huge and imposing man. Ruggedly handsome. Tattoos from neck to toe covered his enormous body. His large hands could crush a windpipe without effort. I knew this from experience. I'd personally witnessed what those hands could do. I couldn't keep my eyes off them now.

He had no family. Just me. And I was not his family.

I immediately sensed when he spotted me. I looked up from his hands into his mesmerizing bright green eyes. I tried to assess whether those eyes held any emotion, but I couldn't tell. It'd been too long. He'd always been good at hiding his feelings. I used to be able to read him. Not today, though.

As he looked at me, he lifted his handcuffed hands and used the fingers of his right hand to encircle the ring finger on his left hand. He then looked down to my hands, but couldn't see them. They were in my lap and blocked by the person seated in front of me.

Would I give him that last consolation? I didn't want to

hurt my husband. But considering I was the reason for Grizz's impending death, I felt the stirrings of an old, old obligation to comfort him in those last moments. At the same time, I felt an uncomfortable thrill in having some control over him. In having the ability to be in charge of something, to be the decision-maker, the empowered one. For once.

Perhaps I was the empowered one all along.

I felt my husband's hand on my left thigh, just above my knee. He gently squeezed. A memory almost twenty-five years old rushed over me of another hand squeezing my leg. A harder, crueler hand. I turned to look at my husband, and even though he was looking straight ahead, he was aware of my glance. He gave an almost imperceptible nod. He'd decided for me. I was okay with that.

I removed my wide wedding band and lifted my left hand so Grizz could see it. He smiled ever so slightly. Then he looked at my husband, nodded once and said, "Let's get this shit over with."

The warden asked if he had any last words. Grizz replied, "I just said 'em."

Leslie had caught the exchange between us and mouthed, "What?"

I ignored her. That was one part of my story that wouldn't make it into her article. Even though I'd vowed to be completely forthcoming, some things, no matter how insignificant, had to remain mine. This was one of them.

Grizz wasn't an easy prisoner, so the guards assigned to him were super-sized, just like him. Much to their surprise, this day he put up no resistance. He lay down and stared at the ceiling as his handcuffs were removed and he was strapped tightly to the gurney. He didn't flinch when the doctor inserted the IV needles, one in each arm. His shirt was unbuttoned and heart monitors were attached to his chest. I wondered why he didn't fight, wondered whether he'd been given a sedative of some sort. But I wouldn't ask.

He didn't glance around. He just closed his eyes and passed away. It took nine minutes. It sounds quick. Less than ten minutes. But for me, it was an eternity.

An elderly woman in the front row started to sob quietly. She said to the woman sitting next to her, "He didn't even say he was sorry."

The woman whispered back to her, "That's because he wasn't."

The doctor officially pronounced Grizz dead at 12:19 p.m. One of the guards walked over to the big window and closed the curtain. Done.

There were about ten of us in the small viewing room, and as soon as the curtain closed, almost everyone stood up and filed out without a word. I could still hear the elderly woman crying as her companion placed her arms around her shoulders and guided her toward the door.

Leslie looked at me and asked just a little too loudly, "You okay, Ginny?"

"I'm fine." I couldn't look at her. "Just no more interviews for the rest of the day."

"Yeah, sure, that's understandable. I have just a few more questions for you before I can wrap this story up. Let's meet tomorrow and talk."

My husband took my hand, stood with me and told Leslie, "It'll have to wait until we get home. You can reach us by phone to finish the interview."

My knees felt wobbly. I sat back down.

Leslie started to object, then noticed the expression on

my husband's face and stopped herself from saying more. She managed a smile and said, "Okay then, until Sunday. Have a safe trip home."

She left the room.

My husband and I were the only ones remaining. I stood to leave and couldn't move. I fell into his arms, sobbing. He gently lowered me to the floor and sat down with me, holding me against him. I lay like that in his arms, crying, for a long time. A very long time.

Chapter One

It was May 15, 1975. A typical Thursday. A day just like any other day, nothing extraordinary or even remotely exciting about it.

But it would be the day that changed my life forever.

I'd gotten up a little earlier than usual that morning and done some chores before school. I didn't have to do chores, but I was used to doing for myself, and there were certain things I wanted done. I had a quick breakfast of toast and a glass of orange juice, then loaded up my little backpack. It wasn't really a backpack, more like a baggy cloth purse with strings that I could arrange around my shoulders and wear on my back for easy carrying. It looked small but could hold a lot.

That morning it would hold my wallet with my driver's permit and four dollars. I wasn't old enough to have an official license yet; I'd just turned fifteen three months before. The bag also held my reading glasses, a hairbrush, apple-flavored lip gloss, two tampons, a birth control packet and two schoolbooks: advanced geometry and chemistry. I'd finished my homework the night before, folded the notebook papers in half and stuck them between the pages of my books. Everything else I needed for my classes I kept in my locker at school.

I wore hip-hugger, bell-bottom blue jeans with a macramé belt, a flowery peasant top and sandals. I had on the same jewelry I wore every day: silver hoop earrings and a brown felt choker that had a dangling peace sign. Even though this was South Florida in May, the mornings could still get a little cool, so I wore a red and white poncho Delia had knitted.

That morning my stepfather, Vince, had driven me to the bus stop. I could've walked, but it was far, so I grabbed rides from Vince whenever I could. He would've taken me all the way to school, but he had to drive in the other direction to do that, and I had no problem riding the bus.

I might have asked Matthew for a ride, but something was off with him. Matthew was a senior I was tutoring, and we'd become close. We weren't a couple, but I knew he was interested. I was also becoming close to his family. I actually spent more time with them than my own. Less than a week ago, he'd kissed me goodnight on my front porch. But now he was telling me he wouldn't need my help with tutoring and he didn't have time to be my friend. Before, he was always offering to give me a lift to and from school. Not anymore, I guess. But like I said, I didn't have a problem with the bus.

"See ya later, kiddo," Vince said as I jumped out of his

rickety van.

"Later, Vince."

That day was a regular day at school. I was spared the awkwardness of running into Matthew. We didn't take any of the same classes and didn't hang with the same crowd. But still, it would've been nice to ask him the reason behind the abrupt halt to our friendship. I was more curious than hurt. I mean, it was just a simple goodnight kiss.

I'd finished all my homework by the time Study Hall ended, which meant I could allow myself to go to the public library after school. If I'd had homework, I would've gone straight home or to Smitty's. But on days I didn't have homework, I loved to go to the county library and immerse myself in books. I'd been going there since grade school, and I'd made friends with everyone who worked there. I'd just need to take a different bus from school. We weren't supposed to swap buses without a signed permission slip each time, but the bus drivers all knew me, and Delia had given her approval earlier in the year. I did it so often they'd stopped asking for a slip.

"Hey Gin, no homework today, I see," Mrs. Rogers, the librarian, said as I walked through the doors. I just smiled and nodded at her as I headed for the card catalog. For a long time I'd been meaning to look up some books on John Wilkes Booth. We were studying President Lincoln's assassination in school, and I'd already devoured the books from the school library. I wanted to see if the local library had anything else to offer on the subject. I was in luck.

By five o'clock it was time to start packing things up, so I hauled my three books to the desk to check out.

"Need to make a call?" Mrs. Rogers asked.

"Yes, please," I replied. They were used to letting me

use the phone to call Delia or Vince for a ride home.

Vince must have been running behind on his delivery schedule and wasn't back at the warehouse yet. I left a message saying I needed a ride home from the library, but that I'd try calling Delia too. Which I did, but there was no answer where she worked. That could've meant a few things: She'd left, or she was talking to a customer and didn't want to pick up the phone, or maybe she was in the back room and didn't hear it. Oh well, this had happened before. No big deal.

"You going to be okay, Ginny?" Mrs. Rogers asked. "I don't want to lock up and leave if you don't have a ride. I'd be glad to take you home."

She was sweet. She offered this every time I didn't have an immediate lift home.

"Oh, no problem, Mrs. Rogers. I'll walk over to the convenience store and get a drink. Vince knows to come by there if the library is closed."

And that's what I did. Like I had done a hundred times in the past. I bought a soda and sat out front with my back against the entrance. I drank my soda and was so engrossed in one of my books I barely noticed when a noisy motorcycle pulled up.

It wasn't until the person driving turned it off and started walking toward me that I realized someone was talking to me. I heard a little chuckle and then, "That must be some good book you got your face buried in. I've been asking you what you're reading since I got off my bike and you didn't even hear me."

I glanced up. He looked like a typical motorcycle guy. Average height. Brown, shaggy hair that just touched his collar. He wore jeans, boots and a white T-shirt under a leather jacket. He smiled then, and I answered with a smile of my own.

"History. Lincoln." That was all I said. I wasn't a flirt and didn't think he required any more than that. I immediately looked back down at the book I had propped up against my knees.

That answer seemed to suit him because he didn't say anything else as he swung the door open and proceeded inside.

He came out a few minutes later with a Coke. He squatted next to me and looked at the book I was reading as he drank his soda. Without any prompting he started to engage me in conversation about Abraham Lincoln and more specifically about Booth. I found what he said interesting so I closed my book and turned to give him my full attention. He was nice and seemed like an okay guy — nothing like what I'd expected a man on a motorcycle to be like.

After a few minutes of discussing John Wilkes Booth the conversation turned personal, but not in a disturbing way. He asked how old I was and seemed genuinely shocked when I told him fifteen. He asked me what grade I was in, where I went to school, my hobbies, stuff like that. He seemed really interested and even teased, "Well, I guess I'll have to come back in three years if I want to take you on a real date or something."

Oh, my goodness. He was flirting with me. I had boys at school flirt with me all the time. They'd say things like, "Gin, how come you're not out there cheering? You're just as pretty as the cheerleaders." They were always offering to give me a ride home or asking if I wanted to hang out after school.

The boy I'd been tutoring, Matthew, had seemed interested, too. At least up until a couple days ago. He was a popular senior and our school's star running back. He went by the nickname Rocket Man. He was cute and sweet and flunking two classes. I was tutoring him in English and math. Truth was, I liked boys, and Matthew was growing on me. I liked the kiss we shared. But I wasn't interested in a serious boyfriend, especially one who would be leaving for college in the fall. I had too much to accomplish before I could get involved in a relationship.

But this was a man flirting with me, not a boy. And I realized I was more than a little flattered that he was taking an interest in me.

Unfortunately, I didn't know how to flirt back, so I reopened my book and just pretended to keep reading while he talked.

After he finished his soda he asked, "So, what are you doing sitting in front of the 7-Eleven? You waitin' on someone?"

"Yeah, my stepdad is supposed to pick me up. He should be here in a minute."

He stood up and looked around. "Well, I can give you a ride home. How far ya live?"

"Oh no, that's okay. I wouldn't want him to show up and me not be here. He would worry."

Actually, that wasn't true. Vince wouldn't see me here and assume Delia picked me up, and he would just go home.

"Can you call him or somethin' and let him know you're gettin' a ride?" Before I could answer he said, "You ever been on a motorcycle before? You'll like it. I'm a safe driver. I'll go real slow and let you wear my helmet."

Again I didn't answer, just looked at him.

He laughed then and said, "It's not like I can do anything to hurt you while you're on the back of my bike. Seriously, it's just a ride home. If you don't want me to know where you live, I can drop you at a corner close to your house. C'mon. Make an old guy's day."

"Why not?" I thought as I tried to mentally guess his age. He was older than me, but I didn't think he was an old guy. I closed my book and stood up.

"Well, I guess it'd be okay. I live off Davie Boulevard, just west of I-95. Is that out of your way?"

"No problem at all."

He tossed his Coke in a garbage can, came back over to me and held my bag open while I stowed my library book away. He made some comment about how my satchel was probably heavier than I was. He walked toward his motorcycle and grabbed his helmet, which had been hanging on the handlebar, and gave it to me. I put my bag on my back, took the helmet from him and put it on. It was loose, so he tightened the strap under my chin.

He swung a leg over the bike, started it up and then stood. I realized he was standing to make it easy for me to get on behind him, which I did with no problem. He revved the engine and I felt a little thrill at being on the back of a motorcycle with an older guy. I wasn't the type to care, but for a second or two I actually hoped someone I knew might see me. How prophetic that thought seemed much later. I yelled that I was going to have him drop me at Smitty's Bar and asked if he knew where it was on Davie Boulevard. He nodded yes.

I guess that was the moment I was officially abducted.

We started out in the direction I'd told him. At a red

light he turned and asked if I was enjoying the ride. I nodded yes and he said very loudly that he was going to take a different route to give me a little longer ride. Not to worry though, he would get me safely to Smitty's. I didn't worry. Not even for a second. I was enjoying myself too much.

It wasn't until we were on State Road 84 heading west and missed the right turn onto U.S. 441 that I felt my first stirring of fear. It was then I realized I didn't even know his name, and that with all the small talk and questions he had for me at the 7-Eleven, he'd never even asked mine. That suddenly struck me as very weird.

I leaned up so my mouth was near his ear and shouted, "Hey, this is the really long way around. I have to be home soon or my parents will be worried."

He never acknowledged that he heard me.

I leaned back against the backrest on the motorcycle. *Don't panic, don't panic, don't panic.* My bag was still on my back, and I could feel the library books digging into me through the thin fabric. It was then that I noticed his jacket for the first time.

It was a skull with a sinister smile and what appeared to be some kind of horns. A naked woman, somehow tastefully covered, was draped seductively across the top of the skull. She had dark brown hair with bangs and big brown eyes. As I peered closer, I saw she was wearing a brown peace choker. I raised my hand to my neck. It looked just like mine. Before I could ponder that strange coincidence I looked lower. To my horror, I noticed the name embossed beneath the morbid design.

Satan's Army.

Chapter Two

I'd soon find out I was nothing more than a thank-you gift after a long initiation ritual.

I sat in the rickety lawn chair and surveyed my surroundings. I clutched my bag to my chest as I tried to adjust my eyes to the dimming light. There was a campfire and a hodgepodge circle of people surrounding it. I can't remember now if I couldn't make out their faces in the waning light or if I was too frightened to notice. I knew where I was but wasn't exactly sure what to do about it. I'd started praying as soon as I realized the seriousness of my predicament. I should've taken my chances when there were more people and cars around. I should've risked jumping off a moving motorcycle. It would have been better than what I faced now.

I remember starting to physically shake when the reality

hit me as we'd made our way west on State Road 84.

These days 84 is updated and modernized, but in 1975 it was an underdeveloped two-way road. Today it runs parallel to a super highway, I-595, that takes you from the Everglades to the beach in a matter of minutes with all kinds of development in between—houses, schools, shopping centers and gas stations. In '75, it was the highway to hell, famous for its head-on collisions. It had little to no turnoffs with the exception of a little bar called Pete's.

When we passed Pete's I felt the nausea rising in my stomach. I knew there was nothing beyond it except the entrance to the deathtrap highway called Alligator Alley that connected the two Florida coasts. I thought the Miccosukee Indian Reservation was out there somewhere, but I didn't have a clue where.

It was getting dark and there were no other headlights in sight. About ten minutes after passing Pete's, we slowed and made a right onto a dirt road. I noticed some dim lights for the first time. Just a little way off the road, and barely visible due to the growing brush, was an old motel.

It was one of those little fifteen- or twenty-unit motels with old jalousie windows. It had an unlit sign identifying it as the Glades Motel. I hoped maybe it was still in business. A working motel might be good. Someone had to be running it. This might be my chance to explain I had made a mistake and ask to use the phone.

I guess it was originally built with the intention of giving travelers a place to stop in the middle of nowhere, but for whatever reason, it couldn't stay in business. As we pulled into the pitted and worn-down parking lot, I saw old gas pumps off to the right. It was obvious they were no longer in use. A couple of rooms had lights on, but what looked like the office showed no signs of life.

As we passed the old gas pumps I looked to my left and noticed a group of people between the motel and us. They were sitting around a dying campfire among the rusty old swings, slide and an antiquated carousel. It looked like a picnic and playground area that had seen better days. On the other side of the playground looked like a pool area. I couldn't tell for sure, but I thought it looked like it didn't have any water in it.

We circled to our left, and I noticed about six or seven motorcycles scattered in front of the units. He pulled up next to one and cut the engine. That's when I heard them.

It was a mixture of laughter, cursing and what sounded like two women arguing. I thought I heard Steppenwolf's "Magic Carpet Ride" coming from somewhere.

He stood up and said, "Get off."

I stood on the foot pegs and swung my leg over. My legs almost buckled, probably from a combination of the ride and fear, but I caught myself. I adjusted my backpack and stood straight. I figured the best way to deal with this was with confidence. I was scared to death, but darn if I was going to show it. He put the kickstand down and got off the bike.

"So, how long before you can give me a ride back?" I asked. I sounded a little too perky even to my own ears.

He didn't reply. He looked straight at me and gave me a smile that was born from pure evil. Was that the smile I'd seen at the convenience store? I couldn't remember. How could I have not noticed it then? The realization of my situation hit me like a lead bullet.

I remembered once when Delia and Vince weren't home and one of his supposed friends stopped by. He'd convinced me to let him in the house to use the phone.

"You can trust me, sweetheart. I'm a friend of Vinny, your stepdaddy."

That should've been a red flag. Nobody called Vince by the nickname Vinny. I'd released the deadbolt and as I was leading him toward the kitchen, where our only phone was mounted to the wall, he grabbed me by the back of my hair and threw me on the cracked linoleum floor. That's when I knew true fear. I'd felt a heat slowly work its way up my spine.

Before anything could happen there was a loud pounding on the front door. It was our neighbor, Guido. That was his real name. Well, that was the name he told us. Vince was convinced Guido was some Mafia guy in the Witness Protection Program. He didn't fit into our neighborhood at all. He was a total bully, and now he was loudly complaining because Vince's friend had parked on his lawn.

That's what Guido did. He sat on his front porch and waited for someone to do something wrong so he could assert himself. Normally I disliked Guido, but at that moment, his big mouth and heavy New York accent were music to my ears.

The mystery man, who never mentioned his name, had flipped me on my back and was sitting on my stomach with one hand over my mouth and the other holding both of my hands over my head. He was yelling for Guido to go away and that he'd move his truck when he damn well pleased. It wasn't until Guido threatened to call the police that the man let go of my hands and jumped off me in one swift movement.

He told me if I ever told anyone what happened he

would come back and finish what he'd started. I told him it would just be our secret. I wouldn't say a word. I wasn't hurt. No harm done. I would never tell. He could trust me.

I told. The minute Delia and Vince got home I told, and they called the police. After I described him and Guido described his truck, Vince knew who he was. Some low-life drifter named Johnny Tillman, who'd been hanging out at my parents' local haunt, Smitty's Bar on Davie Boulevard. He wasn't a friend of Vince's, but he'd had enough conversations with him to learn his name. How he'd known about me, I had an idea. I'd never seen him before, but he may have seen me. When I couldn't get a ride from my friends, sometimes I'd walk from the school bus stop to Smitty's to wait for Delia or Vince to give me a ride home. They could be counted on to stop in for a beer most days. The owner was a real nice lady. I'd sit in the corner and do homework, and she'd give me an orange soda and French fries on the house.

Now, standing in the middle of nowhere, Steppenwolf playing and motorcycle guy still smiling evilly, I was so paralyzed with fear I couldn't even remember her name. But one thing I wish I could forget was Delia's remark after that incident: "How can someone as smart as you do something so ridiculously dumb?"

Back then, I'd tried to reason my way out of it: "But Delia, he knew Vince." I'd even tried to convince myself the man seemed familiar. But that was a lie. She was right. It was the stupidest thing I'd ever done.

Until an hour ago.

Now all I could think was, "You're on your own, girlie. No Guido here this time."

Motorcycle guy grabbed me roughly by the arm and

pulled me forward. "C'mon, time to meet your new family."

Family? I was in too much shock to try to decipher that remark. We walked toward the group of people sitting around a campfire, the noise from earlier slowly fading. As we approached, I heard a long, low whistle and comments coming from all directions.

"Oooh, look what Monster brought us."

"Hey Monster, thought you liked blondes and gigantic titties."

"That one'll bring in a pretty penny. Help pay the bills."

Then a shrill female voice hissed, "Don't know what you think you're doin' bringing that piece of trash here."

A very articulate male voice retorted, "What's the matter, Willow? Afraid Grizz might be interested? Everyone knows he likes brunettes, and I'm pretty sure he's had his fill of you."

"Fuck you, Fess, and your momma and your daddy. She's too scrawny for Grizz and ugly, too."

Good, let them think I'm scrawny, ugly. Anything to get me out of here.

A gravelly male voice added, "No, she ain't none of that, Willow. But don't you worry, honey. You've been with Grizz going on two years now. He ain't ever lasted that long with one woman. I guess it's really love with you guys."

That seemed to placate Willow. The exchanges were so quick and the campfire so dim I couldn't put a face to a voice. My captor roughly plopped me down in a scratchy lawn chair within the group, then took the one beside me. I leaned forward, took my backpack off and placed it in my lap. I realized I wasn't wearing my poncho and the most ridiculous thought popped into my head that at least my poncho was safe and sound at the library. I wrapped my arms around my bag and started to look around, assessing my surroundings.

That's when my captor spoke. "Where's Grizz?"

Monster. I think that's what someone called him. Monster. God help me.

"He's here somewhere. Just went in to make a call, I think," someone answered.

"Why? What you need Grizz for?" snapped Willow.

Monster leaned forward in his chair as if to emphasize his point. "Well, bitch," he spat, "I want to show Grizz my gratitude for letting me be a member. You know, like with a thank-you gift. And this here is it," he said, waving his hand in front of my face.

I felt like a prize on some cheesy game show, and Monster was the model showing off the goods. Of course, I couldn't have been any further away from a soundstage somewhere in California than I was at that moment.

"It being what? Her?" Willow snarled.

My eyes had somewhat adjusted to the dim light, and I finally saw the source of the irritatingly shrill voice. Willow picked this moment to stand up and point at me, the campfire illuminating her. She was small. I couldn't guess her age, but she was probably younger than she looked. She had mousy blonde hair that hung limply around her face. There was nothing really special about that face, although I thought maybe she'd been really pretty at one time. She had smudged dark makeup under each eye. Her eyebrows were pencil-thin and overly arched, which added to her sinister look. She probably didn't need expressive eyebrows to achieve that, though. Hard living, probably including some serious drug use, had aged her. Even in the dim light I could see traces of slight acne scars, and her cheekbones were almost too prominent. They stuck out in sharp contrast to the hollowness that had likely been full cheeks at one time. She was wearing a purple tube top and ratty jeans that rested on her bony hips. And she called me scrawny? She had an assortment of dirty macramé and beaded bracelets on both arms. Almost every part of her skin that was showing was covered in tattoos with the exception of her face and hands. I looked down and saw she wasn't wearing any shoes. Her feet and toenails were filthy.

This was Grizz's woman? Whoever this Grizz was, I wondered if he was into dirty feet.

"Yeah her, Willow. I saw her sitting at the 7-Eleven and thought she looked like the girl on our jacket. Then I saw the damn choker and knew I had to get her for Grizz. Got a problem with that?"

"Damn right I do. He ain't gonna want her and you and your stupid ass should know better than to bring her here."

"Well why don't we let Grizz decide."

"Let Grizz decide what?"

I was so busy watching the exchange between Willow and Monster I didn't notice the large man walk up. Startled, I turned my head to the left and was eye level with the zipper of a pair of blue jeans. I slowly raised my eyes and my breath actually caught in my throat.

I thought Monster and his evil smile were something to fear. The man who stood next to me was not only large and impressive in appearance, but I could feel his raw energy and aggression radiating like a beacon. This was a person of authority. This was a person you didn't mess with.

This was Grizz.

He was the reason I was abducted, and I feared I now belonged to him.

At that moment my mind went in a million directions. I remember hearing snippets of conversation as to why I was there. Apparently Monster, the newest member of this group or gang or whatever they were, had just finished an initiation ritual. This final part wasn't required, and from what I later learned rarely, if ever, carried out: Kidnapping someone to be presented to the leader as a thank-you gift to do with whatever they wanted.

That was me. The thank-you gift. Now that I thought about it, Monster's leather jacket looked brand-spanking new. He couldn't have been part of this group for very long.

Just then my eyes reached Grizz's, and he was looking down at me. I couldn't read his expression. He wasn't classically handsome, but he wasn't ugly either. He was rugged, hard. Even in the semidarkness I could see he had compelling eyes. He was wearing a T-shirt that had the sleeves ripped off. He was muscular and covered in tattoos. His hair looked dirty blonde or maybe light brown, a little long and unkempt. I couldn't guess his age. For someone with such authority, he seemed like he should have been older than he looked. But I couldn't tell.

The dim light and my own fear caused all reason and clarity to leave my brain. I suddenly couldn't think or feel. I was numb.

He didn't smile. He didn't frown. He just continued to stare down at me with those eyes. Willow's voice broke the spell.

"Stupid asshole here thinks you're gonna want this little scrawny piece of shit, Grizz. I told him you wouldn't like her. Right, baby? You don't want her, do ya? The guys can have her, huh? If she's a gift to you, you can do whatever you want with her, like give her away. Right, baby? And he should know better than to bring someone here. Gonna kick his ass, aren't ya babe?"

He looked up then and stared at Willow without saying anything. I could see her face, and it had a pleading look. She wouldn't take her eyes off of him. Just stared with that look of someone who knows they've just lost.

She then turned her anger on me. She lunged at me with her hands outstretched. She was going for my neck.

Before she reached me, Grizz grabbed her by the throat and lifted her off the ground with one hand. He had her suspended, and she was kicking her feet. She had both her hands wrapped around his one hand and was trying to pry his fingers loose. Gurgling sounds came from her throat. Without saying a word, he tossed her, and she fell onto one of the flimsy lawn chairs, crushing it beneath her.

A figure rose from the group and went to her. I recognized the gravelly voice from earlier.

"It'll be okay Willow, honey. He'll play with her a couple of days and be back in your bed before the weekend is over." The man tried to help her up but she brushed him off.

"Shut the fuck up, Froggy," Willow barked. "You don't know nothin'. I'm supposed to feel better knowing my man is sleeping with that white-trash piece of shit? You just leave me alone. Stop touching me! I can get myself up."

She stood up and brushed herself off. She stuck her nose in the air like a queen and started to walk toward the motel.

"I'll be in our room, Grizz darlin', waitin' for ya, honey. Just come on home when you're done and I'll show you how a real woman feels underneath ya."

I watched her walk to the motel, open one of the doors and walk in. I looked back up and he was staring down at me. Without taking his eyes off mine he said, "Moe, take her to number four. Settle her in. Stay with her."

Take who? Me?

A tiny person rose from the ground. She'd been sitting close to the fire and had been staring into it during the whole scene. At first I'd thought she was a young boy. I remember thinking they had kids here so it couldn't be too bad. Now that hope was gone. She had short, jet-black hair. She was wearing a Black Sabbath T-shirt, black jeans and combat boots. As she rose and walked toward us, I could see her face was done up with black eye makeup to the extreme. She probably had a pretty face under all that paint. As an adult I would see young girls made up during the Goth craze, and I would think none of them held a candle to Moe. The original Goth girl.

Without saying a word she walked over to me and just stood there. She didn't meet my eyes, but looked at the ground. I looked to my right where Monster was sitting. He wasn't even looking at me. Sometime during the last ten minutes (or had it been an hour?) he'd gotten a beer and was sitting there with his head thrown back, chugging it. To his right was the man called Froggy, the one who tried to help Willow. He was looking down at the broken lawn chair. Maybe he was trying to see if he could fix it. I don't remember anyone else, although I know they were all there that night. Sitting around the campfire, watching, waiting, obeying.

I stood up and Moe slowly walked toward the motel. I clutched my bag to my chest and looked straight ahead as I followed her. Without turning around I knew with certainty that those mesmerizing eyes would watch me until I was behind the closed door of room number four.

Chapter Three

I followed Moe as she approached the unit with the fading number four on the door. There was a noisy air conditioning unit that made sounds similar to human coughing and sputtering. At least it would be cooler inside. I hadn't realized it, but I'd been eaten alive by mosquitos.

When we approached the door, I noticed two huge black dogs for the first time. They were lying on the sidewalk, one on each side of the door, and they raised their heads inquisitively as we passed them. When they determined we were not a threat, they went back to their naps. I didn't know it then, but those two creatures would become my jailers and eventually my protectors. They were large black Rottweilers named Damien and Lucifer.

I had an idea of what the inside of unit four was going to look like, but I couldn't have been more wrong. It was like walking into a different world. Where there should have been a dilapidated old bed, worn carpet, ancient furniture and the smell of decay, I found instead a totally modern living area. It looked like two rooms separated by a small kitchen. It was clean, cool and tastefully decorated. Was this some kind of dream?

Apparently, two units, maybe even three, had been remodeled to offer the occupant some modicum of comfort. I didn't have to guess as to who that occupant was.

My first thought was to find a phone. But Moe must have been reading my mind. We both spotted the phone on the kitchen counter and looked at each other at the same time. She just shook her head slowly. I sized her up. She was little. I wasn't too big myself, but I was strong and I was pretty sure I could take her down if I had to. I would save that for later if I needed to. I decided to try to warm up to her. Get on her good side. Get her to feel sorry for me. To want to help me.

"Wow, it's really nice in here. Are all the rooms this nice?"

She didn't answer me but gave me a look that said "Are you kidding?"

I sat on the edge of the small sofa. She sat on the edge of an oversized recliner and just stared at me.

"So you're supposed to get me settled in? What exactly does that entail?"

No answer. She got up and walked to the small kitchen area. Opened the refrigerator and took out a can of soda. She popped the top, walked over and handed it to me. I thanked her and sat it on the little coffee table without taking a sip. On second thought, my mouth was as dry as the desert. A sip would probably taste good. So I sipped my drink.

I guess she noticed me scratching at the mosquito bites because she got up again and passed through the kitchen into what I assumed was a bedroom with a bathroom. She quickly returned and wordlessly handed me a bottle of antiseptic and one cotton ball. She nodded at my arms and I realized she was trying to offer some kind of comfort for the bites. My immediate thought was, "Okay, so she's not a horrible person. Only a nice person would be concerned about some stupid mosquito bites." I don't think it ever occurred to me that she was being nice because there would be hell to pay if she wasn't.

I continued with the small talk as I dabbed at the bites with the medicine-soaked cotton. Moe still refused to answer me no matter how hard I tried to engage her. I'd never seen someone so loyal to her leader. There must have been some unspoken rule about not fraternizing with the prisoners.

Oh man, I hadn't thought of that word before, but that's exactly what I was. A prisoner. Held against my will. I had to get to that phone. I had a plan. Not a good one, but if I acted casually enough I might just pull it off. Who knows? Maybe I'm not really a prisoner, I reasoned to myself. Maybe I'm overreacting. This isn't real. This is the kind of thing you see in the movies.

I chugged my soda. When the can was almost empty I casually stood and said, "All done, thanks. Is the garbage can in the kitchen?" Without waiting for her answer I walked to the small area pretending to look for the trash. I walked to the sink and started to pour out what little soda was left in the can. With my left hand, I casually reached for the phone on the counter. Before I could lift it off the receiver I felt her behind me. I stopped dead. One hand on the receiver, one hand still dangling the soda can over the sink. Tiny, quiet little Moe was holding a knife to my neck.

"Whoa, Moe, no need for that. I just wanted to make a call. Let my parents know where I was. They'll be worried and all."

She removed the knife and I turned around and saw that she was giving me the same look she gave me when I asked if all the rooms were this nice. No, little unassuming Moe was no dummy. She was small and she was quiet, but she had my number. Heck, maybe she was me a few years back. I didn't know.

I stammered an apology. "I'm just scared. I don't know what's going to happen to me. Do you know? Why won't you say anything to me? If you could just tell me what's happening or what I can expect I think I could handle it better."

She was shorter than me, but we were standing so close I was able to get a really good look at her face. She had pretty eyes, even with all the makeup, and I could tell she had beautiful skin. I hadn't seen her smile yet so I couldn't comment on her teeth.

She showed no emotion as she stared back at me. I was lost. I was alone. This little would-be friend was not a friend. She was doing her job.

She opened her mouth slightly as if to say something. Finally, maybe an answer. A word of comfort. Anything.

It was then that I noticed Moe didn't have a tongue.

Chapter Four

For the first time in my life, I uttered a word that had never before crossed my lips: "Mom." I wanted my mother.

I was born on Valentine's Day 1960. My mother named me Guinevere Love Lemon. Yes, that's my real name. In order to understand how I got that name you would have to understand my hopelessly romantic, hippie mother, Delia. And before you consider judging her for giving me such a ridiculous name, know that my name is what would ultimately lead to the fall of Satan's Army.

Delia Lemon got pregnant with me while living in a commune and never cared to try to identify my father. She met my stepfather, Vince, at a war protest when I was around six years old, and they were married three years later at Woodstock. Oh yeah, I went to Woodstock. I say they were married, but I don't know if it was legal. She continued to use her own last name, Lemon.

She was way too cool to be a mom, so I grew up calling her Delia. Delia Lemon was quite the character. I like to compare her to the mother from the Jeannie C. Riley song, "Harper Valley PTA." You know the song—the PTA sends a note home to the little girl's mother saying they objected to how she was raising her daughter. That mom goes to the next PTA meeting and basically rips everyone a new one.

The problem with that comparison is I think the mom from that song cared more about her daughter and her reputation than Delia cared about me. Delia wasn't a bad person. She was just indifferent to rules. She truly didn't care what people thought. She was the ultimate flower child. She would just go with the flow.

I still remember my first grade teacher's horror when she discovered I didn't call my mother "Mommy." I called her by her first name. Always had. I remember asking Delia once who my mommy was, because all my friends had mommies, and she brushed it off with a laugh explaining she didn't believe in labels. I was too young to understand what that meant.

Delia worked at a health food store before health food stores were popular. She grew her own herbs and her own pot. She took in stray animals. She never wore a bra and her wardrobe consisted of tank tops, tube tops and long, billowy skirts with stretchy waistbands. She went barefoot as often as possible. She had dirty blonde hair parted down the middle that she always wore in two braids that almost reached her waist.

She made sure I was fed and always had clean clothes to wear to school. Well, most of the time. Wrinkled, but clean. That was the extent of her mothering.

Our home was filled with plants hanging in homemade, elaborate macramé hangers. Scented candles and incense were always burning. Despite working in a health food store, Delia smoked a pack of cigarettes a day until Vince finally convinced her to quit. I used to light the candles to cover up the smell. Later it became a habit I continued long after she quit.

Vince drove a beer delivery truck. He had the same job for as long as I can remember. He was an okay guy. I can't say anything bad about Vince.

Delia and Vince never beat or abused me. I don't remember them ever yelling at me or punishing me. They just didn't care enough. I wasn't loved or nourished emotionally.

I guess they mostly ignored me. I have no memory of Delia or Vince helping me with homework. I don't remember them ever attending any school pageants or volunteering for fundraisers. I do remember always taking care of myself, even at a young age. I still recall standing on a kitchen chair so I could reach the stove to boil water for macaroni and cheese. That was one of my favorite things to make. Unfortunately, I had a few too many meals of the same type, and to this day I cannot stomach macaroni and cheese, tomato soup or any kind of cherry-flavored drink mix.

By the way, Vince and Delia were serious alcoholics. Thank God they weren't mean ones. Waiting for them at Smitty's Bar after school felt normal to me at the time. It was the routine. This was back when Fort Lauderdale felt smaller and people knew each other. That's where I grew up. Fort Lauderdale, Florida.

When I was in grade school I was what people called a

latchkey kid. I walked home every day from Parkland Elementary School. I would let myself in and lock the door behind me. Delia didn't even require a phone call from me telling her I made it home okay.

I was a loner but never lonely and was an excellent student. I buried myself in my books. I showed a real talent for working with numbers. I loved numbers. I still love numbers. I love how they never lie. They always fit. There is always a constant.

By the time I was thirteen I had completely taken over the family finances. Believe it or not, both Delia and Vince would cash their paychecks, keep what they wanted, and give me the rest. I rode my yellow ten-speed bike to the local bank every week to make a deposit. I paid all the bills, forging Delia's signature on the checks. I reveled in feeling like I was an integral part of something. I liked to play chief financial officer for our small family.

I really felt important, too, when Vince would ask me, "Hey Gwinny, my boots are wearing out. Think I can keep back twenty for some new ones? You gonna have enough to pay the bills?"

It was a small empowerment, but it was better than nothing, and the fact that I was managing a family budget gave me confidence and a feeling of importance. I mattered to this family. I had never felt that way before.

I was Gwinny when they were drinking, which most times. But by the time I was ten I'd started to insist that instead of Gwinny, I be called Ginny. I felt like Gwinny was more suited to one of the stray kittens Delia adopted. It was a baby name and I didn't like it.

Eventually, Ginny was shortened to Gin. Yes, Gin, just like the alcohol. Some things are just plain ironic, aren't they?

Chapter Five

Moe smiled. I couldn't tell if she was amused that I noticed she had no tongue, or embarrassed by it. Just then the door opened and the man they called Grizz walked in.

My first instinct was to pelt him with questions. But something held me back. I didn't have any experience with men, but my inner voice was telling me to keep my mouth shut. I wondered if that was why Moe didn't have a tongue; did she say something wrong and it was cut out, or was she born that way? For the life of me I couldn't remember ever hearing about anyone born without a tongue.

Without saying a word, Grizz strode to the small coffee table and picked up my backpack. He turned it upside down and emptied it onto the sofa. The heavy library books landed on top of everything else, so he tossed them aside and picked up my birth control pills. He tossed them aside too. Then he moved his hand over the rest of the contents. When his fingers brushed over one of the two tampons I said in an unnaturally high-pitched voice, "I have my period. And I'm only on the pill because I get bad cramps. They're not for birth control."

There. I put a couple of things out there, but truth be told, I wasn't sure if they would help or hurt my cause. Who wanted to rape a girl who had her period? I had no earthly idea what motivated a rapist. Or in this case, what might deter one. And second, I tried to let him know that I was on the pill because of period cramps. That was true. I was not sexually active. But what if he wanted a virgin? I had no idea where I stood with him.

He didn't comment, but picked up my wallet. He opened it and spotted my Florida driver's permit.

"Guinevere Love Lemon?" he asked with a smirk.

"Gin. I go by Gin," I retorted.

He didn't look at me. "You will never go by that name again. Got it? You tell nobody your name. Ever. Is that clear?"

I didn't answer so he flashed a quick look at me. I nodded yes. But I wouldn't let the moment go. Deep down, I was defiant to the core. Just because I was playing it safe while being scared out of my wits didn't mean I was okay with my predicament. I didn't want my defiant nature to show, but I think it did.

"Well, now Moe knows," I said with just a little attitude.

He tossed my wallet back on the pile of my few belongings and slowly walked toward me. *Don't shake, don't shake, don't shake. Look him in the eye, Gin. Head up. Not too bold, but don't be a wimp either.*

He was standing so close to me that I had to tilt my head

up to continue looking him in the eyes. That's when I noticed the color: a clear, bright green, and even more compelling in the light of the motel room than around the campfire. He raised his right hand and softly caressed my cheek. I was in shock. Even though I didn't flinch, I'd been prepared for a blow.

In almost a whisper, he said, "And who's she gonna tell, huh? Last time she ran her mouth she paid for it." After a brief pause, he added, "You don't look surprised, girl. You already figured out why Moe doesn't talk?"

"Did you do it?" I whispered back.

"Yeah, I did it. So any more questions about your old name?"

"What are you going to call me?"

"Nothing, for now."

He walked back over to my pile of personal possessions. He picked up my wallet with my I.D. and four dollars in it and tossed it to Moe.

"Burn it."

Chapter Six

It didn't take long for me to acquire a new name. I wasn't addressed much by the gang anyway; when I was, it was usually Willow referring to me as "the ugly bitch." That didn't last long, though.

I had only been there a few days and was starting to know some of them by name. One afternoon, a few of us were sitting at one of the rundown picnic tables eating. Well, I wasn't really eating. I had no appetite for obvious reasons. I was sitting on Grizz's left, and Willow was on his right.

That's how it had been the last couple days. I was always with Grizz. Never out of his sight except to use the bathroom. Willow couldn't stand for me to always be with him and she made the most of every opportunity to be near him, too. She would've slept in his room on the floor if he'd let her.

So we were eating and Willow started to say, "So, ugly bitch, when you gonna—"

Grizz backhanded her so hard she would've flown backwards off the bench if Grunt, who was on her other side, hadn't stuck his left arm out to catch her.

Grunt was the youngest of the group. He didn't appear to say much and I couldn't gauge his age, but he had to be only a little older than me. I always felt like he watched me, but when I would look at him he wasn't looking at me.

Willow's hand flew to her mouth. When she pulled it away, she was holding her left front tooth. Blood was running out of her nose and mouth. It wasn't a casual slap. Grizz's hand had been curled into a full fist, and the blow had been powerful enough to knock out that tooth and maybe even break her nose. If I thought Willow hated me before, then this only upped her level of animosity.

A couple of the others laughed. Moe just stared expressionless, but I thought I caught a hint of a smile before she lowered her head back to her plate.

Chicky, who was sitting across from Willow, said, "Gee, Grizz, you going all soft, sticking up for your 'gift'? Since when do you care what Willow calls her?"

The instant she said it I could see regret in her eyes. But apparently Grizz didn't react the way she thought he would, because after a few seconds she looked relieved. He finished chewing his food, and after swallowing it he casually said, "Just tired of hearing it."

Willow was trying not to cry, but she was trembling. She shot up and quickly struggled to get herself untangled from the picnic bench. It was awkward because she was between Grizz and Grunt, and she had to step backwards to get out.

Grunt started to help her, but proud person that she was, she just shooed him away without saying anything and stomped back toward the motel.

She must have sought out Froggy, who was not at the picnic table, because a few minutes later we heard a bike start and saw the two of them slowly ride past us and onto State Road 84.

This was the second time I'd seen Grizz abuse Willow. I'd already known she was sleeping with Grizz, or had been until my arrival. I hadn't had to sleep with him yet, though. I don't think anyone knew that. I still couldn't come up with a reason why he hadn't raped me. He certainly seemed like the type. Maybe he was waiting for me to get over my period. I didn't know. He was obviously a cruel person incapable of feeling much, except for anger. But other than his seeming indifference to my situation, he had yet to lift a hand to hurt me.

I couldn't tell if he cared what the others thought of how he treated me. It was probably new to them, seeing their leader stick up for a fifteen-year-old gang prisoner. I got the impression he let everyone fight their own battles. They could kill each other and he probably wouldn't intervene or care.

I would see his brutality unleashed on many people over the coming years, regardless of their sex, age or physical ability. It didn't matter. I wondered if getting beaten or having your tongue cut out was just run of the mill for his women. I would later see that he never abused anyone for the sake of abuse. He didn't enjoy it. It didn't please him to hurt people, but he never seemed to show any kind of remorse when he did. As far as he was concerned, they got what they asked for. They knew the consequences of defying him in even the slightest way. In all the years I spent with Grizz, only once did I ever hear a word of regret from him.

His stance was that he demanded obedience no matter what the issue. You didn't obey, you paid. There were many instances during my time with Grizz when I would see a lot of folks pay in horrible ways for disobeying him or just doing something he didn't like.

I would see someone pay that very night.

It was around sunset, so I assumed someone had lit the fire in the pit like they had the prior few nights. That's what they called the area where I encountered them on my first night at the motel: The pit.

I was in Grizz's room reading one of my library books. I had tried acting as casual as possible over the last few days. But the truth was, I was just staring at the page. My mind was in constant turmoil trying to think of a way to escape.

For the first time since my arrival, Grizz actually wanted me out of the room. There was something he needed to do. Maybe make a phone call? I didn't know.

He strode over to the door, opened it and yelled, "Grunt. Come here." He stood there with the door open until Grunt appeared. Grizz nodded toward me and said, "Take her to the pit. I'll be a few minutes."

I looked up, surprised. This was new. I shut my book and put my sandals on. I hated going barefoot. Which was kind of funny since I grew up with a mother who hated wearing shoes.

I remembered how cool the nights could get, so I asked, "Can I have a jacket or something?"

"Yeah. Grunt, give her your jacket."

Grunt took his jacket off without saying a word and

handed it to me. I put it on and followed him to the pit.

We sat side by side in two lawn chairs. Willow and Froggy were nowhere to be seen. I didn't know Froggy's motorcycle well enough to know if it was parked with the others. They may have never gotten back from that afternoon. Moe was sitting on the ground in front of the fire just like the first night I was there. A few others were sitting in lawn chairs with their legs stretched out. Everyone was drinking beer.

Grunt saw me looking at the others and asked if I wanted a beer. I told him no, but maybe I should have taken one. It would probably have relaxed me, but I hated beer and how it tasted.

Grunt went over to the cooler, got himself a beer and sat down next to me. I noticed he slapped at his arm. Mosquitos.

"Thanks for giving me your jacket," I told him.

"Didn't think I had much of a choice." He didn't say it in a mean way, just as a matter of fact. I started to take his jacket off and he immediately put his hand up and said, "No, you wear it. You better be wearing it when he comes out, okay? You can give it back to me tomorrow."

"What, you think he'd hurt you if I gave you your jacket back?"

"You're the one who asked for the jacket. Just wear it. He won't be mad at me. He'll be mad at you because you told him you were cold and he fixed it so you weren't cold. So if he comes out here and you're cold, he'll probably be pissed."

"Why would he even care about something so ridiculous?"

By now, the others around the pit had stopped their own

conversations and were listening to our exchange.

Before Grunt could answer, a loud motorcycle interrupted our conversation. Monster. I wondered where he had been all day. Not that I really cared. People seemed to come and go here as they pleased. Everyone except me.

After Monster parked and cut the engine, conversation resumed. But I let the jacket question go. I was curious about certain things, but I also figured the less I knew, the better. I wanted my freedom. If I constantly asked questions and knew too much about this small group, maybe it could influence the decision as to whether or not to let me go.

Monster walked over to the pit and got a beer from the cooler before sitting down. He popped the top and took a big swig. Then, one-handed, he took a pack of cigarettes out of his jacket and lit one up. He downed the rest of his beer in less than thirty seconds, belched loudly, then stood. "Forgot, I got another present for Grizz. Well, for Grizz's hounds actually."

"You don't got another chick hidden on your bike somewhere, do ya?" someone asked. There was a round of laughter.

He didn't answer as he walked back over to where he had parked his bike. He had everyone's curiosity, so all eyes followed him. He opened one of his saddlebags, reached in and pulled something out. It was hard to tell what it was since it was almost dark, but it was small, and he carried it with one hand.

He got back over to his lawn chair, and we still couldn't tell what he had. He plopped down and with his cigarette dangling from his mouth, he held up the prize.

It was a tiny black kitten. A kitten? Would Grizz want a kitten? Then I remembered he said it was for Grizz's hounds. Was he going to give the kitten over to the dogs to be mauled to death? Oh no. I didn't think I could handle that.

Someone, I think it was Blue, said, "What the hell is Grizz gonna want with that?"

"I thought he might wanna feed it to his hell hounds," Monster laughed. He still had it by the scruff of its neck and the poor little thing just hung there without making a sound.

"I'll tell you right now, you're wrong. Get rid of it before he comes out here," Blue warned.

"Why would I wanna get rid of a perfectly good squawk box like this?" Monster asked.

"What do you mean by squawk box?" Grunt asked.

Without answering, before anyone could have stopped him if they'd wanted to, Monster took the lit cigarette and pressed it to the kitten's side. It howled in pain and tried to wrestle free. He just laughed.

"See, squawk box! Hell, anyone wanna know if its eye will make a sizzle sound like when you fry bacon or something?" More laughter from him.

No one was joining in his laughter at this horrible display, but I was too upset to notice. I jumped up and started running to the room. Grunt was on my heels, but I fought him off.

"Just leave me alone! Leave me alone!" I was screaming at the top of my lungs. "You're all sick. Something's wrong with all of you if you think this is fun."

Grunt was trying to stop me from reaching the room, and he was saying something I didn't hear. I was too hysterical.

Just then, the door of Grizz's room opened and he came

out. "What the hell is going on out here?"

"What's going on? I'll tell you what's going on. Your sick friend Monster is getting his kicks out of torturing a poor, helpless animal, that's what. You're all sick. I can't believe this is happening. I can't believe people get off on this kind of crap. I've gotta get outta here!"

By then, Grunt was behind me, using both hands to hold my arms at my side. I was waiting for the blow from Grizz. I'd seen him get mad for lesser things. This would surely warrant at least a slap in the face. But it didn't come. He looked past me and Grunt toward the pit and said, "Take her in. Stay with her."

"What, so you can go join the fun?" I taunted. "Is that what you're gonna do? Big, tough guy, huh? Gonna terrorize a kitten. Gee, how brave!"

While I was yelling Grizz was moving toward the pit so I didn't know how much he heard, thank God. Grunt kept telling me to shut up. Then with a strength I didn't know he had, he picked me up and threw me over his shoulder. He took me in the room and shut the door before letting me down on my feet.

He'd knocked the wind out of me, and I bent over, gasping for air. He kept telling me to calm down while he led me to the couch. Then he flipped on the TV, turned up the volume and faced me.

"It's not what you think," Grunt said. "It'll be okay. Try and take a breath."

I couldn't reply. For the first time since my abduction, I broke down and started to cry.

He started to sit next to me and put his arm around me, but jumped back as soon as he did it. Instead, he sat on the small coffee table and faced me, just watching me as I sobbed.

He went in the bathroom, brought back a cold washcloth and handed it to me. I put my face in it and cried harder.

I looked up when the door opened and Grizz walked in. He looked at me, then at Grunt.

"Leave."

Grunt nodded and got up, walked past him and out the door. I looked down at my lap. I felt so defeated, and the hysterics had made me physically exhausted. I could tell Grizz was walking toward me. Before I could look up, he gently laid the kitten in my lap.

I was stunned. I looked up at him, and he must have read the question on my face.

"Blue told me what Monster did. What he was planning on doing."

I didn't know what to say.

"It's gonna need some fixing up. You can keep it in here and take care of it, but you gotta keep it away from Lucifer and Damien. I don't know what they'd do. I mean it, though. You figure out a way to take care of it. I find one pile of shit in here and I'll have Grunt take it to the pound. Got it?"

I could only nod.

"You'll never talk to me like that again. Got it, Kit?"

"Yes. Thank you." I said in a whisper. "Did you yell at Monster? Did you let him know to stay away from it from now on? That it's mine?"

"No, I didn't yell at Monster, and no, he won't bother it again."

Three things happened that night. That was the night I got my new name. Kit. That was the night I saw a different side of Grizz. And that was the night the others around the campfire would come to disagree about what they witnessed.

Some said, "Yeah, an eyeball does make a sizzling sound like bacon frying." Others said, "No, it don't sound nothing like it."

But they all agreed on one thing. It was hard to tell for sure what kind of sound they heard over Monster's shrieks of pain.

Chapter Seven

That night I slept with the tiny kitten curled up against my chest. Like every night I'd been there, I slept on top of the covers of an extremely comfortable king-sized bed. Grizz's bed. He slept on top of the covers, too, in his T-shirt and jeans. Our backs almost touched. Every morning when I woke up, I would find a blanket draped over me.

I didn't see Monster the next day. I was surprised that everyone acted like everything was normal. As horrified as I was over what Monster had done to the kitten, I was even more appalled at what Grizz had done to him.

I was sitting on the bed the next morning playing with my kitten when Blue came in. Blue was second in command of this group and Grunt's older brother. He told Grizz that Monster had taken off and they weren't sure if he was coming back. I secretly hoped he was angry enough with

Grizz to go to the police about my abduction. No such luck.

He rolled in later that afternoon like nothing had happened. The only evidence of the night before was a patch over his eye.

I was still under the watchful eye of Grizz and never had a minute to myself to get near the phone. He saw me eyeing it one day and told me not to bother even trying to leave or call for help.

"I would be stupid not to try to leave here."

"No," Grizz countered. "You would be stupid if you did try."

"Really? Why's that?"

"Because if you leave, your family gets hurt. That's why."

I already knew what Grizz was capable of doing. I'd seen him abuse Willow and knew what he'd done to Monster. Still, I couldn't help myself. I had to challenge him.

"What would you know about my family?" I asked a little too mockingly.

I knew he'd burned my driver's permit, and there was no way he'd memorized the address on it that night when he glanced at my name. And as far as my name was concerned, Lemon was not in the phone book. Our telephone was in Vince's name.

"Don't push it, Kit," was all he said.

I pushed it. I actually taunted him. Surprisingly, he wouldn't answer my charges that there was no way on this earth he could know anything about me, and therefore had no way to take it out on my family. After a few minutes I noticed the vein in his forehead throbbing.

"You want proof, Kit? Is that what you're asking for?"

"Yes, that's exactly what I want. Know why? Because I

know you don't have it. I was just some stupid, random thank-you gift that Monster happened upon at the convenience store. I was nowhere near my home."

He stared at me for a few minutes without answering. Finally, he said, "Maybe you need a lesson in believing without proof. Maybe you need to learn exactly who you're dealing with."

He said it in such a calm and even voice it scared me. I relented.

"Okay, you're able to hurt my family if you want to." My voice was quiet. "Fine, I believe you. I won't try anything stupid."

That was the end of the conversation. Thank God I heeded my own advice and didn't try to escape or use the phone. I spent the rest of the day in the bedroom with my kitten and three library books.

That night as I reluctantly followed Grizz out to the pit, I stopped dead in my tracks. Fear trickled down my spine like a dripping faucet. There it was. The proof that I told Grizz he couldn't provide. There, leaning up against the dilapidated slide on the playground, was my most prized possession: My guitar. The last time I'd seen it, it was propped up against a rocking chair in my bedroom. How? How could it be here? There was only one way. Grizz knew where I lived. He could hurt Delia and Vince. And even though I didn't love them the way most kids love their parents, I cared about them and didn't want to see them hurt.

I returned to number four that night shaken by fear and completely defeated. I picked up my kitten and cuddled her. I felt so stupid. When Grizz first brought her to me I secretly vowed to escape and take her with me. I was going to be this tiny little creature's savior. Who was I kidding? How was I going to save a kitten from these people when I couldn't even save myself?

She needed a name. That much I could do for her. Since hers had already been given to me, I gave her back the only name I could think of that would also be my last connection to home. It wasn't a happy home, but it was the only home I ever knew.

I named her Gwinny.

Chapter Eight

I'd gotten over my period a few days after I arrived, and a week or so after that Grizz still hadn't tried anything sexual with me. Willow continued to hate me, but from a distance. By the end of the first week I'd even started sleeping through the night. Before that, I'd had a hard time falling asleep and would wake up all night long.

I worried Grizz was going to try something with me, but he never did. I figured after I started sleeping through the night that he was getting up while I was asleep and going to one of the other women's rooms. Good. I hoped that's what he was doing. I sure didn't want him to take out his pent-up desires on me.

I'd also managed to nurse Gwinny back to health. It wasn't hard. The only remnant from that awful night was a nasty blister that had since formed a scab. She was a lively little thing and showed no fear even after the abuse Monster inflicted on her. I was still a prisoner, but allowed to roam the motel freely and without Grizz. He wasn't always with me like in the beginning. I obviously wasn't going anywhere.

Magically, everything I needed was provided for me, including a year's supply of birth control pills. In my mind I tried to deny it was an indication of how long I could be there; regardless, I still didn't know for what purpose. Would they farm me out as a prostitute? Would I work at a topless bar like Chicky and Willow?

I didn't know then how Grizz acquired everything. Slowly, items would just show up outside his room. The day after I got Gwinny, I found a litter box, food and a cat toy outside the door. I kept the kitten inside with me and made sure the litter box was cleaned as soon as she used it. I didn't want to give Grizz any reason to take her away from me.

Another day, five pairs of new underwear, a toothbrush, a sweatshirt and a pair of sneakers showed up—all in my size. Up until then, I'd been hand washing the same pair of panties and letting them dry overnight. I would sleep in one of Grizz's T-shirts and my jeans, which I hadn't washed, and I usually started my days wearing damp but clean underwear.

Another day brought with it new jeans, a couple nightgowns and shorts. Within the month I had a complete wardrobe. It was nice, stylish stuff, too, with the store tags still attached. Almost everything fit perfectly. I wondered if it was bought or stolen. I never asked, but I'm pretty certain it was Chicky and Moe who got everything for me. If it was up to Willow I had no doubt I would have spent my days in a used burlap sack.

I knew for certain Moe got my pills. Moe had a friend who worked for a gynecologist, and this friend had a serious drug habit. Since Grizz made sure all the girls stayed on birth control, Moe would take her friend her drug of choice, and her friend would supply the group with pills from the stash of free samples they got regularly at the doctor's office.

My days were routine and I was bored to tears. Strangely, though, I was no longer frightened. I don't know why. I should've been. But I wasn't required to work at the topless bar like the other girls. I wasn't required to have sex with the guys. I wasn't asked to cook, clean or do laundry. But I had to do something to keep myself from going crazy. I'd done chores in my own home. I decided to try to do some here just to keep busy.

That was how I learned that Damien and Lucifer were my jailers. As if the death threat to Delia and Vince hadn't been enough. Up until that point, the dogs had left my kitten alone. They were allowed in Grizz's room whenever they wanted. They were extremely well trained dogs and never got on the furniture. They slept on dog beds on the floor. They ate their dinner, went to the woodsy area beyond the motel to relieve themselves and pretty much came and went as they pleased.

One day I decided to mop the floor in number four. When I was finished I carried the bucket of dirty water outside, but I didn't want to dump it where someone might walk and track it back in. So I headed for the edge of the motel grounds near the woods.

As I got closer I noticed that bordering the property was what looked like a swamp. I'd forgotten I was in the

Everglades. Wait. Weren't there alligators in the swamp? Before I could ponder that question, I'd reached the edge of the motel lawn and was lifting the bucket to pour it out. Suddenly, both dogs were there—one behind me and one to my left. I held the bucket in midair as they both got into attack stance and growled. I froze.

Oh, my gosh. They thought I was trying to leave and they were stopping me. I couldn't believe it. How did they know to stop me there? I'd seen some of the guys go right to the edge of the lawn to pee, and the dogs never went after them.

I stood there, paralyzed with fear. Then I heard Grizz whistle to them and shout a command as he walked toward me. The dogs trotted off, happily wagging their stubby tails like they were little pups. When Grizz got to me, he took the bucket and poured it out.

"I wasn't leaving, you know."

"Didn't think you were. But they did."

"Your dogs are trained to attack me if I try to leave?"

"Not attack you. Just stop you. But see, you were smart enough to stop. Just keep stopping and it won't be a problem." His tone was matter of fact.

"You would want them to hurt me?"

"No, I don't want them to hurt you, and they wouldn't have attacked. They would've stopped you."

"By attacking me?" My voice started rising, and I couldn't control it. I realized my feelings were actually hurt. I thought Damien and Lucifer had warmed up to me. They certainly had warmed up to Gwinny, letting her swat at them and chew on the nubs of their tails. Sometimes she would even try to chew on their ears while they slept. They never flinched.

"Kit, quit overreacting. They're also your protectors. If anyone ever so much as lifts a hand to you, they'll kill 'em."

"Really? They would do that?"

"Yeah. If they'd been there that night when that scumbag tried to rape you in your parents' house, they would've ripped his balls off."

My head snapped up to meet his eyes. I could see by his expression he hadn't meant to say it.

"That was over a year ago," I said, my heart thudding. "How did you know that? Grizz, how did you know about that guy?"

He started walking back toward the motel. I was carrying the empty bucket and trying to keep up with him. I continued to fire questions at him about how he could possibly have known about that incident. He didn't answer. He just kept walking.

I followed him inside number four, and when I shut the door behind us, I quietly said, "Please. Please tell me."

Grizz spun around then and stared at me, like he was trying to decide whether to tell me. We hadn't had many conversations up until then. He didn't talk much, and I couldn't tell if he was going to say anything at all. The seconds ticked by. Finally, he gestured toward the couch. I sat down and put my hands in my lap. Gwinny jumped up on my shoulder and started playing with my hair. I barely noticed.

I couldn't believe what came next.

Monster's random abduction of me was not random at all, I learned. It was a direct order from Grizz. As far as the rest of the group knew, I was a "thank-you gift," like Monster said.

It all started in October 1973. I was thirteen. Grizz was in my neighborhood when he saw me get off the school bus. I was in eighth grade, and the bus dropped me almost at my door.

He explained how he'd been sitting in Guido's driveway when I passed him, walked up to my porch and let myself in the house. (Guido? He knew Guido?)

Guido's real name was Tony Bono, and he worked for Grizz. Something with drugs. Grizz saw me and instantly wanted me. He didn't know I was only thirteen, but when Guido told him my age, he decided on a plan. Guido was to watch me and report anything strange or unusual. It was an order, and Guido was only too happy to cooperate. He reported the Johnny Tillman incident, plus many other details about my life and my family.

As I listened, something else occurred to me.

"It was you, wasn't it?" I asked, realization dawning. "You were the reason Matthew broke off our friendship."

Grizz clenched his jaw, not looking at me. "He was becoming too interested in you. Have you been with him? That kid. Did you do anything with him?"

"Not that it's any of your business, but no. We never got beyond the kiss on my porch."

"Good thing for him."

"Why's that?"

"Because I told him if I ever found out he touched you, I would go back and cut his balls off."

"Why would you do that?" My cheeks were hot. "He wouldn't have defied you. He immediately ended our friendship. So why did you still have Monster take me?"

"I couldn't risk you being with someone else. You look a lot older than fifteen. I couldn't chance it."

Matthew would tell me many years later that he

regretted never speaking up when I disappeared. He was certain he knew who was responsible. He apologized for not going to the police to tell them about Grizz. He said he was just a kid and he really believed the guy would come back and hurt him. I told him not to feel guilty, and I meant it.

He was right to be scared. Grizz would have gone back for him.

Now my head was spinning. I was actually dizzy from racing thoughts. Mine wasn't an arbitrary kidnapping. It was a well-planned and carefully executed one. He then explained how my guitar got to the motel. It hurt so much to hear that Guido paid five dollars for it at one of Delia's many garage sales—that particular sale being held shortly after my disappearance.

"So that first night when you looked at my license and laughed at my name, it was an act. You already knew my name." It wasn't a question.

"It wasn't an act. I didn't know about the 'Love' part."

I now had no doubt that it was my image on their gang logo. He'd long been obsessed with me. I think I was more frightened at that realization than when I first figured out I'd been abducted.

Grizz went on to explain that after seeing me the first time he knew he would come back for me one day. That I would be his. He admitted that even with Guido keeping an eye on things, he would personally check on me once in awhile. He'd even been at Smitty's when I was there. He'd quietly observed me for almost two years. But he insisted he was no child molester or pervert and that he'd been waiting for me to get older.

I stopped him. "But I'm still only fifteen."

"You're old enough. And I'm tired of waiting."

My head swam and I fought to keep tears at bay. "So what is my purpose for being here? Am I going to work like the other girls? How do you expect me to earn my keep? What's going to happen to me when you get tired of me?"

Grizz eyes turned very serious. "You will never work. You will earn your keep by staying with me. And no man, I mean no man, will ever touch you. No man but me."

So there it was: He was going to rape me. Why hadn't he?

Before I could ask, he added, "The last man who tried to touch you paid for it. So will anyone else who comes near you."

"The last man?" I asked. "Not Matthew, right? Please tell me you didn't hurt Matthew."

"The kid? Nah, I didn't hurt him. The guy that tried to rape you."

"Johnny Tillman?"

"Yeah, Johnny Tillman."

"He knew my stepdad from Smitty's. We called the police and my parents were gonna press charges, but he skipped town so fast that the police never even got to arrest him. Found his truck in front of a supermarket. Figured he hitched a ride out of town."

The part I left out was that I felt the only reason Vince and Delia called the cops was because they were worried Tillman was going after Delia's pot stash. Of course they didn't tell the police that part. They just wanted him arrested so they didn't have to worry about him showing up again. I think there was some sincere concern on their part about him trying to hurt me, but Delia's pot stash was what they were really worried about.

Grizz looked at me then, and I read something in his

expression. I knew immediately.

"He didn't skip town, did he? Did you beat him up and chase him off? Is that what happened to him?" Shock filled me.

"No, I didn't chase him off, but I did beat him up, and when I was done with him, he was begging for me to put him out of his misery."

"Okay, so where is he?"

"I don't know where he is, but I can tell you where he was."

I rolled my eyes. "All right, so where *was* he?"

"About three feet from where you were tossing your dirty water."

Chapter Nine

I'd been at the motel for about a month when Grunt told me everything that happened the night Johnny Tillman was brought to the motel. Even I felt sorry for him after hearing what happened.

It was simple and completely awful. Johnny Tillman was basically relieved of every projecting body part. His ears, his lips, his nose, even his testicles. Grizz slowly cut him to pieces until, like Grizz told me earlier, he was begging for death. Grunt wasn't sure if he was dead or passed out from the pain. Grizz gave the order for him to be tossed into the swamp and the alligators did the rest. That was the end of Johnny Tillman.

When Grunt finished telling me the story I was numb with shock. I couldn't believe it. Who was this person who could hack a man to pieces one day and save a kitten the next?

I'd been sitting on Grunt's bed talking to him. He had invited me in to listen to his albums. I was a little surprised that Grizz said it was okay. He'd seemed so jealous when he asked me about Matthew and told me what he did to Johnny Tillman. I don't know, maybe I read him wrong. Or maybe he just trusted Grunt. Nevertheless, I sat on Grunt's bed, cross-legged, drinking the soda he had offered me. In the background The Moody Blues serenaded us with "Nights In White Satin." It was the first time I'd been in his room, and I was really surprised. It wasn't as fancy as Grizz's. It actually looked like a motel room, but it was neat and clean.

The most surprising thing of all, though, was the books. Where a normal motel room might have two double beds, Grunt's room only had the one bed, and the wall that separated the room from the bathroom had a massive bookshelf that was so full of books, you couldn't see the wall behind it. Books took up every available space on the shelf. And they weren't crammed in randomly, either. When he noticed I couldn't keep my eyes away from the bookshelf, he explained they were sectioned off by genre and then alphabetized by author last name within each genre. I turned to look at him, surprised. Who was this young motorcycle guy? He told me I could borrow any book I wanted.

I noticed a chess set on a TV tray in the corner.

"You play chess?" I asked.

"Yeah, do you?"

"No, but I'd like to learn. Who do you play with?"

"I play Grizz. Sometimes Fess. But it takes too long between Fess's visits for us to play a regular game. I have a game going now with Grizz. You want me to teach you?"

"Definitely." Why not? I thought to myself. It could help pass the days until I could get away from here. Grunt eventually did teach me to play chess. I became good enough to occasionally beat Grizz. Grizz was a good player, and I think chess may have been his only passion aside from the gang and me. I never did beat Grunt, though.

Grunt told me all about himself that night, including how he came to be part of the gang. He told me everything I wanted to know except for one thing. His real name. It was the gang's code: no real names.

Grunt was the youngest of three children. He was born in Miami in 1959. He was only a year older than me. He was raised in what now would be called a dysfunctional family. His father died after he was born. It was an accidental drowning. Up until that point, his mother was a housewife, and according to Grunt she was a useless waste. She resented being left with three kids to raise. Actually, two kids, since Blue wasn't really home all that much.

She worked as a waitress at a local hot dog joint. They were famous for steaming their hot dogs in beer. After she was finished with her shift, she would hang out at the restaurant all night with her divorced girlfriends and spend her tips on beer.

She left the raising of baby Grunt to his older brother and sister. It wasn't long before Blue was getting in trouble with the law, mostly for stealing. His sister, Karen, wasn't much better. He remembers her locking him in his room while she had boyfriends over. She was supposed to be watching him, and he was lucky if he got a peanut butter and jelly sandwich every other day.

If it wasn't for school lunches, he probably would've

starved to death. His neglect didn't go unnoticed by the neighbors, and child welfare was called in several times over the years. Sometimes they removed him from the home and placed him with a foster family.

He didn't have a horrible experience with the foster childcare system. The problem was being pulled in and out of the system and being placed with families in different school districts. His life was constantly being uprooted.

Karen married her twenty-two-year-old boyfriend practically the day she turned eighteen and immediately applied for sole custody of Grunt. Unfortunately, it wasn't because of her kindness and love for her little brother. He was only nine. She was under the impression she was going to get paid to keep him. What she didn't know was that she was not applying as a foster mother; therefore, the state was not going to give her child support.

After she realized this, she tried to force him back on their mother. But by now, his mother had skipped town with an abusive alcoholic trucker she'd met at work. They never heard from her again.

Grunt didn't know then that Blue was still very much in his life. He didn't realize Blue was coming around and giving Karen and her husband money to provide for Grunt. Blue always came at night when Grunt was sleeping. Blue thought Karen and her husband, Nate, were nurturing their little brother, and Blue didn't want to interfere.

It was just by chance that one night, when Blue was there with some cash for his sister, a then-ten-year-old Grunt woke up and came out to the kitchen for a drink of water.

Grunt told me he remembered the look on his big brother's face that night. What Blue saw was a ten-year-old who looked like he was seven. Grunt was wearing only his pajama pants, and he was so thin he had to hold them up by the waistband so they wouldn't fall off his scrawny body. But that wasn't what Blue noticed first. Grunt's body was covered in bruises and blisters from cigarette burns. This was clearly a child who had been abused on a regular basis.

Karen's first reaction was to defend herself. She said Nate was the one who hit on the kid. She never hit him. That didn't matter to Blue. What mattered was that she never stopped Nate.

Just then, Nate got home from work. If he had been just ten minutes late it might have saved his life. That was the night Grunt witnessed his first murder. Two murders, actually. Without saying a word, Blue took out a gun and put a bullet between his sister's eyes. Nate had turned in an attempt to run out the front door, but Blue was too quick. He put one in the back of Nate's head before he took two steps.

He looked at his little brother and told him not to be afraid. He was going to take care of him from now on. Grunt told him he wasn't afraid. Blue smiled and took his jacket off. He wrapped it around his little brother's broken body and carried him out the front door.

Grunt had been with the gang at the Glades Motel since that night.

As I sat there on Grunt's motel bed, I couldn't believe he had shared this with me. It dawned on me that I wouldn't be leaving here after hearing these stories of brutality, and I instantly pushed that thought to the back of my mind.

"So did you get your name, Grunt, because you were the youngest and had to do all the crappy work, the grunt jobs?"

Grunt laughed. "No. The name is a shorter version of my original nickname, when I first got here. I was little for my age, so some of the gang started calling me runt. Like the runt of the litter. As time went by, the group started noticing my smarts. Some said I was the most grown-up runt they'd ever known. I guess I wasn't an average ten-year-old. Grown-up runt was eventually shortened to 'Grunt.'"

I laughed at this description. He was smart. That was interesting. I wondered if he had the mean streak I'd seen in the others, especially Grizz.

"So you're Grunt. I like it. Especially now that I know what it means," I teased.

"Yeah, I guess it's easier than 'Grown Up Runt,' but it's kind of an oxymoron if I ever heard one."

"An oxy what?"

"An oxymoron. Here, look it up," he said as he tossed me a dictionary.

I didn't know then, as I innocently perused the dictionary looking for a word I wasn't sure existed, that I hadn't been invited to Grunt's room to listen to records. I'd been invited to Grunt's room to lose my virginity.

Chapter Ten

Grizz was ready to sleep with me. The problem was he didn't want to force himself on me. He didn't want to be the one to cause that initial hurt. I was going to be his, and he didn't want every time he had sex with me to be a reminder that he'd taken my virginity. So he ordered Grunt to do it.

How he ordered Grunt to do it sickened me, but more than that, I was baffled by it. It would take me awhile to discover the reasoning behind Grizz's strange request. But as time passed, it would make more sense.

Earlier that day, he'd called Grunt into number four. I don't know where I was. Probably outside with Gwinny. He told Grunt to bring me into his room that night and slip me some kind of drug to make me pass out, and to take my virginity. But not with his body. He handed some kind of billy-club to Grunt and told him to cover it with some lotion or something and take care of it. He wanted me to be asleep. He didn't want me to remember it.

Looking back now, it makes sense that Grizz didn't ask one of the girls to do it. He didn't want them to know he hadn't been sleeping with me. As for the comment that no man would ever touch me, he wasn't thinking of Grunt as a man. Grunt had been there since he was ten. Grizz just didn't notice that he had grown into a healthy, virile, sixteen year old. He didn't see Grunt as a threat. As to why Grizz didn't do it himself, it was simple. He couldn't bear to hurt me.

So I was there to be drugged and raped by someone I thought was my new friend.

I was getting drowsy. Grunt had offered me a soda earlier and I'd been drinking it as we talked and listened to his records. I didn't recognize the drowsiness for what it was and stood up and told him I had to go back to number four. I was getting really sleepy.

He stood up and gently grabbed my arm. "Don't leave yet, Kit. Stay here with me."

"Why? I don't think Grizz would like me to take a nap in your room, Grunt."

He looked uncomfortable then, and I immediately sensed something was up, but I never imagined how deplorable it was.

"Please just sit down. Actually, lay down. You can fall asleep here. It'll be okay. I promise."

My senses were on alert and adrenaline kicked in, temporarily killing the buzz.

"What is this? Tell me what's going on, Grunt. You have to tell me. Oh!" My mind went into overdrive, and I started to panic. "You're going to kill me in my sleep, aren't you?

He's decided he doesn't want me, and he can't let me leave. I'm going to die tonight, aren't I?"

"Kit, I'm not going to kill you. Grizz doesn't want you dead. I want you to sleep because I don't want you to have an awful memory. Please don't ask me anymore, just sleep. Trust me. You're not going to die." Grunt fisted his hands. "Fuck! I wish he'd handle this himself."

"Handle what?" I blinked my eyes open, willing myself to stay coherent. "And no, I'm not laying down. Not until you tell me. I'm going to make myself stay awake. You put something in my drink, didn't you? Well, I didn't finish it and I'm not going to. You have to tell me."

He sighed and walked over to his dresser. He pulled out the bottom drawer and removed what looked like some kind of stick. He told me it was an old billy-club. It was on the smallish side and had a strap at one end so it could be held on one's wrist.

"You're going to beat me with that stick?" If he was going to kill me it would take a lot of blows. I felt nausea rising in my stomach.

"No Kit. Grizz wants you to lose your virginity tonight. He didn't want to do it. He told me to do it. With this." He looked down at what he was holding. His face was flushed.

"And you have to do everything he tells you?" My voice rose.

"What do you think? If you'd just fallen asleep you would've woken up a little sore. I would have done my best not to hurt you."

I sat on the edge of the bed and looked at the floor. He just stood in front of the dresser still holding the offensive object. I wasn't going to be able to stay awake forever. I had to make a decision.

"You do it." I said to him. "You personally, not with the stick. Please, Grunt. I can't lose my virginity to something so vile. You do it."

"He would kill us both if he knew."

"He'll never hear it from me. I swear. Please, I can't stand the thought of you sticking that in me. It's awful. Please. We'll never talk about it again after tonight. Please, Grunt."

He didn't say anything, so I added, "I'm on birth control so I won't get pregnant. He'll never have to know."

Well, this was certainly something I never expected. Here I was begging to be raped. I still can't get over the irony of how that happened, but it did.

He walked over to me then, and I stood up. Then he did something I never expected. He hugged me. He held me close to him for almost a full minute. I was shaky on my feet, and he eventually let go.

I started to undo my jeans and he undid his. I laid back on the bed and struggled to pull my pants off. The adrenaline was wearing off, and I was starting to get drowsy again. He helped me pull my jeans and panties down. I knew he took his off too, but I didn't look. He reached for some hand cream that was on his nightstand and coated himself with it. Again, I didn't look, but I could tell by his movements.

He was on top of me now and gently spread my legs with his knee. I just looked at him. We made eye contact then, and I said, "Can you call me by my name, just once? Can you call me Ginny?"

"I'll try not to hurt you," and then after a pause, he softly whispered, "Ginny."

"Please. Please tell me your name. I'll never tell. I

swear," I pleaded.

"I can't do that. You know that. You shouldn't have even told me your name."

I was starting to pass out now. I could feel him slowly entering me. I closed my eyes. I opened them as he entered me fully. I registered some discomfort, a burning sensation, but no real pain.

I was starting to go under again. I quickly opened my eyes in an attempt to stay awake. But to no avail. They were slowly closing. As they were closing for the last time and I was losing consciousness, I was certain I saw tears in his eyes.

And I heard him say, "Tommy. My name is Tommy."

Chapter Eleven

I don't know how long it was before I woke up, but when I did, Grizz and Grunt were standing at the foot of the bed talking.

"What the fuck do you mean she was awake? She wasn't supposed to know anything. Damn it, Grunt!"

"She didn't drink enough and wanted to go back to your room to go to sleep."

"So she was awake and felt it. You hurt her?"

"Fuck, I don't know, Grizz. She was starting to pass out. I don't know what she'll remember, if anything."

I stirred then and realized I'd been covered. I could tell Grunt must have managed to get my underwear back on me. They must have sensed I was awake because they both stopped talking and looked at me at the same time.

"I hate you both," is all I said.

As I got myself off the bed and reached for my jeans, I noticed Grunt wouldn't make eye contact with me. Grizz had no problem, though. With an expression on his face that I couldn't read, he said, "You'll be okay," and left the room.

I wouldn't look at Grunt as I fidgeted with my jeans. I slipped my feet back into my sandals and said "thanks for the drink" with as much sarcasm as I could muster. I left the room. It was dark out. Exactly how long had I been in Grunt's room? Well, it didn't matter now. I'm certain that was one room I would never be seeing again.

I walked toward number four and found myself pausing just as I was ready to open the door. What if Grizz wanted me now? I wasn't in pain, but I was sore. I closed my eyes, took a breath and opened the door.

He was on the phone when I went in. I saw Gwinny cuddled up in a corner of the couch. I went to check her litter box, and since it didn't need cleaning, I went to the couch and picked her up.

Something occurred to me. What if I smelled like Grunt? He wore some kind of cologne. I thought he smelled good the few times I'd been around him. I needed to get a shower, but the last thing I wanted to do was take my clothes off anywhere near Grizz. I would just have to do it quickly.

I made a dash for the bedroom quickly shutting the door behind me. Once inside I stripped bare as fast as I could and went into the bathroom and started the shower. When it was warm enough I stepped in and started to wash myself. Just then the bathroom door opened and the shower curtain was pulled aside. I tried to cover myself with my hands. It was Grizz, and he just stared at me.

As far as I know, this was the first time he had seen me naked. What I saw in his eyes scared me to death. It wasn't a violent look like I remember seeing on Johnny Tillman's face. It was the look of a man that desired a woman. Grizz didn't want to hurt me like Johnny, but it was obvious that he wanted me. I just stared back at him.

"You sore?"

"Yes, very. It hurt."

"You remember then? You were awake?"

"I remember a little. I started falling asleep as it happened."

That seemed to satisfy him because he didn't say anything else and left the bathroom. I finished washing and dried off. I went out into the bedroom with a towel wrapped around me and got some clothes out of the dresser. I started to walk back toward the bathroom to change when he said, "You change in front of me from now on. No need to be hiding anything."

He was letting me get dressed. So what if it was in front of him? I doubt he would be letting me get dressed if he intended to have sex with me.

I slipped my underwear up underneath the towel. Then I struggled to pull a nightshirt over my head while trying to keep the towel up. It wasn't easy. I was shaky. I don't know if it was nerves or the drug wearing off. Probably a combination of both. I reluctantly dropped the towel, put on the nightshirt as quickly as I could and went back into the bathroom to brush my teeth and comb my wet hair.

When I came out I noticed a small duffel bag on the bed. What was this? I could hear him talking outside the bedroom. I thought I heard Blue's voice. Just then, Grizz came back into the bedroom and picked up the duffel bag.

"You have three days to get over being sore. I'll be back on Wednesday. Blue is in charge. I told him Grunt could take you off the grounds. Same rules apply. You have any notions of getting away from him just know that I will find you, Kit. Have no doubt about that."

I couldn't believe it. I was getting a reprieve from sex with him and I was going to be allowed to leave the motel? This was the best thing to happen since he let me keep Gwinny.

"Where are you going?"

"Business." he said as he walked to the bedroom door.

He stopped and turned around. He walked over to me and lifted my chin up to look in my eyes. He didn't say anything right away, and I wasn't sure if he was going to say something or maybe even kiss me.

"What I made Grunt do was for the best. You are never to tell anyone what he did to you. You hear me? And don't forget Kit, you're mine. Only mine. And I will have you when I get back."

With that he kissed me lightly on the forehead, spun around and walked out the bedroom door. As he approached the front door, he yelled back to me, "Don't forget to feed my dogs," and then he was gone.

Chapter Twelve

I slept like a baby that night. I'd had number four to myself before, but Grizz was always still nearby. Now I had three whole days to myself. The next morning, I got up and pretty much played housewife. I wouldn't let myself think about the night before. I pretended I was in my own little apartment as I did all the chores. I had started doing most of them anyway, and I think Chicky and Moe appreciated it, but Willow didn't. Taking care of Grizz was the one thing she liked to do, though I think she was feeling somewhat self-conscious after losing that front tooth. She visited the pit regularly, but eventually stopped coming by number four. I busied myself with dusting, sweeping, scrubbing the bathroom. One of the units had a washer and dryer. I did some laundry. I even cleaned out the refrigerator.

After an hour and a half I was bored stiff. What was I

going to do with myself? I knew Grizz said I could leave the grounds with Grunt, but I didn't know if I could face him. My feelings were so conflicted.

But the more I thought about it, the madder I got. It occurred to me that maybe the only reason Grizz said I could leave with Grunt was because he didn't think I would. After all, I'd told them both I hated them when I woke up. That was it. Grizz was certain my hatred wouldn't let me take him up on the offer to leave. Well, I would show him.

I certainly wasn't happy with Grunt. I mean, let's face it. Was I supposed to thank him for "raping me nicely"? It sounded ludicrous. But my boredom and restlessness won out over anger and pride, and I found myself knocking on his door by ten o'clock that morning.

He answered wearing nothing but a pair of jeans. I was speechless. I don't know what I expected, but it wasn't Grunt wearing only his jeans. I had never seen him with his shirt off before, and I guess I expected a skinny kid body. He wasn't big, but he wasn't skinny by any means. He was toned and had a taut stomach that showed his abs. His arms were not as gigantic as Grizz's, but they were definitely muscular.

I hadn't given much notice to Grunt's looks before, but as I stared I realized he was really a good-looking guy. He was about five foot nine inches tall. I'd say he weighed around a hundred and seventy pounds. He had dark hair and brown eyes that had green flecks. He had a tall forehead like me, which had always been my reason for wearing bangs, but on him, it was nice. For the first time, I noticed two small silver hoop earrings in his left ear. I was certain he'd never worn them before. Grizz had an earring, too. I'd seen guys with earrings at Woodstock, but in the seventies it still wasn't that common. Especially two.

But what caught my attention the most, though, was his tattoo. Grunt's arms and neck weren't covered in tattoos like everybody else's—even the women. Grunt had one tattoo. It was of a huge bird, its head facing down the side of his right arm, not quite reaching his elbow. Its wings were fanned out down the inside of his arm and across his chest. They were massive and covered most of his chest in a sweeping arrangement. Right below the bird's wing was a serious scar; I wondered if it was from his childhood abuse.

He didn't say anything to me, just turned and walked back into the room. I followed and couldn't help but notice the tattoo continued onto his back. It was like this bird had its wings wrapped around him. It was beautiful.

"Wow. Your tattoo is really nice," I managed to say. He didn't answer me but walked over to his stereo and turned it off. I hadn't noticed anything was even playing. I had been so distracted by his body and tattoo.

He looked at me then. "You okay?"

"Yeah, I'm fine I guess." Before he could say anything else, I added, "Grizz said you could take me out. Off the motel grounds. Did you know that?"

"Blue told me."

"Will you? Will you take me out somewhere? Anywhere?"

"I don't know. It could turn bad. Probably not a good idea."

"Look, I thought we were friends. I thought we made a connection."

He raised an eyebrow at this. "Thought you hated me."

"I thought I did too when I woke up. Look at it from my standpoint, Grunt. I woke up and you and Grizz were standing there. I knew you must have dressed me and covered me up. It was humiliating. But can't we just forget it and move on? I'm dying to do something. Anything. Please?"

He smiled then and said to give him ten minutes to shower and change. He told me I could look through his albums and put on whatever I wanted.

Grunt had a ton of albums, and I settled on something from Fleetwood Mac. I sat on the edge of the bed and started to look around the room. The first time I was there I was fascinated by the bookshelf and didn't pay much attention to anything else. Now my eye caught a stack of mail on his nightstand. Mail? He gets mail here?

I could still hear the shower running so I went and picked up the letters. They were all addressed to Michael Freeman. Michael Freeman? That's his name? I could have sworn I heard a different name when I was losing consciousness. I noticed they all were from different educational institutions and addressed to a post office box in Davie. Davie wasn't really developed back then. It was more like a little country town for people who loved horses. It was as rural as you were going to get in South Florida and was just east of where I was now. So Davie had a post office and that's where he got his mail. My mind filed away the information. Interesting.

I didn't realize the shower had turned off. I didn't even hear him open the bathroom door and come out. When I realized he was watching me, I jumped and laid the mail back on his nightstand.

"Your real name is Michael Freeman? I thought you said it was—"

"It's not Michael Freeman," he said quickly, cutting me

off. "It's an alias, Kit. I needed to have an alias to be able to still exist. I couldn't use my real name because, well, you know we don't use real names here, but also because I'm the kid who's been missing for six years. Probably presumed kidnapped and murdered by the person who killed my family."

"Why do you need an alias, anyway?"

"Well, I could hardly apply for college with the name Grunt, could I?"

"College? You're applying to college? How are you going to do that?"

"After I became Michael Freeman, I finished high school through a correspondence course."

"How could you finish high school? What are you, in tenth or eleventh grade, maybe?"

"Well, I should be in eleventh grade, but I'm not. I'm a junior at Cole University."

"Are you kidding me? You're *in* college? You already go to college?"

"Yes, I go to college and yes, I'm young for that, but I've always been pretty smart and I want to make something of myself."

"How can you be that smart? You told me what your childhood was like. How did you live like that and still flourish?"

Again, the raised eyebrow. He walked over and picked up the stack of letters and pulled one out. He opened it and handed me one single page. I'm certain my mouth dropped open as I read what was neatly typed. It was from a testing facility, congratulating Michael Freeman on his IQ test scores.

Apparently, my new buddy Grunt was a real honest-to-

God genius.

Chapter Thirteen

Before we left Grunt's room, he asked me what I was wearing the day I was abducted. After I described the outfit and he was satisfied I wasn't wearing anything from that day, not even my peace choker, he picked up a baseball cap that had been sitting on his dresser. He had me tuck my bangs up under the cap and put my hair in a ponytail that came through the back. He then picked up a pair of sunglasses and told me, "You can wear mine until we get you your own."

As we were leaving, I noticed his jacket slung across the back of his desk chair. "Aren't you going to wear your jacket?"

"No reason to call undue attention to the group." He picked up a wallet and a set of keys off his dresser, and we walked out.

I followed him around the side of the motel where the office was located. I'd never really explored over here before. When we got around the side, I saw two cars. Really nice cars. One was a black Corvette, which I knew was Grizz's; he must have taken one of his bikes for his business trip.

We headed toward the other one. It was a light blue Camaro. I wasn't sure of the year, but I knew it was an older model. Just old enough to be stylish.

"We're not going to take your bike?"

I think I was disappointed. For some reason, being on the back of a motorcycle behind Grunt was appealing. Where was this coming from?

"Don't have a helmet for you yet. I don't think you want to borrow one either," he laughed. "Actually, that's something we can do. Let's go get you a helmet."

"I don't have any money."

"You don't need any."

He unlocked the passenger side of the car and let me in. After he got in and started the loud engine, he turned on the air conditioner. Then he took an eight-track tape and stuck it in the player. We were listening to Simon & Garfunkel as we pulled onto State Road 84. Simon & Garfunkel? I laughed to myself. I was beginning to think Grunt might be a nerd.

We didn't talk as we made our way east on State Road 84. He made a left on U.S. 441 and we headed north. I was so close to home I could almost smell it. It was so strange passing by familiar places. After a few miles, though, we were out of my territory, and I started to feel less anxious.

"Where are we going?" I leaned my head back on the seat, trying to relax.

"Little shop up near Riverview. They have helmets."

I watched the scenery fly by, feeling calmer by the minute. "So just out of curiosity, where does the gang have their meetings?"

He looked quickly over at me. "Meetings? You mean when they gather in the pit?"

"No. You know, the satanic rituals and stuff. The gang is named after the devil. Even Grizz's dog's names are pretty bad. I figured maybe you use one of the old unused rooms at the motel. You know, to worship."

He threw his head back and laughed. "Kit, we don't worship the devil."

"It's on your jacket." I think I blushed.

"Yeah, to scare the shit out of people. It's not a religion."

"You're not devil-worshipers?" I'd worried about this for awhile and had even secretly wondered if Grizz had let me keep my black kitten for another, more sinister, reason.

"Hell, no!" He was laughing hard now.

"But you believe in hell, though. I mean, if it's your logo and stuff."

"No, Kit." He shook his head, still smiling. "I don't believe in the devil or hell. Don't believe in anything, really."

"What about God?" I turned to look at him. "You believe in God, don't you?"

"No, don't know much about anything that has to do with religion."

"For all of your studying and schooling, you've never taken a class on religion?" My eyes were wide. "You know, world religion, religious philosophy, anything?"

"Nothing." He paused, then asked, "That thing you do, before you eat, is that religious?"

"You mean blessing myself?" Being a Catholic, I'd

always made the sign of the cross prior to saying grace before a meal.

"I don't know what it's called."

It was my turn to smile. "You said you would teach me to play chess. Will you let me teach you something?"

He hesitated. "Yeah, sure. Why not?"

And so began Grunt's lessons in religion, specifically Christianity.

I let myself enjoy the rest of the ride as we talked. I even convinced him to turn off the air conditioning and roll down the windows. I felt oddly exhilarated. We got to the shop and I picked out a helmet fairly fast. The guy who worked there knew Grunt and never made any indication that he expected us to pay. We walked out of the shop less then fifteen minutes later.

I wasn't really familiar with this part of town. To get to the shop, we had turned off U.S. 441 and were now on some shady-looking backstreets. It was an odd mixture of businesses and old houses, kind of like someone messed up badly with the zoning ordinances. Next to the shop, I saw a guy building a wooden fence. I wondered if it was his fence or if he was the hired help. He had given me a disturbing look on the way into the shop.

Now as we were coming out, he yelled, "Hey, sweet thing. You wanna spend some time with a real man, why don't you come on over here? Tell your baby brother he can come back for you in an hour. Make that ten minutes." Then he gave this awful laugh that turned into fits of coughing. What a creep.

I looked over at Grunt, who just ignored him. Well, that's good. If I was with Grizz, I'd probably be an accessory to murder. Honestly though, if I was with Grizz, I bet Mr.

Build-A-Fence wouldn't have said a word. Still, it was probably a good thing I was with the youngest of the group. I didn't want any trouble.

After we got inside the car, Grunt said he wanted the air conditioning on this time. We rolled up the windows, and he started the car and turned on the A/C. He took the Simon & Garfunkel eight-track tape out and stuck in Pink Floyd. Then he turned to me.

"Stay here. Do not get out of this car for any reason. You got it?"

Before I could answer, he blared the music really loud and got out of the car. He started walking toward Mr. Build-A-Fence. Oh no. Oh, dear God. Grunt is going to try to act all tough and get the crap kicked out of him. I looked around, wondering what in the world I was going to do if something happened.

They disappeared behind a part of the fence that was already built, so I couldn't see anything, and with the music up so loud, I couldn't hear anything, either. After a few nervous minutes, I decided maybe I should turn down the music. But before I could, Grunt came walking around the side of the fence. He looked okay. He didn't look hurt. Maybe he told the guy someone was going to come back and kick the crap out of him. Grunt jumped in the car, and before I could say a word, we took off. I decided not to mention it.

We spent the next couple of hours running errands—picked up some groceries, got gas, went by the drugstore. I even got some new sunglasses. Grunt was careful to pick out-of-the way places. By mid-afternoon, we got back to the motel, and he went to his room. I went to number four to check on Gwinny and make sure the dogs were fed. Grunt reminded me I could borrow any of his books any time I wanted. I thanked him for the day and I told him I would definitely take him up on his offer.

As evening approached, I decided to stay inside. The pit had no appeal for me, and I made myself a bowl of cereal and sat on the couch to watch TV. I decided to watch some local news. I was always hopeful of seeing something about me, but too much time had passed and I'm pretty sure my abduction never made the news in the first place. I was certain the police didn't take it seriously, anyway. One visit with Delia and they would have assumed me to be a runaway. Of that I had no doubt.

I flipped impatiently through the few channels we had. Those were the days before cable and you watched what was in your viewing range. The volume was turned down, and I thought I saw a reporter standing in front of a familiar place. I turned it up.

"We're at the house of Raymond Price," the attractive reporter was saying. "Earlier today, Mr. Price was rescued by a couple walking their dog who heard muffled screams. When they investigated, they found Mr. Price had been brutally attacked. He was found standing with his back to a fence with his hands stretched out on each side." The reporter paused here for effect. "Mr. Price's hands were nailed to the wooden fence he had been building. There were several nails in each hand, making it impossible for him to get himself free without ripping his hands to shreds. A rag had been stuffed in his mouth making it difficult to call for help."

The reporter then squinted as she listened to someone asking her a question from the small crowd that had gathered.

"I've just been asked if Mr. Price could identify the person or persons who assaulted him," she said, her pretty face frowning. "In a strange twist, the Riverview Police Department told us Mr. Price has refused to tell them anything. They're concerned he might have been threatened and is afraid of retaliation. Police say this particular area is well known for motorcycle gangs. One gang in particular has been known to frequent this shop next door."

The camera panned over behind the reporter, and my stomach roiled. I now saw why the scene looked so familiar. Right there on TV, I could see the shop where we had picked out my helmet that afternoon, and the newly constructed fence dividing it from the house next door.

I couldn't believe what I was seeing. My heart pounded thickly. I swallowed and took a deep breath.

I had read Grunt all wrong. He was no defenseless runt.

He was one of them.

Chapter Fourteen

Just then, the door flew open and Blue came in, walking straight toward me.

"Get up. Now. You're coming with me."

Before I could ask anything, he walked past me to the bedroom and found my backpack hanging on a hook behind the door. I followed him into the bedroom, pelting him with questions about what was going on. He was too focused to talk. He kept looking around the room.

"Where's your stuff, Kit? You got anything personal here? Like if you were going to stay overnight somewhere, what would you need?"

My hands were shaking. "Where am I going?"

"I don't have time to explain anything to you. What would you have to have with you?"

Without answering him I went into the bathroom. I took

my birth control pills, my toothbrush and my hairbrush. I opened a dresser drawer and grabbed some underwear and a nightshirt. I opened another dresser and grabbed some shorts and tank tops. I still only had my one bra, which I was now wearing. I guess that was one article of clothing I needed to try on for myself. I quickly stuffed everything into the bag.

"Good girl." He saw my new helmet sitting on the coffee table and picked it up. "Get your shoes on. We gotta go. Now."

I dashed to the kitchen counter and picked up my reading glasses. I shoved them in my bag along with a magazine as I slid my feet into sandals. I was still wearing what I had on that day. A pair of jeans and an unremarkable top. He carried my helmet and I followed him out.

"Gwinny!" I shouted, remembering the cat.

"She'll be okay. Moe will take care of her and the dogs. Let's go!"

We were on his motorcycle and I was still fastening my helmet when we sped out of the motel and onto State Road 84. My arms wrapped tightly around him as we drove off into the night. We took State Road 84 east and turned right at Pete's. This was Flamingo Road, and as it was the seventies, just like on State Road 84, we were in totally undeveloped territory. Flamingo Road was mostly pastureland.

Fear began to fade. At one point, I even laughed to myself as we passed an old two-story house with a big sign in front of it. The owner had spray-painted in big, black letters on a piece of plywood propped up on his second-story porch: "Wife wanted. Must cook and clean. Husband will pay bills." That particular wannabe husband has since sold that property. I'm pretty sure a shopping plaza is there now.

We headed south on Flamingo until we got to a little town called Pembroke Pines. We turned left onto Taft Street and were suddenly in a beautiful and tastefully landscaped housing development. After a few more turns, we pulled up to a very nice house. Someone inside must have heard the motorcycle, because the garage door opened as if on cue. Blue pulled the bike in and cut the engine.

As I lifted myself off the back, I noticed an attractive, tall and very tanned brunette standing at the door that led from the garage into the house. She had her finger on the garage door opener, and as I waited for Blue to get off his bike, the door went down. She walked toward me then and held out her hand.

"Hi. I'm Jan. Blue's wife," she said, smiling warmly. "You're just in time for dinner."

I couldn't have been more surprised than I was the day Moe showed me into Grizz's room. Blue's *wife*? It had never occurred to me that Blue, or any other member of the gang, could have been married or actually lived somewhere other than the motel. I just hadn't paid enough attention to what everyone else was doing.

Blue and I followed Jan into the house. Just then, two little boys ran toward Blue and grabbed him around his legs. They were both wearing matching overalls without a shirt underneath. They were young, and it looked like the smaller of the two was wobbly on his feet. He was probably just a little over a year old. His older brother was maybe three.

"Daddy! Daddy! Play with us," the oldest roared.

"Let him have some dinner, boys, and then Daddy can

spend time with you," Jan told them, laughing.

"Who that girl is?" the oldest asked.

"This is Kit," Blue said gently. "She's my friend. You boys be good while we eat dinner and I'll come see you in a little bit."

They bounded away happily toward what looked like a very comfortable family room. The TV was on and toys were everywhere.

"I already fed them." Jan explained. "C'mon. Let's eat."

Since my dinner of cereal and milk was interrupted, I was eager to eat the meal set before us. I made the sign of the cross and said a mental blessing. Then, while Blue talked, I thoroughly enjoyed the homemade meatloaf, mashed potatoes and green beans. He explained the reason for our abrupt departure from the motel.

Moments before I had seen the news clip about Mr. Build-A-Fence's attack, Blue was getting paged at work by Grizz. Grizz had been tipped off that the police were going to be visiting the motel. Apparently, Grizz had people everywhere, including the various police departments in South Florida.

Not everyone had pagers back then. They were relatively new, but I wasn't surprised to know Grizz and some in his group had them. The key to communicating through a pager, though, was you had to find a phone to call back the number the pager digitally displayed. It was easy enough for Blue to call Grizz back. He was on top of a telephone pole doing a repair. He'd tapped into a line and called Grizz immediately.

This was also something I'd been clueless about. Blue worked for the telephone company?

"But why would the police be coming to the motel?" I

asked, pushing my other questions aside.

"After the little stunt Grunt pulled, there would definitely be a police visit," Blue said, shaking his head.

"But how would they know it was Grunt?" I asked, confused. "We didn't have a motorcycle. He wasn't wearing his jacket. Heck, we never even paid for my helmet so it's not like there's a receipt to trace. And anyway, how did *you* know it was Grunt?"

"Grizz has eyes everywhere." Blue said. "And it doesn't matter if it was Grunt or not. Just the mention of a motorcycle gang and there are certain police departments that jump on any excuse to come out to the motel and try and shake things up. They know our base, and Grizz wanted you out of there."

Jan passed over some more mashed potatoes. "I saw the news. I could have guessed your baby brother had something to do with that," she said to Blue with a smile. "Grunt is quite the creative tormentor."

She said this with the attitude of a proud mother as she then helped herself to more green beans. I looked up from my plate. Creative tormentor? What an odd description. I looked over at Blue, who was watching Jan with an expression I couldn't read. Before either of us could say anything or question her comment, she started talking about something cute one of the kids did earlier that day. I looked toward the family room where those two sweet little boys were playing. *Yes, Mrs. Misplaced Pride, your son is the one responsible for blowing up that building. You should be so proud.* These people were a mystery.

I shook my head in disbelief. "Will Grunt get in trouble with the police?"

"No." Blue sounded casual. "There's no doubt the guy

won't identify him. There's nothing to tie him to the scene. Even if his car was identified, it won't matter. They'd never think a kid could do that to a grown man. They'll just go to the motel with their warrant and look around and try to dig up anything they can on Grizz. He's the one they want anyway."

"What about Grizz, though? Will Grunt be in trouble with him?"

"Don't know. He'll have some explaining to do. It's up to Grizz."

I didn't understand. "But aren't you scared or worried for him? I mean, he's your brother."

Blue just shrugged and spooned some more green beans onto his plate. "Grunt's old enough to face the consequences. He knows what he can and can't get away with. At some point, you have to let people fight their own battles and take responsibility for their choices."

That night, as I tucked myself comfortably into the bed in Jan and Blue's guestroom, I couldn't help but worry about Grunt. My friend.

It turned out the police did raid Grizz's rooms that night. If circumstances were different, I might have been rescued. If someone had remembered the girl who went missing was talking to a guy with a motorcycle out in front of the 7-Eleven. If someone had remembered seeing me climb on Monster's bike, even if they didn't see his jacket, it might have sparked some recognition in the officers who were combing through Grizz's rooms. If there was even a hint that I could have been abducted by a motorcycle gang, then the police officers that searched Grizz's rooms might have noticed some clues.

Like the three county library books sitting on top of the

dresser with my brown peace choker draped across them.

Chapter Fifteen

But they didn't notice. They weren't looking for a kidnapping victim. They were looking for drugs or some other type of connection to Grizz's illicit dealings. I wasn't even on their radar.

The next morning Blue told me he would take me back to the motel before he went to work. It was clear. The police were gone.

Jan made a counter offer. "You know, Kit, you're welcome to spend the day with us. I mean, Blue has to work, but the boys and I are home by ourselves. We could hang out and lay by the pool while Timmy and Kevin play. Just have some girlfriend time, if you want."

I looked over at Blue to get his approval. Before he could say a word, Timmy started jumping up and down and yelling, "Kit! Kit can stay with us. Kit can swim in the pool and be here and be friends with mommy!"

Timmy looked like a miniature version of Blue. I glanced at the youngest, Kevin. I imagined this was how Grunt looked at his age. I could definitely see a family resemblance.

I smiled down at them. Grunt never told me he had two adorable nephews. As an only child myself, I was anxious to accept Jan's offer. But it would be up to Blue.

Blue seemed hesitant at first, but then said, "Sure. I can bring you back tonight or send someone to get you. Just don't leave the house, okay? We've had enough drama."

He kissed Jan on the lips, then bent down and kissed each child on the head. He then ruffled their hair and went out the door. I didn't hear the motorcycle start, and I walked over to the front window.

"Surprised, aren't you?" Jan asked. She must have been reading my mind. "It's not all about the gang, you know. A lot of them have families, like Blue. It's not always about the motorcycles, either."

She nodded at something out the window, and I noticed Blue driving away in a small gold pickup truck. I hadn't noticed it when we pulled in yesterday.

She smiled at me then and said, "Want to help me get these monsters fed? I have a couple of things to do around the house, and then we can spend the rest of the day out back by the pool."

I was only too eager to help, and before I knew it, we had fed the boys and cleaned up the kitchen. She told me to watch TV or relax while she did some chores. She took the children in the family room and went to a closet.

"Okay, boys, special toy time," she said as she pulled what looked like a large laundry bag out of the closet. She proceeded to dump a huge pile of blocks on the floor. Timmy and Kevin were excited. They obviously loved playing with these blocks, and they jumped up and down and clapped. Jan smiled at me. "It's amazing how just keeping back a little something from them makes it more special. They will spend hours stacking these blocks, knocking them down and then starting all over again."

I decided I really liked Jan. I asked her if I could help do anything. I'd seen enough TV. I wanted to start some girlfriend time. We spent the morning chatting. We alternated between small chores and spending time with the kids. I would fold laundry while she ironed a couple of Blue's shirts. I swept the kitchen floor while she emptied the dishwasher. I watered her houseplants while she stripped down the boys' beds. It was an amicable and comfortable morning. She shared some things with me I should have known but never really gave much thought to.

For instance, I hadn't paid much attention to the comings and goings of the gang. I was under the assumption almost all of them lived at the motel and their job was whatever gang activities they participated in. I was wrong. The only full-time residents of the motel were Grizz, Grunt, Moe and Chowder.

I interrupted her. "What about Willow? The first night I was there she said something to Grizz about waiting for him in their room." Jan explained that Willow didn't live at the motel full-time, but had use of the empty rooms whenever she wanted. They all did.

Chowder was a quiet, unassuming part of the gang. I'd not given him much thought. I'm not sure I ever even heard him speak. No, I wasn't worried about his tongue. I'm pretty sure he was just a quiet guy. He was a master carpenter by trade, and he was the one responsible for remodeling Grizz's units. He was the motel handyman and maintenance person. He took care of the yard and anything else that needed fixing—clogged toilets, broken windows, fuse boxes. He even made sure the light bulbs were replaced when they blew out. Of course, it was a rundown old motel, and there was only so much fixing he could do. It wasn't necessary for him to concern himself with things like the playground equipment, the old gas pumps or the empty, cement pool.

Jan couldn't tell me a whole lot about Moe. I tried to fish around for information on why she lost her tongue. I wasn't going to outright ask so I tried dropping subtle hints about my curiosity. Either she didn't take the bait, didn't know or decided she wouldn't be the one to tell me. She breezed over Moe and went right to her favorite of the group: her brother-in-law, Grunt.

Jan was really fond of Grunt. She told me how he had always been welcome to live with her and Blue, but had decided not to. He'd been so young when Blue had brought him to the motel. Blue used to live there then. Grunt was only there a year when Blue met Jan and moved out.

"Wasn't he worried about leaving his little brother with Grizz?"

"No, never," Jan said, her pretty brown eyes thoughtful. "Grizz was always good and fair to Grunt. I don't think Grizz has any family, and just like that kitten of yours he rescued, he watched over Grunt when Blue wasn't around. Yeah, I heard what happened with the kitten," she said as I gave her a curious look.

She continued, "Grunt has always been an old soul. I think he'd been disillusioned with domestic life from his home experience and then foster care. I really believe he likes being on his own. But he's always welcome here. I've loved him dearly from the beginning."

From the little I knew about Grunt, I had to agree with her. An old soul? Delia once told me I was an old soul. I'd never heard anyone else ever called that before.

The chores were finally done and the little ones went down easily for their nap. Jan told me they were only thirteen months apart. They sure were cuties. She took me in the master bedroom and opened a dresser drawer and started pulling out bathing suits. "Let's find you something to wear," she said. "Pick out anything you like and try it on. I've got my favorite drying over the shower rod. I'll be out in a few."

She went into the bathroom and shut the door. I looked through the pile of suits and settled on a yellow bikini that tied at the hips. It was adjustable so it should fit. Jan was tall and slender. I was short and slender, but maybe just a little curvier. I put the bathing suit on. I was tying the straps at my left hip when she came out.

Jan stopped and looked at me. "How old are you again?"

"Fifteen, why?" I was starting to feel a little self-conscious.

"You don't look fifteen."

I turned and looked at myself in the mirror over their dresser. I could see what she meant. The bikini bottom fit me perfectly. The top; however, was a little too small. I guess I had a bigger chest than she did and my breasts looked like they were struggling to break free of the yellow fabric.

"You look better in that than I do. You can keep it."

I thanked her as we got some towels and headed for the backyard. We laid in the sun the rest of the afternoon. Jan left the boy's bedroom window cracked, and when we heard Timmy and Kevin waking from their nap we went in and made them some lunch. Then we changed them into their swimming trunks and brought them out back. They were too small to go in the built-in pool by themselves, so they played in a little blow-up pool in the grass next to the concrete. When Jan and I wanted to cool off, we each took one in the pool with us.

I really enjoyed myself and was sorry when Blue got home. I guess Jan hadn't realized the time, because she kept apologizing, saying she was sorry she didn't think to fix me some dinner before I had to go back to the motel. I told her it was no problem. I had plenty to eat back there. She told Blue she would have dinner ready after he got back from returning me to the motel.

I went into the guest room to change. I was packing my bag when Jan knocked lightly and walked in. I smiled at her and told her I thought I'd gotten everything, but if I forgot something, maybe we could spend another day together and I could get it then. I was smiling at her and waiting for her to say something.

But Jan just stood there in her bathing suit, the towel wrapped tightly around her.

"Blue told me he sees Grunt watching you." An icy look matched the tone in her voice. "You better not be leading him on. If you do anything, I mean anything, to make Grizz think there is anything between you and Grunt, and he hurts Grunt in any way, I will personally see to it that you suffer."

I was so shocked by her change in personality, I couldn't

even respond.

She continued, "I know what you think. I've seen your kind. You think because you're with that hulking ape you can get away with anything. Well, just know things don't last. It won't be long before Blue is running that show and your ass will be grass then. And if you're even thinking about telling Grizz we had this conversation? Well, let's just say, Kit"—she practically spat my name—"that accidents happen all the time. You understand? You know now who you're dealing with?"

Yeah, I knew who I was dealing with. Psycho woman of the century, that's who.

I'd had enough drama for one month. I picked my bag up and slung it over one shoulder. Then I looked her right in the eyes and with a tone that said she was nothing more than an ant to be stepped on, I said, "Fuck you, Jan."

I walked past her, and as I headed down the hallway toward the front door I couldn't resist one last parting shot.

"You know, Jan," I said in as sweet a voice as I could muster. "If Blue's late for supper, I'm sure it's because he's getting one of those fantastic blow jobs Chicky is famous for."

And with that, I picked my helmet up off the bench by the front door and walked out.

Chapter Sixteen

Blue was revving his bike in the driveway. I put my helmet on and jumped on the back. We sped off. I didn't look back.

It took us almost thirty minutes to get back to the motel, and I battled my inner demons the whole way. Who was that girl who'd spouted profanities at Jan? Did Jan deserve them? Absolutely. Was I the type to deliver them? No way. I didn't even *think* curse words. That was not who I was.

As far as the Chicky comment was concerned, I had no idea of her specialties in or out of the bedroom. I made that up. If being with Grizz for one month had this kind of effect on me, what was being with him forever—as he had indicated more than once—going to do to me?

It didn't matter. I'd had a lapse in judgment brought on by the shock of her sudden change in personality. I certainly was no mental health expert, but it was obvious that she had problems. Poor Timmy and Kevin. Poor Blue. The irony that I was feeling sorry for a man who'd killed his sister and her husband without a second thought wasn't lost on me.

But then again, maybe Jan didn't suffer from any mental illness. Maybe she was just a witch. Well, she picked the wrong girl to victimize with her maliciousness and threats. I was no victim. Never had been. Never would be.

I'm certain someone would look at my situation and disagree. I had two major indiscretions in my past. One was letting Johnny Tillman in the front door. The other was climbing on the back of Monster's bike. But each time, I'd known the risk and made a conscious choice. Both times, my brain had calculated the odds of something bad happening as a result of my choice. I'm not saying they were the right choices or smart ones. But I'm saying I knew the risks I was taking at the time. The odds ended up not being in my favor. I accept that.

I was also not the naïve virgin someone might think. I was sexually inexperienced by choice, yes. But I was definitely educated about the most intimate details of a sexual relationship. Remember, I'd lived with Delia. I had been at Woodstock. I'd seen things there that would make even Grizz blush.

Delia had encouraged me long before Grizz came along to explore my sexuality. She thought I should have a lover. She insisted I go on the pill. Yes, the birth control pill really did help with cramps, but that wasn't Delia's motive. I think what she really wanted was for me to be out of the house. The sooner I had a guy in my life, the sooner I wouldn't be her problem. Well, I guess she got that wish.

Something else occurred to me as Blue and I barreled along Flamingo Road back toward the motel. I wondered if

Grizz swooped in and took me when he did not because of Matthew, but because of Delia? Did he realize how flighty she was and that my virginity may have been in peril?

Well, I knew it wasn't in peril. You might be surprised to know I'd planned on waiting until I was married. I wanted a life completely opposite of the one I had with Delia.

I was also a Christian. No thanks to Delia there, either. I first started going to church with a neighborhood friend, Cathy, when I was in the second grade. Delia loved it because that gave her and Vince Sunday mornings to stay in bed, get high, make love and do whatever else they wanted. Don't get me wrong, they did that when I was there, too, but maybe she just liked the freedom of Sunday mornings. My absence caused her to forget for a few hours that I was her responsibility.

After a few years, Cathy moved away. I started riding my bike to the closest church in the neighborhood, Sacred Heart. It was a large, impressive Catholic church near my elementary school. I attended Mass every Sunday by myself until the day Monster took me.

No, I wasn't the type of girl who'd lash out at someone's crazy wife. Yet I had.

I snapped back into the present as Blue rolled into the motel. I looked for Grizz's bike. It was still gone. *It's only Tuesday night. I guess he'll be back tomorrow like he originally said.* I think I was actually disappointed that he didn't return sooner.

Blue let me off the bike first. He got off, too, and was walking me toward number four when he stopped.

"Aw, shit." He was looking down at his pager.

I kept walking. He followed me into number four and to the phone, dialing a number. I could hear his side of the conversation as I went to the bedroom and started to unpack my things.

"Calm down, Jan. No, she didn't say anything to me. What did you say to her? Shut the fuck up and tell me what you said." A pause. "Because I have no doubt that you opened your fucking mouth first." Another longer pause. "No, Chicky is *not* going to blow me."

I moved so I was standing in the bedroom doorway facing him. He glanced over at me as he talked; I couldn't tell if he was angry with his wife or with me. I didn't care. I walked past him and into the small living room and started picking up the remnants of my dinner, which I had left on the coffee table less than twenty-four hours ago.

After some more yelling, Blue hung up. I felt him watching me.

"You wanna tell me?" is all he said.

"Yeah." I set my bowl on the kitchen counter. "I'll tell you."

And I did. I told him everything that was said, word for word. I apologized for the Chicky comment, because I felt some guilt at involving her without her knowledge.

Blue sighed and ran his hand through his hair. "Well, I guess you know the real reason Grunt doesn't live with us."

I didn't respond.

"You gonna tell Grizz?"

"Why wouldn't I? Sounds to me like with all the precautions this group takes to remain anonymous, your wife is the biggest threat to that."

"Well, you wouldn't be telling him something he doesn't already know."

This surprised me.

Just then, Moe knocked and walked in. She was holding

Gwinny, and Damien and Lucifer were behind her. She motioned to me that she'd already fed them. I thanked her and took Gwinny from her. She left as quickly as she had come in, and the two dogs went with her.

Damien and Lucifer loved Moe. She always brought them in her room and spoiled them with treats. They would even sleep with her sometimes. She let them lay on the bed with her, and they loved that.

After Moe left, I turned back to Blue. I couldn't tell where I stood with him. And as I looked at him, I decided that, quite frankly, I didn't care.

I excused myself to go get a shower, and I heard him leave as I went into the bedroom. The shower was long and hot, and I tried to luxuriate in it, doing my best to erase the memories of the past few days: the loss of my virginity, Grunt's attack on the fence guy, Blue's psychotic wife.

When the hot water ran out, I reluctantly got out of the shower. I dried off and put my hair up in a towel. I wrapped another towel around me as I went into the bedroom.

And I stopped short.

Grizz was there. He was sitting on the bed. He was leaned up against the back of it, watching me, and he wasn't wearing a shirt. As a matter of fact, I was certain he wasn't wearing anything. The white bed sheet was pulled up just enough, and barely covered his hips.

I took in his physique. He was so big and muscular, and his chest and arms were covered in different tattoos. He had a smattering of light blonde hair across his chest. His skin was tanned. Light from the bedside lamp glinted off the gold hoop earring in his left ear. He had the same expression from the first time I met him: He didn't smile. He didn't frown. He just looked at me with those green eyes.

"Kit, it's time. Come here."

With a lump in my throat, I replied in barely a whisper, "No."

Chapter Seventeen

"It's not why you think," I quickly added, face flushing. "I just got my period and don't have any tampons. I was going to go and find Moe, maybe see if she has anything."

Before he could answer I lifted one edge of the towel wrapped around me and showed him the light pink smear. I didn't bleed heavily the first day of my period, but I still would need something.

"Fuck!" Grizz yanked off the sheet and jumped up, stopping me. "You can't go out looking for Moe in a towel."

I looked away as he stepped into his jeans and pulled them up. But not before I noticed what was under the sheet. I guess it was true, at least in Grizz's case. Big man, big— well, you know. The little billy-club was actually smaller than him. I shivered.

He quickly returned with a partial box of tampons, and I

retreated to the bathroom. I subconsciously knew I would have my period around now. I'd finished up my birth control packet, so I knew it was coming. But in all the excitement of the last few days, it was the last thing on my mind.

I came out of the bathroom dressed in my nightshirt. Thank God Grizz wasn't waiting for me on the bed. Good— me having my period wasn't appealing to him. Hopefully, that meant another week's reprieve.

I found him in the little living room. He was sitting in his recliner flipping through the few TV stations available.

"You're back early. How was your business?" I asked, perching on one arm of the sofa.

He turned the TV off and looked at me. "Heard you had a bit of drama while I was gone."

"Yeah, about that. I want to tell you why Grunt—"

"Doesn't matter. I talked to Grunt. The guy had it coming."

I was relieved. I was still a little angry with Grunt because of how he handled the situation. It was a cruel thing to do. But Grizz seemed to think it was justified, so I dropped it.

"I got to meet Blue's wife," I said instead, giving him a level look. "What a sweetheart. Thanks for asking him to take me home. I think I would have been better off if he'd locked me in the lion's cage at the zoo."

Grizz started laughing then and suddenly I couldn't help myself; I laughed with him. I plopped down on the couch, and after a few minutes he filled me in on Jan.

Blue had met Jan about five years earlier. He had been involved with another woman at the time, but she was "crazy," according to Grizz, and Blue broke it off. Poor Blue.

What was it with him and women with emotional problems? He met Jan at a bar a few months later, and it was love at first sight. I could understand that. Blue wasn't as attractive as she was, but I think she found the tough guy persona appealing.

They had a very quick romance and married soon after. They bought a little house in an older section of Pembroke Pines. I knew where he was talking about. It was called Summer Wood. They were older and smaller homes, but it was a nice neighborhood that appealed to young families just starting out.

It wasn't long after they married that Blue noticed the change in her and immediately regretted the hasty decision to wed. She was quick to lose her temper. She would pick fights with him. She would dare him to lay a hand on her. She constantly provoked him until he would walk out. When he got home, she went into fits of hysterical crying and begged for forgiveness.

Eventually, she started picking fights with the neighbors. It got even worse when she started threatening the neighbors with her husband's status as second in command of a motorcycle gang.

Word got back to Grizz, and he told Blue to take care of it. I wasn't sure what he meant by that. But it didn't matter. She pulled an ace out of her sleeve just in time. She was pregnant.

So Blue settled for moving her to a nicer part of Pembroke Pines. I wasn't a real estate expert, but I was certain a telephone lineman's salary wasn't equal to the upscale home I visited. I guess that's where his extracurricular activity with the gang came in, enabling him to afford it. She saw a doctor and was taking medications that seemed to help. The only time they had trouble with her was when she got pregnant again and stopped taking the medications. Blue practically had to monitor her 24/7, and Chicky, Willow and Moe spent a lot of time with her when Blue was working.

"So she freaked out on you, huh? I wonder if she's pregnant again and off her meds?" Grizz looked thoughtful.

"I don't know. She didn't say anything and she didn't look pregnant." I told him everything she'd said to me and what I said to her in return.

He chuckled. "You really said that to her?"

"Yes, and I can't say I'm proud of myself. You've obviously had a terrible influence on me."

He just laughed. "Well, if it's anything like before, she'll have a meltdown and start crying and wanting to see you to beg for your forgiveness." He didn't seem the least bit concerned with his status as leader of the gang or the threats made to me.

Grizz and I spent the rest of the night watching TV and went to bed. I no longer slept on top of the covers, but I still slept with my back to him. He no longer slept on top of the covers either.

But he also never slept in his jeans anymore. I knew he was nude, and prior to earlier that evening, I had never looked. I'd made it a point to pretend to be asleep if he got up before me. If I got up before him, I just made sure I wasn't in the room when he woke up.

Chapter Eighteen

I woke up the next morning in a pool of sweat. Oh my goodness, it was hot.

Grizz wasn't next to me, so I got up and went looking for him. I peeked out the door and saw him in conversation with Chowder on the walkway a few units down. He heard me open the door and called out, "A/C unit is on the fritz."

So that explained the heat. This was June in South Florida, and it didn't matter that it was nine o'clock in the morning. It was blazing. The humidity alone could suck the life out of a room.

I went back to the bedroom and dressed in the coolest outfit I owned: a pair of cut-off jean shorts, the yellow bathing suit top from Jan and my sandals. I made a piece of toast and sat on the couch to eat it. I had finished and was rinsing out my orange juice glass when Grizz came back.

"C'mon, let's go," he said, standing over me.

"Where?"

"Just c'mon, and grab your helmet and sunglasses."

We walked to one of several Harley-Davidsons parked in front of the motel. He took a dark blue bandana off the handlebar and wrapped it around his head, then straddled the huge bike and started it. He put his sunglasses on and looked at me. Staring at him, I had to admit he was a magnificent specimen. He was wearing the same thing he'd worn the first day I met him—blue jeans, biker boots and a T-shirt with the sleeves ripped off. His hair had gotten longer in the last month. I put on my helmet and sunglasses and jumped on the back.

Grizz took me down to the beach. State Road 84 was a straight shot toward the ocean. We made a left on Federal Highway, then headed up to 17th Street Causeway. A right on the Causeway, and then we were going over a big bridge that spanned the intracostal. On our right, all kinds of huge ships, cruise and military, were docked. The left harbored personal yachts.

I loved this part of Fort Lauderdale. We followed the Causeway down toward the beach where it meets A1A. We slowly rode north on A1A, which parallels the Fort Lauderdale beach. It was summer and the beach was packed.

I immediately realized we were noticed, especially by the girls. I have to admit I sat a little taller and wrapped my arms around Grizz a little tighter. I rested my chin on his shoulder. I was never the type of person who craved the spotlight. Before, I was always content to sit in the shadows and do my own thing. I think that's because I was so completely satisfied with knowing myself. No soul-searching for me. I knew who I was and what I wanted out of my life.

Until now.

Being on the back of Grizz's bike was a new experience for me. I'd now ridden once with Monster and twice with Blue. It was nothing like I felt with Grizz. My whole demeanor changed. I liked that I was envied. I liked how he gently squeezed my thigh just above my knee as we idled at a crosswalk. I liked how he lifted one of my hands to his mouth and softly kissed the inside of my wrist. And I especially liked that I could read the "I wish that was me look" on every female who walked by.

It occurred to me that several days had passed without me thinking about going home. I remembered the first night Monster had brought me to the motel. He'd told me, "Time to meet your new family." Maybe he was right. Maybe I was meant to be with Grizz.

The realization stunned me.

We finally turned left at Sunrise Boulevard, passed Birch State Park, over the intracoastal again and then south on Federal Highway. Grizz pulled up to a rundown tattoo parlor. We parked and got off the bike, and I hung my helmet on the handlebars. He told me to leave my sunglasses on until we got inside. Good thing I was allowed to take my glasses off when we got inside because it was so dark I couldn't see that Grizz, who was walking in front of me, had stopped. I walked right into his back. He turned around and grabbed my arm to steady me.

"You can take your glasses off now, Kit. Eddie? Where are you?"

A small, tattooed man came out of the back room.

"Grizz, my man," Eddie said as he walked toward us. I

could smell the alcohol on him before Grizz could reply.

"Need an I.D." Grizz gestured to me.

"Sure, man. Stats?"

Grizz told me to tell him my height, how much I weighed.

Then Eddie asked, "How old?"

I opened my mouth to answer when Grizz cut me off. "She just turned eighteen in March."

"You got it, Grizz. C'mon back here."

We followed him to a back room. Eddie had me stand up against an empty wall. He was getting ready to take my picture when Grizz stopped him.

"No bangs."

Eddie went to a desk drawer and pulled out a headband. I secretly thanked God that he didn't pull out scissors. I put on the band so my bangs were pulled back. A quick glance in the mirror showed me I looked a little less like myself. More like some other girl. An older girl. Different. The kind of girl who might like sitting on the back of Grizz's motorcycle, his hand casually squeezing my thigh.

Eddie took the picture and said, "Give me an hour."

As we walked out the door, Grizz grabbed a pink bandana off a pile by the cash register.

"We're going to lunch," he told me when we got to the motorcycle. "When we get to the restaurant, I want your helmet off and replaced by the bandana as quickly as possible. Leave your sunglasses on, even in the restaurant. Got it?"

I got it.

We went to a little place called Southside Raw Bar. We sat outside on the docks that overlooked the water. I remember not being able to read his expression after I blessed myself and said a quiet prayer before eating. He'd watched me do this before and had never commented. I don't remember what we ate. We chatted comfortably about a lot of different things, purposely leaving my abduction and anything to do with the motel out of the discussion.

The conversation only turned personal in regards to our likes and dislikes. Standard stuff. Music, movies, books. It was lighthearted and casual conversation.

Then it occurred to me. "Hey, we didn't tell Eddie my new name."

"We don't get to," Grizz informed me. "Eddie has been in this business for years. He's very organized and has his own list of pre-approved names."

"Really? Sounds like the people that name the hurricanes."

He smiled at me. My stomach fluttered. He really had a beautiful smile.

"Yeah, I never thought about it, but I guess it kind of is like that."

"I'm really curious what name he's going to give me."

"Don't worry, Kit. Nothing could ever be as bad as your real name."

Chapter Nineteen

Grizz was wrong.

"Priscilla Renee Celery?" I shouted. "You cannot be serious. There is no way in this world I am going to use the name Priscilla Celery."

I looked up at Grizz, who was smiling. What an awful last name—and going from a fruit to a vegetable? Forget it.

"She's right, Eddie, it's pretty bad. Give her a new one."

Less than thirty minutes later I was the proud owner of a Florida driver's license that identified me as eighteen-year-old Ann Marie Morgan. The physical address on my license was in Pembroke Pines. I wondered if it was Blue's.

I liked the name and told Grizz I thought Annie would make a cute nickname. He told me nobody would ever call me Annie. The driver's license was just a formality in the event I needed it. More back-up ID would be mailed to the post office in Davie. A false birth certificate and Social Security card arrived within the week.

I asked him if he had an ID, and he told me he was Rick O'Connell. Of course, I never once heard anyone refer to him as Rick, so I knew what he meant about me never having a different nickname. I was Kit.

Chowder had fixed the A/C unit by the time we returned to the motel. I thought it was a little noisier than before, but it was cool inside and I couldn't wait to take a shower. My shoulders were sunburned and the water stung, but I was oddly elated. I guess I was still a little high from the ride.

The next two days passed uneventfully. I rarely went to the pit in the evenings. I honestly had no use for anyone in the gang, not to mention the dirty looks I got from the other women. There were always women coming and going. Other than Grunt and Moe, I'd still not warmed up to anyone. Besides, I didn't want to see Willow. She still came around quite a bit, but thankfully, she stayed away from me.

I caught myself starting to fantasize about my life with Grizz. I guess that afternoon on the bike had something to do with it. I still had my period and Grizz still had not tried anything in bed. That was okay. I knew I needed more time.

One night, a small crowd had gathered at the pit. I was bored. I went out and found Grunt.

"Do you mind if I go in your room and listen to some records?" I asked him.

I had only seen Grunt a handful of times since the day we got my helmet. I got a few chess lessons from him and he was impressed with how quickly I took to the game. He was always coming and going. It was summer, so I wasn't sure if he was taking classes. Grunt looked over at Grizz who gave a nod. I wanted to roll my eyes, but didn't. Grunt jumped up and said, "Sure, c'mon."

"I didn't mean to take you away from the pit," I stammered as we walked away. "You don't have to come with me if you trust me to be in your room."

"No problem. Bugs are eating me alive anyway. Let's go."

I followed Grunt to his room and spent the next couple of hours listening to his albums and continuing with my chess lessons. While we talked and played chess, I perused his bookshelf and settled on two books to take back to number four with me.

Grunt was the perfect gentleman, and I found myself a little disappointed that he didn't flirt with me. I didn't flirt with him either, though. I don't know if it was a growing loyalty to Grizz or my embarrassment of our night together, or a combination of both. I told myself I was glad he didn't like me that way because it would certainly complicate things.

It was starting to get late. I was actually surprised Grizz hadn't come looking for me. I yawned and picked up my books.

"Thanks for the books and for putting up with my record choices tonight."

"You can borrow any books you want any time. And remember, you picked records from my stash, so I liked listening to everything you picked out. Need me to walk you home?" he teased.

"No, I think I can get there all by myself." I answered. We both laughed, and I was still smiling as he closed the door behind me. I got to number four and went in.

I almost dropped my books at the sight that greeted me.

Grizz was laying back on the couch with his eyes closed.

And Willow was crouched between his legs with her head bobbing frantically.

Chapter Twenty

Neither one had heard me open the door. I guess that's because the A/C unit was much louder than before. To my right was a shelf unit that held the TV. I slammed my books down as hard as I could on it.

Grizz opened his eyes, and Willow stopped and turned around to look at me. Grizz grabbed her by the hair and said, "Finish."

She gave me a toothless smile and went back to what she was doing.

I turned around and ran out the front door, and before I even knew where I was heading, I was pounding on Grunt's door. He opened it and I fell into him, wrapping my arms around his back. I wasn't crying, but I was on the verge of tears. I didn't know why.

Why should I care what Grizz and Willow were doing? I

certainly hadn't done anything like that with him, and I had been telling myself for the last month I didn't want to. So why this feeling of betrayal? No matter what I told myself, the truth was it stung.

"Hey, hey, hey, what's wrong?" Grunt asked as he held me closely. "Kit, what's wrong, what happened?"

All of a sudden something dawned on me. There was no way in the world I was going to tell Grunt, or anyone for that matter, that catching Willow performing oral sex on Grizz bothered me. Absolutely no way. I caught myself then and stood back. Thank goodness there were no tears yet. He had his hands on my shoulders.

"Nothing's wrong really." I stammered. "I walked in on Grizz and Willow and I'm embarrassed, is all."

He gave me a look that said he knew I was lying, but being the gentleman he was, he didn't press.

"You know, he's been waiting for you awhile. I'm the only one who knows that. I don't even think Blue knows. Grizz is very prideful. And he's only human and she's only too willing. Besides, he was drinking before you even came out to the pit. He's probably pretty hammered by now."

"I know. Like I said, I'm just embarrassed. Let's forget I even came here." I paused. "Ummm, how long do you think I should wait before I go back?"

My inexperience was showing and I started to blush. Before Grunt could answer, his door flew open and Grizz came in.

"Thought I'd find you here. Let's go." Grizz nodded toward the door.

I immediately pulled myself together and said a little too haughtily, "Just wanted to give you some privacy."

With that I strode past him and was reminded of my

first night at the motel. The night I replaced Willow and she'd proudly flounced away from the pit.

I went back to our unit and changed into my nightgown. I washed my face, brushed my teeth and hair and climbed into bed. I'd taken the borrowed books into the bedroom with me. I picked one up and pretended to read. I looked away as he undressed and slid in next to me.

"It shouldn't have bothered you, Kit."

"It didn't bother me," I replied too quickly. "I was just embarrassed to interrupt, that's all."

I was lying on my back and he was on his side facing me with his head propped up on his right hand. He raised an eyebrow.

"Didn't bother you, huh? So I guess I could've been getting head from Willow this whole time and it wouldn't have bothered you?"

I looked straight at him. "How do I know you haven't been doing that with her this whole time? What's it to me? None of my business. I'm sure you do what you want anyway."

"Damn right I do what I want."

I didn't say anything and continued to feign interest in my book.

"Look, she followed me back to number four and asked to use the phone. You know how Willow can be. I guess she had something to prove and I was horny enough to let her. That whore doesn't mean anything to me."

"I don't care if she means anything to you." I looked at the pages of my book coolly. "Of course, it was really rude of you to let her do that while I could have been in the other room."

"But I knew you weren't. I watched Grunt's room all

night. I knew you hadn't come out."

"How convenient for the two of you." I kept my tone even. "Well, like I said, I don't care. So keep doing what you want. Doesn't matter to me."

I turned back to my book and tried to concentrate on the pages.

"Doesn't bother you, huh?"

"Nope. Doesn't bother me at all."

"You sure about that?"

"Yes, I'm sure, Grizz. Why would you even think something like this would bother me?" I asked a little too smugly.

"Because your book is upside down."

With that I slammed my book shut and sat straight up to face him. "Gosh, Grizz, of all the girls, it had to be *Willow*? I mean, even Chicky and Moe would've been easier for me to handle because they don't hate me. I'm sure she thinks she has one up on me now. Not that I care. I don't know. I guess it's a woman thing. I don't expect you to understand."

"So it would've been okay if you came in and it was Chicky or Moe?"

I didn't answer. I couldn't fathom my own reasoning. Was I upset he was engaging in sexual activity with another woman, or was I upset because the other woman was Willow, a woman who had become my instant enemy?

"You want Willow gone? If you want her gone, all you have to do is say so. You'll never see her again."

"Yeah, Grizz," I said quietly. "I want her gone."

That was the end of the conversation. We both fell asleep, and when I woke up the next morning he had his arms wrapped around me. I had my back to him and I started to gently lift one of his heavy arms off of me. Then I stopped myself. I closed my eyes and fell back to sleep.

Grizz was true to his word. I never saw Willow again.

Chapter Twenty-One

Grizz became a little bolder in the bedroom after that night, but he still never pressed me. He also started insisting I sleep in the nude like him. I always made sure I had a towel wrapped around me as I climbed into bed, and once I was under the covers I would take it off. This didn't provoke or anger him, though. He thought it was funny and would just shake his head as he wrapped his arms around me and pulled my backside up against his front.

I actually slept very comfortably in Grizz's arms. Maybe a little too comfortably. One particular night, not long after the Willow incident, I was enjoying an especially erotic dream.

I was dreaming about the night I lost my virginity to Grunt. The only difference was that I was not drugged and I was thoroughly enjoying our lovemaking. "Nights In White

Satin" was playing in the background. He was on top of me and inside me, and his thrusts were rhythmic and I was meeting him each time. I felt his breath at my ear and he was saying to enjoy it, to let go. I had a quick and powerful orgasm. So intense it actually woke me up.

I was disoriented at first, not remembering where I was or who I was with. I was on my back and looked over to my left. And there was Grizz, smiling like the cat that ate the canary. He had his hand between my legs and was still touching me.

I pushed his hand away and sat up, aghast. "Stop it. What do you think you're doing?"

"Lighten up, Kit. It's not the end of the world if you let yourself enjoy it a little. Was that your first one?"

"That is none of your business!" I spat as I lay back down and rolled onto my side.

He pulled me against him, and I could hear him chuckling as I tried to fall back to sleep. But I was worried. Why was I dreaming about Grunt?

I spent the rest of the week in a crush-induced fog. I couldn't get that dream out of my head. I found myself making excuses to be near Grunt. I continued to borrow books, play chess and ask to listen to his records. He would let me hang out in his room when he wasn't there, and once or twice I tried on his jacket and checked myself out in the bathroom mirror.

It was funny. I felt so differently than I had the first night I tried on Grunt's jacket. The night I got Gwinny. It was different now. I liked how I looked in it, and I wondered if I would ever get to ride on the back of his bike. I even started to fantasize I was there to be with him, not Grizz.

After a couple of days of making excuses to be in Grunt's room to listen to his music, I found a brand new stereo system set up in number four. Grizz told me to borrow some of Grunt's records until he got me my own. You would think I would be excited to have my own stereo, but I found myself disappointed that the main reason I had to hang out in his room had been taken away.

The fog lifted soon enough. It was a Saturday morning a few days later. Grizz told me he had to spend the day away from the motel. He said I could go off the grounds again with Grunt, but not to familiar places and to make sure I wore the baseball cap and sunglasses.

I was elated. This was perfect. I would ask Grunt to take me to the beach. With the thousands of girls my own age, I was certain I would blend in even if I didn't wear the baseball cap and sunglasses. I put on my yellow bikini and cutoff shorts, slipped my feet into sandals and put my hair in a high ponytail. I headed for Grunt's room.

I had my hand raised to knock on his door when it swung open. I stood there with my hand still in the raised position. Grunt was coming out of the room and stopped short when he saw me.

"Hey, Kit. You here for books, albums or chess lessons?" he said, laughing.

Grunt was not alone and I had obviously interrupted a private joke. He had his left arm slung around the shoulders of a girl.

Before I could answer him he said, "Kit. This is Sarah Jo. Jo, this is Kit. Kit lives here with Grizz."

I thought I saw a flash of recognition in Sarah Jo's face. Did she place me as the girl who went missing back in May?

She held out her hand to take mine and said, "It's so nice

to meet you, Kit. I cannot believe how much you look like my best friend, Kelli. She just moved to North Carolina. I'm supposed to go visit her sometime this summer. You could be her twin sister."

As she spoke, I sized her up. She was tiny. I mean, all the women at this motel seemed to be of small stature, except for Chicky who was on the voluptuous side, but this girl wasn't little. She was miniature. She must have been only four foot eleven. She had a cute figure and seemed very well proportioned for someone so small. She had brown hair with gold highlights, blue eyes, a nice tan and a sprinkling of freckles on her nose.

She was adorable. It was hate at first sight.

"Jo is Fess's daughter." Grunt was saying. "She's your age. You should have a lot in common."

She giggled then and looked up adoringly at Grunt. "Can Kit go with us to the beach? We don't have to take your bike. We can take your car."

"Yeah, sure. Kit, wanna come? Looks like you've already got your bathing suit on."

"Uh, no, I was actually just coming down to pick out some books if it's okay," I stammered.

"Oh, please come, Kit. It'll be fun," Sarah Jo begged.

Was she really this sweet or was it an act? I'd already been fooled by Blue's wife, Jan. I wasn't sure how I was feeling and didn't trust myself to spend the day with them.

"Maybe another time. I've got a bad headache and the sun probably wouldn't help," I lied.

"Well, don't read too much, then." Grunt gave me a funny look that said he wasn't sure if he believed my excuse. "Reading won't help a headache. But I don't keep the door locked. Help yourself."

Then he turned to Sarah Jo. "C'mon, Littlin. Got your helmet?"

"Right here," she said as she held it up with her left hand. Her right arm was draped around his waist. She waved to me as they started to walk away. "I'm sorry you don't feel good. Maybe another time?"

"Yeah. Sure. Definitely." I answered as they walked off, leaving Grunt's door open.

Definitely never, I thought, staring through the open door without going in as I tried to figure out what I was feeling.

I wasn't really troubled by her cuteness. I was cute too. Her blue eyes and bubbly personality didn't really bother me either. I was always receiving compliments about my big, brown eyes. People always told me how smart I was. I closed Grunt's door and continued to think about it as I made my way back to number four. I heard Grunt's bike start.

And I stopped dead in my tracks. That's what bothered me so much. Sarah Jo was wearing his jacket.

I spent the rest of the day keeping myself busy, grateful I hadn't made a fool of myself in front of Grunt. He had a girlfriend. I don't know why it'd never occurred to me that he might.

I had Chowder help me hook up some hoses, then took Damien and Lucifer down into the empty pool and bathed them. They loved it. Moe showed up sometime around one o'clock and I asked her if she could take me shopping. She looked at me skeptically and I told her Grizz had given me permission to go with Grunt. I didn't see why it wouldn't be okay if she took me to a couple of places. She motioned that she would and to give her ten minutes. That was enough time for me to go back to number four, check on Gwinny, change clothes, grab my hat and sunglasses and get some money.

Grizz had recently showed me where he kept some cash in case I ever wanted any. This was the first time I'd used some. My eyes widened when I realized the amount of money I was holding and had no choice but to take a hundred dollar bill. There was nothing smaller.

I met Moe back at her car. She drove a Volkswagen Bug. Naturally, it was black. I told her I needed bras. That was one article of clothing that hadn't shown up at the motel. I also wanted to get another bathing suit. We headed north to the Pompano Square Fashion Plaza, which was north of Fort Lauderdale and not really familiar to me.

I went to JC Penney for the bras and was surprised that I found a bathing suit there, too. It was late June, and the bathing suit selections were usually picked over by this time of year. I settled on an orange and turquoise bikini that fit my top better than the yellow one Jan had given me. I encouraged Moe to try some things on, too. I had never seen her wear anything other than black T-shirts and black jeans. She just smiled and shook her head.

I asked her if we could find a grocery store on the way back and she nodded and took me to a small, family-owned store. It wasn't in a really good part of town but I wasn't afraid; I was just worried what Grizz might think if he knew where we were. Was I subconsciously trying to please him? But the grocery shopping was quick and uneventful, and before I knew it, we were heading back toward the motel.

We were back on State Road 84 heading west when she

took a left. I realized we were heading into the small town of Davie. I asked her where we were going, and she reached into her ashtray, took out a small key and dangled it. Then it occurred to me. We were going to the post office to check the mail. I found this very interesting. I was curious to see if anyone else received mail besides Grunt.

Soon enough we pulled up and parked at a small building. I asked if I could go in, too. She shrugged her shoulders like "why not?" and I followed her in. We were in a small vestibule area that housed the boxes. I leaned up against a counter that was there for customers to use. I turned around and noticed there was a bulletin board above it. I took note of the lost dogs, horses for sale, babysitters and cleaning ladies for hire.

I heard Moe approaching and was just turning to follow her out when something caught my eye. It was an old missing persons flyer, yellowed with age. The girl in the picture seemed familiar. She had long black hair, parted down the center. Other than that, I couldn't tell what it was that made me think I knew her. Then it dawned on me and my jaw dropped as I read:

$25,000 REWARD
Missing Person
Last Seen November 12, 1969
Miriam Parker
Aged 20

It was Moe.

I completely forgot about spying on the mail Moe had picked up. I followed her out to the car and got in. I must have been unusually quiet because she kept glancing at me as she started the car. I was speechless. I couldn't think of what to say. That poster was printed six years ago, and it said she was twenty years old then. So she was twenty-six now. Her real name was Miriam Parker. I think that and her age were the first personal things, other than her missing tongue, that I learned about Moe.

There was a huge reward offered for her return. That amount of money is a lot today. It was really significant back then. That told me she was loved. That someone missed her. How many times had she been at this post office to get the mail? Surely she knew that poster was there. Maybe she didn't. It was crammed in between a lot of different flyers. I wondered if she was from Davie. If she was, would she feel comfortable going in the local post office? Of course, with her short hair and heavy makeup, I doubted she would be recognized. Had she been kidnapped? Was her family threatened like mine?

I wanted so bad to ask Grizz, but wasn't sure if I should. I could always ask Grunt, but I was still dealing with mixed emotions concerning him. If she had been with the gang since the time she went missing, that meant she would have arrived at the motel about the same time Grunt did. I wonder what he knew.

We drove off and she took some side roads. We were really in the heart of Davie now, and we turned off onto an unpaved road. We followed a fence for what seemed like a long time. On the other side of the fence was beautiful, green pastureland. I noticed horses in the field.

We pulled over at a shady spot. There was a gigantic ficus tree on the other side of the fence, and two horses were under it. She smiled and pointed. I looked at the horses and then at her.

"You like horses?"

She nodded and smiled. Then her smile faded and she didn't look sad, but wistful. Like she was thinking about the past.

"Did you used to have horses?" I asked, pressing further.

A small nod this time. She never took her eyes off the big brown one.

"Did you have a horse that looked like that one?"

I looked from her to the brown horse and back again and I instantly knew. She didn't have a horse that looked like this one. This one had been hers. We had just stepped into her past and I was honored and saddened at the same time that she had let me be a part of it. Again, I didn't know what to say. She shifted the little bug into drive and made a sharp U-turn. We headed back to the motel.

As I carried my groceries into number four, I told her I was cooking dinner and she was invited. She carried my JC Penney bags for me and left them on the couch. I didn't hear her leave.

I put the change on the dresser and went to feed the animals. After that, I put away my new bras and bathing suit and set to work in the kitchen.

I don't know if I mentioned I could cook. As I got older at home, I'd taught myself. I was pretty good. I guess it was survival instinct. Vince and Delia usually ate something at Smitty's or brought home take-out from a fast food restaurant. Early on I'd grown tired of macaroni and cheese, tomato soup and take-out, so I experimented. I knew I was a good cook based on Vince and Delia's occasional requests.

This was the first time I found myself wanting to do

something nice for someone at the motel. Up until this point I'd made small meals for myself, sometimes Grizz. He never asked me to cook for him and he lived mostly on take-out from one of the many bars he owned. I'd give Moe a small grocery list and she provided the basics every week. I'd been living off of cereal, grilled cheese and BLT's. I was ready to cook again.

So here I was at the motel, whipping up spaghetti and meatballs from scratch. I made everything except my own pasta. I hadn't thoroughly surveyed Grizz's kitchen, so I realized too late that I didn't have a strainer for the pasta. I found Chowder and he quickly made me a homemade strainer with some leftover screening. It was crude, but it worked. I thanked him and told him dinner would be at seven.

That's how Grizz found the three of us. Moe and I were sitting on the couch. Chowder was in the recliner. We were holding our plates and eating and laughing at something Chowder had said.

"What smells so good?" Grizz asked as he laid some paperwork on his desk.

"Best damn spaghetti and meatballs I ever ate is what smells so good," Chowder replied.

"From where?" Grizz asked.

Chowder now had a mouthful of food and motioned toward me with his empty fork.

Grizz looked at me. "You had somebody take you for take-out? Hope you saved me some."

"I made it. Moe took me grocery shopping. There's plenty. Help yourself."

"Good, cause I'm half starved," he said as he headed into the kitchen.

Chowder started to get up to let Grizz sit down, but Grizz motioned him back and indicated for me and Moe to scoot over. We made room for him on the couch. The four of us sat there in companionable silence and enjoyed the homemade meal.

Chowder and Moe eventually went back to their rooms, and I started to do the dishes. I thought I heard Grizz fiddling with the stereo. I was right. Before I knew it, Barry White's sexy voice was belting out a tune. Grizz wanted to listen to Barry White? I stiffened for just a second then let myself relax. I had my hands in the hot, soapy water and was really enjoying the music when I felt Grizz come up behind me. He slipped his arms around my waist and softly kissed the side of my temple.

"Kit, I don't know how much longer I can wait for you, honey. I've tried to be patient. To give you space. Just so you know, that's not like me."

My hands stilled. "I'm a little scared, Grizz. Actually, more nervous than scared." I tilted my head up to him, hands damp. "I know you have experience. I have none. I'm afraid you've built me up in your head to an ideal I can't live up to. I don't want to disappoint you."

Until that very moment I didn't even know the extent of my feelings. But I recognized there was truth in what I said.

I was falling for Grizz.

I still can't explain the Grunt thing. Maybe it wasn't real. Maybe it was all in my head because of the dream. I didn't know. It didn't matter.

Because while I was talking, Grizz was kissing my neck and I was letting myself enjoy it. I closed my eyes and leaned into him.

"You could never disappoint me, baby and I don't want

you to have experience. Everything you need to know you'll learn from me," he said as he turned me around and kissed me. "Only me."

I wasn't a very practiced kisser, either, but I was able to take his lead and kiss him back the way he wanted. I was leaning into him now, and if what was pressed against my stomach was any indication of his feelings for me, then I must have been doing something right.

"I'll go real slow with you, baby. I promise."

I was heady with emotion. I didn't think about Grunt. I didn't think about Sarah Jo. I didn't think about the kidnapping, Johnny Tillman, fence guy, Moe. I was lost in the man that was holding me and kissing me.

I stopped him, took him by the hand and led him back to the bedroom. He was right.

It was time.

Chapter Twenty-Two

My experience with Grizz was better than I ever expected. He was gentle, he was caring, he was patient. So different from the man I watched lead a notorious motorcycle gang.

The rest of the summer passed uneventfully. I signed up for the same high school correspondence course Grunt took. I fell into a domestic routine of cooking and cleaning. I spoiled the animals. Every evening after dinner, Grizz and I played chess on a little set that I bought on one of my shopping trips. Afterwards, he'd go to the pit while I read, did homework or practiced my guitar.

I never asked Grizz about his business and he never offered up any information, either. I rarely, if ever, went to the pit at night, but I knew he had to. In addition to just hanging out there, a lot of business was conducted around the fire. There were always people coming and going.

Two or three times I went with Moe to get the mail in Davie, and we made the same stop under the ficus tree each time.

I think I was happy, but restless. Something was bothering me. I struggled with my faith. There was serious guilt about having sex out of wedlock. I didn't realize how much it bothered me until one evening in August.

Grizz and I were in bed and we were getting ready to make love. He was on top of me and kissing me. He slowly started to make his way down my body teasing me with his tongue and light kisses. Every time he went lower, I scooted lower, causing him to have to inch his body lower. Just as he was making his way below my belly button, he stopped what he was doing and looked up at me.

I was leaning up on my elbows, eyes wide. I'd been watching him.

"Damn it, Kit, what are you trying to do?"

"What do you mean? I'm not doing anything. What are you doing?"

"I'm trying to get to your pus—"

"Eh, stop it! Don't say it. I hate that word. It's so vulgar. Just don't, please."

"Kit, I'm laying here with my ass hanging off the end of the bed. Would you mind telling me why you won't let me down there?"

"It's just too personal."

He looked at me strangely and started to crawl up to face me. "What do you mean too personal?"

"Look, I just think that you having your face in my...my—" I could tell he was getting ready to finish my sentence. "Don't say it!"

With my right hand I absently played with the earring in

his left ear and continued. "Having your face there is the most personal thing I can think of between a man and a woman. Even intercourse doesn't seem as intimate compared to that."

There, I finally said it.

I had avoided oral sex with him ever since that first night, after the spaghetti dinner. It was never an issue. He was true to his word about taking things slowly with me, and he never pushed me. When I thought he might try something like this, I purposely distracted him. When I had my period and thought he might want oral sex, I avoided him. I guess it was a miracle I'd held him off this long. I was very good at providing distractions. I didn't fully understand myself the reason why until this moment. I did my best to explain.

"Look, Grizz. Thanks to Grunt, I will never be a virgin on my wedding night."

He interrupted me before I could continue. "Kit, I've never told you how sorry I am about that. I never should've had Grunt do that to you. I wasn't thinking straight. You know, I'm bigger than that damn stick. I thought it would hurt you less and I didn't want to hurt you even a little. That's why I let Grunt take care of it. I never cared about a woman before."

He looked away from me then, and I realized how much it cost him to say that. That was the first and last time I heard Grizz express regret for anything.

"That's not what I'm trying to get at here," I said, cheeks flushing. "What I'm trying to say is I need to save something of myself for when I do finally get married one day. There has to be something I can give my future husband that is his alone. Does that make sense?"

I looked at him pleadingly and he didn't say anything. An emotion showed on his face I had not seen yet. I was unable to read him. He dropped his forehead so it rested on mine. I wrapped my arms around his back and started to kiss him.

We made love that night and I fell asleep grateful he didn't press the issue.

I thought the matter was dropped until two days later. He told me he was taking me somewhere special and to dress nicely.

I didn't have any dress clothes, so I wore a nice sundress and sandals. He wore new jeans and a dress shirt. We got in his Corvette and headed for the beach. I pestered him the whole way. What were we doing? Why the surprise?

I was a little disappointed when we pulled up in front of Eddie's tattoo parlor. I told him I didn't mind waiting in the car, but he said to come inside. His business here had to do with me.

It had to do with me, all right. Apparently, Eddie was also an ordained minister.

That day I became Mrs. Richard David O'Connell. I was six months shy of my sixteenth birthday.

Chapter Twenty-Three

There were two customers in the shop who served as witnesses. Ann Marie Morgan was eighteen and didn't need parental permission to get married. I was in too much shock to even remember the ceremony.

I remember telling him I didn't have a ring for him, and he told me not to worry, it was being handled. I watched nervously as Eddie used his tattoo gun to create a beautiful ink wedding band on Grizz's left ring finger. It was my name, Kit, and it had vines weaving in and out of it. Then it was my turn.

"I can't, Grizz," was all I could say.

"What do you mean you can't?"

"I can't." My voice shook. "I hate needles. I fainted when I got my ears pierced. Twice! Delia did each one with an ice cube and a sewing needle, and I fainted after each one."

Eddie interrupted. "It's not that bad, Kit. How about I draw it on first and let's see if you like it? Huh? How about that?" he asked as he held up an ink pen. "Your finger is so small it's not gonna take a lot of ink."

I reluctantly sat down. Grizz held my right hand and kept telling me it wouldn't be that bad.

True to his word, Eddie used an ink pen with a really fine point to start drawing Grizz's name on my finger. He was talking to me as he was doing it, trying to ease my anxiety.

"Then we'll go right here and make the bottom of this 'z' like a vine, to match Grizz's finger, and then we'll—"

I didn't hear the rest. I fainted. When I woke up, Grizz was standing over me with a big grin.

"Didn't feel a thing, did you?"

I was so humiliated. I'd fainted before they even used a needle. That had to be a first. I stayed passed out during the whole tattoo process. I know I was beet red and just wanted to crawl into a hole.

"C'mon, Mrs. O'Connell, let's go home."

We stopped at a really nice Italian restaurant on the way home. He teased me the whole time about fainting. I finally saw the humor in it and laughed at myself.

"I just don't get it," I said to him while waiting for our dinner.

"What, baby? What don't you get?" he asked me as he buttered a roll.

"Why me? It's obvious you can have any woman you want. Why do you want *me*, Grizz? Truthfully. Why?"

He got very quiet and placed the now-buttered roll back on the plate. I didn't think he was going to answer me. I couldn't fathom the depth of his feelings for me. I'd done nothing to call attention to myself when I lived next to Guido. It just didn't make sense.

I asked again, "Why me? I mean, I tell you I'm uncomfortable having oral sex and you marry me. Who does that?"

It was then that Grizz told me a story. I sat in stunned silence as he told me about a lonely biker and a little, neglected girl with a sloppy ponytail and two missing front teeth.

I didn't completely understand it, but yes. It now made some sense.

When we got back to the motel there was a bigger than usual crowd around the pit. I started to walk to number four, but Grizz told me to come with him for a few minutes.

As we stood facing the group, he said, "I have an announcement to make."

Just then, Grunt came out of his room and walked up to us. He was standing off to Grizz's right waiting for the announcement.

"I just made it official. Meet the new Mrs. Grizz."

As he said this, Grizz held up my left hand showing my ring tattoo with his name on it. It was so small and hard to see that some people jumped up and came over to take a closer look. I was overwhelmed by the hooting and hollering and looked at Grizz to let him know I was done and going back to number four. He nodded at me to go.

I turned to walk toward our room when I saw Grunt standing by his door. Now that I thought about it, he wasn't

one of the people who came up to congratulate us. I
changed direction and started to walk toward him. I don't
know why, but I felt the need to explain this to him. I was
looking down and trying to figure what I was going to say
and wondering why I felt I needed to say anything. I had
almost reached his door.

But when I looked up, he was gone.

I knocked on Grunt's door and went in when he yelled, "It's
open." He was standing near his stereo flipping through
albums.

"Hey," I said.

"Hey." His voice was casual, unreadable.

I took the plunge, blurting out in a rush, "Grunt, I don't
know why, but I feel like I owe you an explanation about
me and Grizz."

"No, you don't, Kit." Grunt shook his head. "You don't
owe me anything."

"Well, then why do I feel like I do?"

"Don't know. Maybe because of our secret?"

"Maybe that's it. I don't know. It was a surprise, you
know? He didn't tell me where he was taking me. I don't
know why it bothers me, but are you okay with this?"

"Yes and no."

I gave him a look that pleaded with him to continue.

"I don't know why he had to marry you. You're really
young. But, it's not just that. I'm concerned for your safety."

I started to interrupt but he held a hand up to stop me.
"Grizz has a lot of enemies, Kit. Yes, he also has a lot of
people who are afraid of him, who do what he tells them to

do. But there's always going to be that person out there looking for a way to get to him. By announcing his marriage to you, he opened that up. It's going to get around, you know? People will hear that he cared enough about a woman to marry her. I'm just surprised he announced it. I'm worried for you, is all."

I didn't know what to say. He didn't say he was upset because I married Grizz, thereby making me unavailable to him. What in the world was wrong with me? I'd been in Grizz's bed for months now. I'd told myself Grunt was with Sarah Jo, and if I harbored any feelings at all for him, I needed to squelch them. So where was this coming from?

"I appreciate the concern. I really do. I don't know if it makes a difference or not, Grunt, but I feel safe with Grizz."

"Just do me a favor, Kit. Stay sharp. Never let your guard down. You just never know with this kind of lifestyle what can come knocking at your door."

"I will. Thanks."

We both moved in for a hug. It seemed like it lasted a little longer than it should have. I looked up and he was looking down at me. We stood there like that for a few seconds, but it seemed like hours. He broke away first and turned back to his stereo. I left and headed back to number four.

Chapter Twenty-Four

Thanksgiving was approaching, and I realized I'd never sat down to a traditional Thanksgiving dinner with turkey and all the trimmings.

Grizz was sitting at his desk doing some paperwork, and I was sitting in the recliner repairing a ripped seam on one of my blouses. We must have looked like the poster couple for wedded domestic bliss. Truth be told, I really was happy. I was rattling on about a menu and cooking my first turkey when Grizz said, "Won't be here. You can go to Blue's with Grunt."

"What do you mean you won't be here? Why not?"

"Nope. Business." He turned around to look at me and rested his arm on the top of the chair. "Sorry, Kitten, I've got to be gone, and I can't bring you with me. Jan does a big dinner every year. You'll like it."

"Ugh. Really? Dinner with Jan? I don't think so." I know my disappointment was evident.

"Look, she's been after Blue for months now to bring you back around. I told you how she gets. She's so full of remorse over how she treated you that she'll probably roll out the red carpet and be on her best behavior to get back on your good side. You really should go. Moe and Chowder go every year."

"No way. I'd rather stay here alone before I go to that house again. Nope. I'm definitely not going."

I went. Grunt coaxed me into going by telling me how he needed me for moral support. He hated going to his brother's, but the truth was he loved the kids, and Jan always was on her best behavior when he was there.

I was at Moe's door knocking to see if she was ready. Chowder had already begged out. He was invited to Chicky's place and said he didn't want to hurt her feelings. I wondered if that was true.

Moe opened the door and let me in her room. I'd never completely walked inside Moe's room before. I was stunned. The walls were covered in beautiful drawings of horses. I noticed one particularly recognizable brown horse.

"Wow. Moe, did you draw these?"

She mouthed "yes" and smiled at me.

"I didn't know you were such a talented artist. These are gorgeous. Can I have one to hang in number four?"

She smiled even bigger and gestured with her hand for me to pick one out. I settled on one of the brown horse grazing under a familiar tree.

"Thanks. I'll leave it in here, though, until we get back from dinner. Ready to go?"

She shook her head "no."

"No? What do you mean no? You have to come. You can't leave me to face Jan all by myself."

She just shrugged her shoulders and mouthed "sorry."

"I can't believe you're not coming. You owe me big time for this," I teased.

She smiled at me and followed me to the door. I told her I would bring her a plate of food and she gave me a thumbs-up.

I found Grunt in his car. I explained that Moe wasn't going and I didn't know why.

"No biggie," he said. "You never know with her. Looks like it's just you and me. Ready?"

"As ready as I'll ever be."

We headed over to Pembroke Pines and I realized I had not been alone with Grunt since the day Grizz and I got married. It wasn't awkward at all, and I found myself falling into easy conversation with him. He told me about his college courses and I told him where I was with my high school correspondence course. I never asked about Sarah Jo, and he never offered up any information about her, either.

We were greeted at the door by Timmy and Kevin jumping up and down and yelling, "Uncle Grunt, Uncle Grunt, pick me up, pick me up!" They remembered me, too, and were soon latching on to me for hugs and kisses.

Just like Grizz told me, Jan was more than accommodating and nice. She fussed over me like I was a long-lost sister. I let myself enjoy the camaraderie, but made sure I didn't get too close. I still had reservations about her sincerity. I even let myself have a couple sips of wine at dinner and felt myself loosening up a little. I'd never drunk alcohol before and was feeling comfortably buzzed. Jan and I were in the kitchen cleaning up.

"Kit, I've been waiting for so long to tell you how sorry I am about the last time you were here."

"It's okay, Jan. Don't worry about it," I said as I scraped leftover food into the garbage.

"No. It's not okay. I know you must've heard why I sometimes do the things I do. When you were here I thought I might be pregnant, so I'd stopped taking my meds. You got the brunt of it. I'm really sorry. If there's anything I can do to make it up to you, please just say it. I'd really like to be friends."

Hmm. I thought about it a minute. "Yeah, actually, there is something you can do," I said.

"Anything. Name it."

"Tell me about Moe."

Moe was raised in Davie. Her stepfather, who married Moe's mother when Moe was about ten years old, was wealthy and eager to spoil his new stepdaughter. That explained the exorbitant reward money. Moe's mother worked for some big airline at the time, and although she made a nice living, she was able to quit her job and be a stay-at-home-mom to Moe. She went on to have three more children with Moe's stepfather. All girls.

Moe had been the recipient of all the attention for about four years before her first half-sister was born. She was fourteen then and completely rebelled. She started running with a fast crowd, using drugs and sleeping around. She lost interest in her beloved horses. She was given a brand-new car for her sixteenth birthday, and it ended up in a lake. Two months after her sixteenth birthday, she dropped out of high school. She was eventually picked up by the police for shoplifting.

Her parents couldn't understand where this was coming from. Why did she need to steal when they gave her everything?

Jan couldn't comment on why Moe's life spiraled out of control. It was just one of those things. She was technically still living at home when she was twenty, although by most counts she was never around. She slept on friends' couches and only showed up at home to borrow money. When her parents finally cut her off, she resorted to breaking into her own home and stealing. I was still curious as to how she came into contact with the gang.

According to Jan, Moe was picked up by one of the members. Jan thinks his name was Chip. He wasn't around anymore. She'd been hanging at one of the gang's local bars, performing sexual favors in exchange for drugs. Chip brought her to the motel and shared her with the guys. I looked at Jan. She knew what I was thinking.

"Yeah, I'm sure Grizz and Blue were both with her," she said.

Jan went on to explain that Moe was pretty much the motel whore. There were other women who came and went, but Moe was a permanent fixture.

I couldn't contain my curiosity any longer. "Why did Grizz cut her tongue out?" I had to know.

"Apparently, Moe had a real mouth on her," Jan said quietly. "She never got over being the spoiled princess and was constantly bragging about how she didn't have to live at the motel like a whore. Her family was rich and she could go home anytime she wanted. There was only one problem with this. She couldn't be trusted. She'd been at the motel and heard too many secrets exchanged. Witnessed too much. No one really took her seriously, but it was still too risky."

Jan said Moe was steadily mocked and abused by some of the regulars. And how does someone cope with abuse? In this case, Moe turned her frustration on the only other person she perceived to be weaker than herself: Grunt. He was only ten or eleven then.

Blue had just met Jan and wasn't at the motel a lot, so Grizz had taken Grunt under his wing. It wasn't exactly clear, but Jan was pretty sure that while Moe had never physically hurt Grunt, she was mean to him. Where the others fondly teased him about his size, she was cruel and started to order him around. She treated him like a slave, getting him to wait on her and do her chores. She was very careful not to do it when Blue or Grizz were around.

But what Moe didn't count on was that Grizz knew everything going on. It was only a couple of weeks after Moe started picking on Grunt that it happened.

Grizz later told Blue he called Moe into his room for sex. She was always willing to accommodate Grizz. Jan thinks she was secretly in love with him. When they got in the room Grizz unzipped his jeans and told her to kneel. She was offended that he didn't want intercourse with her. He just wanted a blow job. She made an off-the-cuff comment about "blow jobs being the runt's work." She probably thought she was being cute and funny, but Grizz snapped.

I was shocked. I couldn't equate the meek and unassuming Moe with the snotty, mouthy, nasty girl Jan was telling me about. I could see why Grizz would be mad at the comment, but to cut out her tongue?

"Wouldn't that just make her more hateful and resentful

of Grunt?"

"You would think so," Jan replied. "But things don't always turn out the way you think they might."

"What do you mean?"

"Well, Grizz left her in the room, bleeding and crying hysterically. No one really cared that she was hurt. That she was maimed. Well, except for one person."

"Who?" But I knew before she told me.

"Grunt. He nursed her back to health all by himself. He was just a little guy, and he never left her side. Even after she had been so mean to him."

I could see Grunt nursing Moe back to health. I'd seen him more than once at the motel stitching up someone who'd been in a fight. I knew Grizz had a doctor on his payroll, and that the physician noticed Grunt taking an interest when he occasionally came to the motel to provide medical care. He'd showed Grunt how to deal with some basic injuries and left medical supplies for him to use. Grunt was smart. He most certainly could've gone to medical school.

I knew instantly the reasoning behind Grizz's insistence that Grunt be the one to take my virginity that night. He saw in Grunt a nurturing, caring person who'd do his best not to hurt me. I still wondered, though—Grunt was the same person who nailed a man to a fence.

I snapped back to the present and my conversation with Jan. I'd felt there was a special bond between Grunt and Moe, but I didn't know what it was. If I was going to be honest, I thought it might've been sexual, but I was wrong. It was so strange to think her comment about Grunt is what caused her mutilation. She could've justified an even more intense hatred of him after that. Yet the simple act of loving concern from a child changed it all.

I was touched.

I was thinking about this and watching Grunt as he drove us home. I had a paper plate full of food wrapped in tinfoil for Moe on my lap. I was feeling a slight high from the wine and had my head leaned back against the seat, but facing Grunt.

We stopped at a stop sign and he looked over at me. I lifted my hand and caressed his cheek. "You are such a good person, Grunt. I'm glad it was you."

He looked at me like he was confused and then realized that I was talking about the night he drugged me in his room. He took my hand and kissed it.

"I'm glad it was me too, Kit."

We were lost in the moment, and the reality of what was happening sunk in. I pulled my hand back and sat up.

"I hope it hasn't caused a problem with you and Sarah Jo," I said quietly. "I mean, I'm assuming she doesn't know, and I don't know if you feel guilty about cheating on her like that. You know? I'm sorry if you do."

He didn't say anything right away, but looked straight ahead and started to drive.   "Sarah Jo's not my girlfriend, Kit."

This got my attention and I looked over at him. "What? What do you mean she's not your girlfriend? I've seen you two together. You sure look like a couple to me."

"Well, we're not. We've been best friends for a long time. Fess didn't like to bring her around, but he liked me and would take me home with him once in awhile. She has two younger brothers, too. They'd lost their mother a year or two before. Breast cancer."

I was stunned. "Stop. Pull over here, Grunt. I want to

talk to you, and I want your attention."

He did as I asked and made a right on Griffin Road. There was nothing but orange groves out there in the seventies, and he easily pulled into one of the rows.

He cut the engine and turned to face me. "She's not my girlfriend, but she is very special to me."

"Do you always act that lovey-dovey with someone who's not your girlfriend?" On the few occasions I had seen them, they were either holding hands or had their arms around each other, but now that I thought about it, I'd never seen them kiss.

"Jo and I are affectionate with each other, but there's nothing to it. She's had the same boyfriend from high school for two years. Stephen somebody."

"You do know I thought you were a couple, right? Grunt. Answer me. You wanted me to think you were a couple, didn't you?"

He didn't say anything, just looked at his lap.

"It's better this way, don't you think?" he whispered.

I couldn't believe what I was hearing? Did Grunt have feelings for me and was trying to hide them? Did he know I had feelings for him back in the summer and purposely derailed them by bringing Sarah Jo to the motel?

I touched his face then and turned it toward me. We were staring at each other. I wanted so badly to kiss him, but I couldn't betray Grizz. I didn't know what to do. My mind was reeling. I remembered how much I had tried to hang around Grunt after that dream. That's when Sarah Jo showed up. Had he done that on purpose to dissuade me?

"What is this, Grunt?" Tears pricked my eyes.

"It doesn't matter." His voice was hollow. "It can never be and we both know it."

I couldn't let it drop. "If it could be, would you want it? Would you want me?"

"Kit, I've wanted you since the first night I saw you. You sat there that night in the pit, so brave and so beautiful in those jeans and that flowery shirt. I was going to take care of you. I didn't know what Monster was gonna do with you, but I would have gone up against him for you. That was before I knew he brought you there for Grizz."

I remembered that night vividly. I remembered the feeling of being watched. I instantly remembered the morning after I lost my virginity. How I went to Grunt's room to ask him to take me out. He'd asked me what I was wearing that first night so I didn't wear it while I was out with him. I might've been recognized. Now I knew it was an act. He knew exactly what I'd been wearing the first night at the motel.

My mind was in turmoil. I didn't know what to say.

I didn't have to say anything. The spell was broken when he started the car. The loud engine snapped me back to reality, and we wordlessly drove back to the motel.

Chapter Twenty-Five

That evening was never discussed again. We fell back into our normal routines like it never happened—no covert glances or stolen looks. We both must have committed to ourselves the same thought: It never happened. It couldn't happen. And it was erased from memory.

There was one positive thing that came from that talk, though—Sarah Jo. Knowing she wasn't romantically involved with Grunt opened up an avenue I wanted to explore: friendship. I was growing to love Moe, but honestly, communication was difficult. Grizz and Grunt were men. The thing with Jan was a disaster. I wanted a girlfriend.

I asked Grunt for her phone number. Grunt and I had gone back to being comfortable around each other like we were on the drive over to Blue's that Thanksgiving. I made first contact with Sarah Jo, and it was instant chemistry.

It didn't start out easy, though. Her father resisted our friendship at first. I think Fess was uncomfortable with her being friends with the underage wife of a notorious gang leader. And who could blame him?

Her father wasn't the hardened criminal one expected to find in a motorcycle gang. He actually fell into it by accident. Fess's nickname was short for Professor. He taught at a local college. Back then, he was juggling his teaching career, three small children and a dying wife. It was all too much for him.

Three months after his wife died, he was approached by the parent of one of his students. The student was failing his class, which would have prevented him from graduating.

Fess didn't have to be bribed. He already felt like he'd let his students down by not being there for them during his wife's illness and ultimate death. He told the parent to not worry; his son would pass.

That parent happened to be a narcotics detective. He told Fess he would make it up to him no matter what. Whenever Fess needed a favor, no matter what it was, he would be his man. Fess got the distinct impression that when he said it didn't matter what it was, he meant it.

Less than a month later, Fess was drowning his sorrows at a bar and met a young, up-and-coming motorcycle gang leader. Grizz.

Fess was not only missing his wife, trying to raise three small children and hold down a job, but he was terribly in debt. His wife's illness was long, and even though he had insurance through his job, it wasn't enough for all the care she required. He needed money. He was going to lose his house.

That's how it started. Grizz's network of inside informants. Fess called in that favor and the parent was only too happy to oblige. Grizz paid well. That's what Fess did. He kept a ledger for Grizz of informants and other people who worked for him in other capacities. Fess kept records of who did what and how much they were paid. He never passed money. He never made contact. He never used his real name. There was never anything to tie him to Grizz.

He eventually bought himself a Harley and would occasionally come out to the motel, but he never wore the jacket. The only reason Sarah Jo was friends with Grunt was because Fess felt sorry for the little boy at the motel. He later became extremely fond of Grunt. Grunt had potential, and Fess saw that.

Sarah Jo confided in me that Fess regularly visited Moe in her room when he was there. Jo knew how much he missed her mother, and he was only human. She thought her father might have feelings for Moe. But if they cared about each other, they hid it well from the rest of us.

Sarah Jo told me she did recognize me when she first met me. But, of course, she knew better than to say anything. She attended my rival school, Fort Lauderdale High School. My school, Stranahan, and her school had been archenemies as long as I could remember. But she had enough friends at Stranahan to know about me: the honor student who'd gone missing. It was assumed I'd run away.

She told me all about her boyfriend, Stephen. She'd been with him for two years and was currently torn between her love for him and the interest a new boy was showing her.

Our friendship was difficult for us in the beginning because of my limitations on where I could go, and neither one of us had a driver's license. We had to rely on Grunt,

Moe, Grizz, Fess or whoever was available to drop us at an occasional movie, the beach or an out of the way mall.

Still, in spite of the obstacles, the friendship flourished. She was my maid of honor when I married my husband. I was hers when she married her husband. She was there when I gave birth to my two children. I was there when she had her three children. She was waiting for me outside the execution viewing room the day Grizz died.

She was, and is to this day, one of my very best friends.

Thanksgiving had come and gone. It was now only a couple of weeks before Christmas. I'd managed to shop a couple of times with Sarah Jo. I had a nice Christmas gift planned for Grizz, but it was going to take some time. I told him it would be late. I think he assumed it was something I was making for him since I had no money of my own and wasn't going to touch his money to buy him a gift. He was more concerned about a gift for me.

One night, I was sitting cross-legged on the bed doing homework. Grizz, who had just come out of the shower and was drying himself, had been pestering me about what I wanted for Christmas. I kept telling him I didn't need anything; I had everything I could need or want.

"There must be something, Kit. Anything you want," he said, a white towel wrapped around his waist as he crossed the room and sat down on the bed next to me, his body still damp. "You name it. It's yours. I don't care how much it costs. I don't care if it's something you think is hard to find. Anything, baby. Anything."

I closed my book, touching his arm lightly. "Really

Grizz. I'm serious. There isn't anything."

He pushed my books out of the way and laid me gently back on the bed. Then in one swift movement he straddled me and brought his face close to mine. "Okay," he said, grinning down at me and kissing my forehead softly. "How about a trip? We can get a house in the Keys for a couple of weeks. Just the two of us."

I just looked at him and smiled, wrapping my arms around his neck and kissing him. And after a few seconds something did occur to me: something I'd been wanting to do.

"You know, yes, there is someplace you could take me."

"Name it, baby. I can have Eddie get you a passport. We could go to Mexico, Paris, anywhere. Name it."

"I want to go to church."

As hard as it may be to believe, I missed church more than I missed my home. I'd come to rely on my faith for survival from a very young age. I missed the feeling and sense of peace I got when I was there—the knowing that I was loved unconditionally, that I didn't have to do anything to earn that love. I wasn't required to cook or pay the bills. I was required to do one thing only: accept Jesus Christ as my Lord and Savior. I did that when I was nine years old.

Grizz scratched his chin and sat up. "I was wondering when you were going to get around to asking that."

I looked at him questioningly.

"I know you went to church every Sunday."

Of course he did.

"Kit, I can't take you to your church. I don't even think it would be a good idea to take you to any church on this coast."

Years later, I found out Grizz's connections had told him

it was my church, and one nun in particular, who'd pushed investigators to search for me. Sister Mary Katherine had taken a special interest in me. She was worried about the young girl who attended Mass every Sunday by herself. She'd become my friend and my confidant. I missed her more than I missed Delia.

When I allowed myself to think about it, I didn't miss Delia at all. I just missed the familiarity of a home. I knew what to expect in that home. Living at the motel was frightening in that it was fraught with uncertainty. I rarely allowed myself to think about what was going on outside the door of number four.

That's how I was able to cope for years with the reality of my husband's criminal behavior: I ignored it. I actually pretended it didn't exist. Of course, there were some things I couldn't avoid or ignore, so I played a little mind game with myself. I called it "that didn't happen."

When investigators refused to cooperate with Sister Mary Katherine, she used Catholic churches up and down the east coast of Florida as a way to keep my disappearance in the spotlight. Even if it was just within the church circle, it was kind of her to do it.

"Why not?" I asked him now. "If we went just a little north or even south toward Miami, I think it would be safe."

"I just think there's more of a risk of you being recognized. But I've got an idea. Trust me. I'll take care of it."

And he did. For many years after this conversation, early every Sunday morning, Grizz either took me himself or had someone else drive me across Alligator Alley to the west coast of Florida. It was about an hour and a half drive. Sometimes, he would take me over on Friday or Saturday and we would get a hotel. He never attended church with me. But he was always waiting for me when I came out. I eventually started attending on my own coast as development migrated west. But he kept his word in those early years.

Christmas and New Year's soon passed, and I was approaching my real sixteenth birthday. I wasn't sure if Grizz knew when it was. I was wrong. Grizz knew everything. Well, almost everything.

I woke up that morning and busied myself like I usually did. Grizz was outside doing something with Chowder. He peeked his head in number four and asked me to come outside. When I got outside, there was a shiny new black Trans Am parked in front of the motel. He was smiling at me.

"Do you like it?"

"You got a new car? Of course I like it! I love it! Take me for a ride."

"No, you take me for a ride," he smiled. "It's yours. Happy birthday, Kitten."

He hugged me and kissed me on the top of the head. I didn't know what surprised me more—the fact that he remembered it was my real birthday, or the fact that he bought me such an unexpected and expensive gift.

"The keys are in it. Let's go," he said. "You drive."

"I can't."

"Why not?"

I blushed. "Because I don't know how to drive."

For someone who knew every detail about my life, this

seemed an important one that he missed.

"I know you don't have a real license, but Ann Marie O'Connell does," he told me; Eddie had made me a new license after we were married.

"But, Grizz, I don't know how to actually drive. You know, steering and gas and all that."

"What do you mean? I saw your driver's permit last year."

"Yes, I took a written test to get a driver's permit last February, but drivers ed classes weren't until summer school. I don't need to tell you why I never got to take them."

The look on his face was comical, and he started laughing hard. "How'd I miss that?"

I started laughing, too. "I don't know, but you did."

"Hop in. Let's go. You're going to learn to drive."

For the rest of the month, I got driving lessons from Grizz, Grunt, Chowder and Moe. Whoever was available took the time to give me lessons. But it was Grizz I spent the most time with. There were certain rules he insisted on. At least in the beginning, I was never to go anywhere by myself. I was never to go anywhere near my old neighborhood. I could live with those rules, but he made one exception that angered me: I wasn't allowed to go anywhere alone with Sarah Jo.

I'd argued back that he'd told me I couldn't go anywhere alone, and if Sarah Jo was with me, I wouldn't be alone. Besides, he himself had dropped the two of us off at the movies a few times. But it was no use—he didn't like it. It wasn't about Sarah Jo; he just didn't like the idea of two young girls riding around in a Trans Am.

"Then you should have bought me an ugly old clunker,"

I yelled.

It was our first real argument, and I fought him tooth and nail. But of course, I didn't win. I stayed mad at him for days. I ignored him. I wouldn't cook for him. I definitely didn't sleep with him. I locked myself in one of the unused motel rooms and did my homework and read my books, only coming out to eat and check on Gwinny. He left me alone, which only made me madder.

Then something happened that I didn't expect: I realized I missed him.

I guess it was because I'd been taken from a home where I'd been virtually ignored. Here, Grizz lavished me with attention and gifts. At this point in our relationship, he'd never denied me anything, other than my freedom. Not counting my first sexual experience with Grunt, he'd never hurt me.

Actually, he spoiled me rotten.

Grizz was quiet. He didn't talk a lot, but he was affectionate. And it wasn't always the sexual affection. He was touchy, always holding my hand whether in public or strolling out to the pit. If I walked out to the pit alone, he would pull me down to sit on his lap. I woke up every single morning wrapped in the warmth and protection of his arms.

I tried to think what I had given him in return. Well, I gave him me, if that counted. I gave him my loyalty. I certainly could've figured out a way to escape and warn Delia and Vince. But was loyalty enough? By then, I'd started feeling guilty, so I made my way back to number four. I didn't know if he would be there or not.

He was there, relaxing in his recliner with his eyes closed. I knew he wasn't asleep. The stereo was on. He was listening to one of my albums. Seals & Crofts. "Summer Breeze" was playing.

I'd accumulated my own record collection by now. It was rare that Grizz and I agreed on the same music. He liked hard rock, and although I liked some, I also enjoyed easy listening: Loggins & Messina, Bread, Paul Davis, ABBA.

I stood over him. "Since when do you like Seals & Crofts?"

"Don't," he said, his eyes still closed.

"Then why are you listening to them?"

"Because you love them and I love you and I missed you."

Did he just say he loved me? My heart thudded.

Grizz opened his eyes then and looked at me.

"Does that surprise you, Kit?" His green eyes were warm. "That I'm in love with you?"

I didn't know what to say. Even after last year's explanation of the reason behind his obsession with me, I'd never heard him talk about love.

So I did the only thing I could think of. I pulled the recliner—and him—into an upright position. Then I sat down on his lap and wrapped my arms around him.

"I love you too, Grizz," I said.

And I meant it. It was probably more of a shock to me than to him.

He kissed me then. "Can you do me a favor, baby?"

"Yes, Grizz, anything." I answered him, smiling. I knew what he was going to ask for, and I was willing.

"I have a bad headache. Can you get me some aspirin?"

I pulled back and looked at him, surprised. "Sure."

"What's wrong?" I said, returning with aspirin and

some water. "Have you been in the sun or something too long? You never get headaches."

"Nah. I think it's from listening to your music."

Chapter Twenty-Six

It was now March, and I was finally ready to give Grizz his Christmas present. We'd just eaten dinner, and he went to sit down and do some work at his desk. I went into the bedroom and brought out his gift. It was heavy.

I sat it on the small coffee table and grinned at him. "Merry belated Christmas!"

He turned around and noticed the present. I must have shocked him. Either he wasn't used to getting gifts or he thought I'd forgotten I owed him one. He just looked at me.

"Are you going to just sit there and stare at me or are you going to open it?" I teased.

Without saying anything he got up and started to pick it up with one hand, but I think the weight of the box surprised him.

"Whoa, what's this?"

"You have to open it and find out."

He picked it up with both hands and sat down on the couch. I sat next to him and pulled my knees up and rested my chin on them. He slowly started to unwrap it. It was a plain brown box. He opened the box and lifted out one of many individually wrapped pieces. I watched his face closely as he unwrapped the first one.

It was a customized chess set, all handcrafted pieces of ivory—skulls and other symbols.

He held up the first piece and looked at me.

"How? How did you get this for me, Kit? If the rest of the pieces are this intricate, it must have cost you a fortune."

"Doesn't matter. Do you like it?" I hugged my knees tighter. "Just tell me you like it. Oh, and the chessboard is under our bed! It was way too heavy to wrap. You like it, don't you?" Suddenly I was worried whether I chose the right gift.

"How did you pay for it?" His eyes were serious.

"That's a terribly impolite question, Grizz. Don't worry, I didn't use your money, if that's what you're thinking."

"I'm not thinking that at all. I just can't figure out how you came up with this kind of money." Carefully he unwrapped every piece, setting them all down in an even line on the coffee table.

I knew the minute he figured it out. I could tell by the expression on his face. It was one of only two times I saw something close to tears in his eyes. The second time was when I showed him a picture of our daughter when I visited him in prison.

In barely a whisper, he said, "You hocked your guitar."

———

He was right. I'd hocked my guitar. It was a special guitar, and I'd received a substantial amount of money for it. Thank goodness Guido had picked it up in Delia's yard sale before she sold it. She never did believe me when I'd told her how valuable it was.

I got the guitar as a gift in 1969. I was nine years old and attending Woodstock with Delia and Vince. The only thing Delia let me bring to keep myself occupied were some magic markers and coloring books. We'd set up our small camp next to a young couple. I wish I could remember their names. The guy had a guitar he would bring out and play when there were no performances. He caught me staring the first day. I think they both felt sorry for me since Delia and Vince were either wasted or asleep. He gave me guitar lessons. He showed me the basic notes and let me practice on his guitar.

It rained that weekend and performances were delayed and it was a muddy mess. The young couple left for home late Sunday night. While his wife was packing up, he called me aside and told me he wanted me to have his guitar as long as I would keep learning to play it. I'd already learned "Jingle Bells," and he said it was good to learn that, but I needed to practice the notes he taught me, too. He said it was an old guitar, but tuned well, and I could keep it. I was thrilled.

The next morning, most of the crowd had cleared out. I woke up to loud music that was so good I was mesmerized. It was Jimi Hendrix playing "The Star-Spangled Banner" on his electric guitar. I tried to wake up Delia and Vince, but they were completely passed out. Before Jimi was finished with his set, I took one of my black magic markers and my newly acquired guitar and hauled myself up to the side of the stage.

"Sorry kid, can't let you back here," some guy with an official-looking pass told me at the gate. He had to yell over the sound of the music.

"My parents are working back there and I've been walking around with my dad's guitar. He's gonna be so mad at me for running off. Please let me back there before I get in trouble," I lied, shouting up at him.

He either believed me or figured a kid wasn't much of a threat. He let me in. I was waiting for Jimi Hendrix when he finally came down off the stage. I barged right up to him and stopped him in his tracks.

"Could you please sign my guitar, Mr. Hendrix?" And before he could answer, "I just learned how to play it this weekend."

I think this amused him because he gave me a big smile. His face was glistening with sweat, and he used his arm to swipe across it. "Sure, gotta pen or something?"

I handed him my magic marker. He wrote "Gypsy Eyes, Jimi Hendrix, WS, 8/18/69" right on the back of the guitar.

"What are gypsy eyes?" I asked him as I tried to make out the words of his hasty scribbling.

"What's your name?"

"Gwinny."

"Well, Gwinny, it's a song I recorded last year, but since you have the biggest, brownest eyes I've ever seen, I think it applies to you today."

I gave him the biggest smile I could muster. "Thank you."

He didn't reply. He just smiled and started walking. I took my newly autographed guitar and headed back the way I came in.

"Hey, your parents are gonna be mad if you take your dad's guitar out there again," the guy at the gate said to me.

"No, it's okay, my parents are out there camping," I said as I sauntered past.

"What? I thought you told me your parents were on the crew."

"I did. I'm sorry for lying. But I got Jimi Hendrix to sign my guitar!" I lifted it up for him to see.

"Nice going," he said with a smile.

When Delia and Vince finally sobered up enough for us to leave I showed them my autographed guitar. They didn't believe it was an authentic signature. I guess it was just sloppy enough that they thought I signed it myself. Either that or they were too hungover to care.

"Yes, I hocked my guitar," I answered Grizz, my eyes on the ground. "You've given me so much, and I just wanted to give something back. I'm sorry it took so long, but it's handmade and there was no way I could get it in time for Christmas."

He stood up and looked down at me. Then he took my hand, pulled me up and caught me in a bear hug that almost took my breath away.

"It's the nicest present that anyone has ever given me, Kit. Thank you. I love it and I love you." He kissed the top of my head.

"Now let's go get your guitar back."

Chapter Twenty-Seven

By now I'd almost forgotten I was a victim of an abduction. I continued to disguise myself when I left the motel, but for the most part I just assumed people had forgotten about me. I was okay with that. I didn't want to be found.

There were always new people coming and going, and I did my best to avoid them. I knew what Grizz was. He was a criminal. So were the majority of the people he associated with. I despised that the man I loved earned a living illegally. The only way I knew how to deal with it was to ignore it. It wasn't always easy.

I'd been living at the motel for almost a year. One day in particular I heard a loud fuss out by the pit—yelling and hooting. Lucifer and Damien were barking. Grizz walked out to see what was happening. When things didn't quiet down, I went out, too. It took me a few minutes to assess what was happening, and when I did I was horrified.

It was a young couple. He was getting beaten and she was getting raped. Grizz was just standing there talking to some guy and ignoring everything that was happening. The dogs had stopped barking because Grizz had commanded them, but other than that, there was still a frenzy of activity and yelling. I almost couldn't believe what I was seeing.

Apparently, this young couple had been tricked into coming back to the motel. The guys who did it didn't want the couple; they wanted the couple's motorcycle. And they made sport of the young guy and his girlfriend for kicks.

I walked right over to Grizz and interrupted him. "Can you please stop this? Do you see what's going on?"

He looked at me hard. "Not your concern, Kit. Go back inside."

I looked around for someone I might recognize, but there was no one. Where was Grunt, Chowder, Moe? I saw Monster, but he was enjoying himself too much. He must have raped the girl before I got out there because he was zipping up his jeans while simultaneously kicking the young guy in the ribs. I was outraged. Not my concern? I was witnessing a rape, for goodness' sake!

"Grizz, please stop this. I'm asking you to stop it for me."

Grizz nodded at the guy he was talking to. I recognized him now. His name was Chico. I'd noticed him at the motel once or twice before. He didn't wear a gang jacket.

"Miguel, end it now," Chico said to one of the guys sitting in a lawn chair. Grizz and Chico went back to their conversation.

Thank God, I thought, willing my hands to stop shaking. Before I could thank him, I watched the man called Miguel walk over to the girl who was lying on the ground and sobbing. I jumped. Miguel then walked over to the young man who had just been beaten and was also lying on the ground.

His way of ending it was by putting a bullet into each of their heads. I'd just witnessed my first executions.

It happened so quickly I couldn't even react. I was in shock but knew better than to show any hysterics to Grizz in front of these people.

I walked quickly back to number four and shut the door behind me. I leaned against it and was taking deep breaths and battling nausea when it opened and I fell backwards into Grizz's arms. He caught me and took me inside.

"You shouldn't have come out."

"Really? Really Grizz? What the heck was that? You were just standing there while a guy was being tortured and his girlfriend was raped?" I struggled to control my rising voice. "How could you let that happen?"

"Wasn't my problem to deal with, Kit."

"This is your place, Grizz. These are your people."

"Chico and his crew aren't my people. Miguel is his guy. They were setting up a delivery. Those kids were collateral damage. Not my problem. Not yours, either." He stepped past me to the couch and sat down.

I followed, hands on my hips. "So what you're basically telling me is you had no problem blinding Monster to save a kitten, but you wouldn't stop the execution of two innocents? Grizz." I paused for effect, my heart pounding. "You nodded your head and two people were *executed*."

"Kit, they weren't mine to deal with," he said and flipped on the TV. "You asked me to end it. Not my problem how he chose to do it. You don't like what goes on out there, then stay inside. Got it?"

I couldn't believe it. I thought I'd seen a different Grizz. A sympathetic Grizz who rescued kittens and listened to my kind of music. Someone who made sure his young wife went to church every Sunday.

I couldn't believe how naïve I was. He was all of those things, but I kept forgetting that he didn't get to be the leader of this gang by being soft. He was hard. He was cold-blooded. He was ruthless in his pursuit of what he wanted.

I took his advice. I stayed inside as often as possible.

———

I racked my brain for days afterwards, trying to figure out if I could've done something different. Of course I could have. I could've walked into that motel room and called the police. But would it have saved those two people? No.

More than likely, Grizz would have received a tip of his own before the police got here, and I might have ended up in the swamp with the others. I didn't really think that would happen, but I couldn't let myself imagine what Grizz would do to me if I really made him mad.

I went over it and over it in my head. If I told, would it save future people from being murdered in cold blood? Maybe. But what else would happen? Did I want to go back to my old life with Delia and Vince? Did I want to see Grizz, Moe, Chowder or Grunt in prison? Did I want to see Blue go to jail and his family fall apart? What about Fess?

The truth was I didn't know the extent of the criminal

activity that went on here, but it couldn't have been worse than murder. Could it?

I tried to engage Grizz in conversation about it, but he never indulged me. "It's better for you if you don't know certain things" is all he said.

After the incident with Chico and his crew, I noticed Grizz was trying to be more accommodating with me, if that was possible. He already spoiled me. But there was something different in the way he treated me after that day. I can't explain it, but I certainly felt it. I think even though he put his foot down and refused to discuss it, he secretly worried that what I saw that day might have put me over the edge. Maybe he was concerned I would stop loving him. I wasn't sure.

But then something happened and I knew my suspicions were correct.

It was a Saturday afternoon a week later. We were getting ready to leave for the west coast for church. I was packing an overnight bag. The weather was supposed to be good, and Grizz wanted to take his bike. He was standing at the foot of the bed and had just asked me if I would rather drive my car. I told him no. I loved my car, but I loved riding with him more. That seemed to make him happy, but quite honestly, it was true.

Just then the door burst open and Moe ran in, frantic. Tears ran down her face. She grabbed Grizz by the arm and pulled him towards the door. She didn't have to do much pulling. We both were on high alert and ran outside as quickly as possible.

When we got outside we followed her over toward the edge of the motel, and that's where we saw him—Damien. The big dog was lying on his side, and Lucifer was prancing around him excitedly, crying and whining. We heard the problem before we saw it.

A huge rattlesnake was coiled and made a lunge for Lucifer. Lucifer was able to avoid it and just kept barking and pacing. As soon as we got close enough, Grizz put up his left hand and waved me back. Before I realized it, he pulled out a gun that had been shoved into the back of his jeans. He killed the snake in one shot.

"Probably protecting her nest," he said. "Otherwise, she would've bit him and slithered off. Not stayed around for a fight."

I didn't know anything about snakes, so I just nodded like I knew what he was talking about.

He told me to get my car. I ran for number four and grabbed my keys. I ran to my car and got in. I started it and drove toward him. He was carrying Damien. He told me to get in the passenger seat. I put the car in park, jumped over the column and waited for him to lay Damien across my lap. Just then, Chowder came out and asked what the commotion was all about.

"Call the vet, tell him rattlesnake bite. Looks like two bites, maybe. I'll be there in ten minutes." Grizz turned to Moe and said, "You can't come."

I think she was already expecting this, but I could tell she was hurt and worried about Damien. It made more sense to me when we drove up to the vet in Davie. Of course Moe couldn't come. If she had been part of a rural community and raised horses, it was likely someone from the vet might have recognized her.

Chowder must have talked to someone, because they were waiting for us when we pulled up. Grizz parked and came around to pick Damien up off my lap. They were waiting with a gurney, but Grizz ignored them. After realizing Grizz wasn't going to lay Damien on the gurney, they ran up the front steps past him and opened the door. We followed the two vet technicians in and passed through the waiting room and into one of the treatment rooms, where Grizz laid Damien on a table. The vet was there and told us to wait outside.

We didn't go back out to the waiting room, but instead sat in two chairs just outside the door. I didn't notice if there were other patients waiting when we rushed in, but it didn't matter. I would think a deadly snakebite would take precedence over the other appointments.

We waited for what seemed like forever, but wasn't really long at all. The vet came out and explained he was treating Damien intravenously with anti-venom and heavy doses of antibiotics. Damien had to stay at the clinic for at least a week. They would watch the area around the bite marks and make sure he continued to respond positively to the treatment. He expected Damien to make a full recovery, but it was still too early to tell. He told us to go home and give him a call in the morning. It was going to be a long week.

Grizz shook his hand and opened the door for me to go out into the waiting room. He stopped at the reception desk and told the girl we would handle the bill the following day. She batted her clumpy mascara eyelashes at him and said that would be fine. We made our way through the waiting room, not really noticing anyone who was there.

Grizz was holding the door open for me to go outside when I heard a voice.

"Ginny? Ginny Lemon, is that you?"

Chapter Twenty-Eight

You always hear about people who think they are dying and how their life flashes in front of them. You secretly wonder, how can that be? A whole life in a matter of seconds? You might hear about someone who witnessed an accident say everything happened in slow motion and they recount every detail.

I never believed those kinds of stories until that day.

That day, I heard a name I hadn't heard in almost a year.

I read the look on Grizz's face immediately. In that instant, I knew he thought he'd lost me. And I also knew I was correct in thinking something had been different about him since the executions.

Grizz knew there would be no going back from what I'd witnessed that day in the pit. He'd worried I might want to leave him, and now he was faced with that possibility. The threat to hurt Delia and Vince would no longer hold water. I wouldn't be trying to escape if someone recognized me. All I had to do was turn around to the person talking to me and say, "Yes, it's me," and it would be done. There would have been plenty of witnesses in that waiting room.

Grizz would have two choices: grab me and drag me out to the car, or take off by himself and hightail it out of there. One choice meant he risked losing me; the other way meant he risked not being able to come back for Damien.

That's when time stood still. That's when, not my whole life, but the past year, flashed before my eyes. I met Grizz's glance and knew instinctively what I was going to do.

Standing in the doorway I turned to see who was talking to me. I recognized her immediately: Diane Berger. She wasn't a close friend, but we'd shared a couple of classes. She was a nice girl. Kind of like me. Not real popular, but not an outcast either.

With an extremely convincing British accent, I answered her, "Me, luv? Are you talking to me?"

That surprised her.

"Uh, yeah. You look like a girl I went to school with. She's been missing. It'll be a year next month, I think. You could be her twin."

"My name is Amelia. I'm visiting my cousin," I lied with my phony British accent.

"I'm so sorry. I just can't believe you're not Ginny. The similarities are unbelievable!"

"No, luv, it's me that's sorry. I wish I was your friend. I hope you find her some day."

Grizz grabbed me by the hand and walked me to the car. He didn't say anything. We headed back to the motel and I spoke first.

"Do you think she believed me?" My voice was quiet.

"Actually, I do. Hell, I think I believed you," he said, incredulous. "Where did you learn how to do an accent like that?"

"Oh, you know how much I love Masterpiece Theater."

"I wasn't sure what you were going to do," he said, giving me a sidelong glance as he drove.

I didn't say anything.

"You know I wouldn't have let you go, don't you? I would have hauled you out to the car and kept driving. I would've taken you somewhere else. No one would have found us."

This surprised me. "What about the motel? Your car, your bikes, your money, your dogs?"

"Doesn't matter. I have a way to get all my stuff back eventually, if I needed to."

"You're telling me that if for some reason I was recognized and there was a chance of me being rescued or found, you wouldn't give me up?"

"Never, Kit. Never."

We drove the rest of the way back to the motel in silence. When we arrived, he asked if I wanted someone to take me to church in the morning. He was going back to the vet to see Damien, but he didn't think I should go with him.

"No, I can miss church tomorrow. I want to be here for you."

I know this made him happy. I put together a quick dinner, and he went out to the pit for a little while. When he came back I was already in bed. He climbed in beside me and pulled me into his arms.

"You awake?" he whispered.

"Am now."

"Good," he replied, nuzzling my neck.

"What do you have in mind?"

"I want you to talk dirty to me."

This was new, and I laughed. "Oh, you do? And what exactly do you want me to say to you?"

"Ah, I don't care. Use your imagination."

"I don't have any dirty talk experience, but I'll try," I teased, my cheeks hot in the darkness.

"Can you do me a small favor?"

"Sure."

"Can you talk dirty to me with that British accent?"

Damien's recovery was quicker than expected and uneventful. Before the snake, I'd never considered the dangers that lurked in the swamp. Other than keeping an eye out for the occasional alligator, I never gave a second thought to other harmful creatures. I did now.

We fell back into a routine, and I stayed busy with my correspondence course. Before I knew it, it was 1977 and Ann Marie Morgan O'Connell was the proud owner of a high school diploma. Ginny Lemon wouldn't have graduated for another year. I was a good driver and was getting to go to most places I set my sights on, but I still had to follow Grizz's driving rules. That would change in a couple of months.

Still, it wasn't enough. I needed more. I was bored. I needed a mental challenge. And I found it quite by accident.

I'd been living at the motel for almost two years. One day, I was sitting on the couch painting my toenails. Grizz was doing paperwork at his desk. I'd never concerned myself with the type of paperwork he did. I figured it had to do with his criminal activity, and like he'd told me more than once, the less I knew the better. I'd just finished my nails and was twisting the lid back on the bottle of nail polish when Grizz slammed his fist down hard on the desk. I jumped.

"Damn it!" he yelled.

"What? What's the problem?" I was glad I'd finished my toes. His outburst was so loud I might have messed up my paint job.

"Just trying to get these damn numbers to work, is all. Numbers aren't my area of expertise."

"Well, what exactly are you doing with numbers?"

"Balancing this fucking bank statement. Hasn't balanced for three months, and I can't figure out why."

I immediately perked up. "Bank statement? Why don't you let me look at it? I can help you. I love working with numbers."

"Nah. I'll figure it out eventually."

"Seriously, Grizz. I'd love to help. I bet I can figure out the problem."

He turned around then and looked at me. I could tell he was weighing his options. He was just frustrated enough to let me help, but he had also been very careful to keep me away from his business.

"I could be like a secretary or bookkeeper. I don't have to know any details or where these numbers come from. Believe me, I'm just interested in the numbers, Grizz. I'd like the challenge."

I knew I'd won when he didn't say anything right away. I jumped up and walked over to him while balancing on my heels, trying not to mess up my pedicure.

"Okay, Kit," he said at last. "All yours. No questions, though. You just balance the checkbook. Old statements are right here." He pulled open a drawer.

I sat down and got to work. I figured out the problem very quickly. An old entry had been calculated as a minus instead of a plus. In addition to about $21.65 in other combined entry errors, I could see why he was having trouble finding the problem. He could have found it easily enough if he'd had more patience.

That's how I started taking care of Grizz's finances. I soon came to learn he had more than one alias. Each one had a substantial balance in their account.

I started diving in a little deeper and casually asked him one afternoon, "Why do you just let all this money sit there and not earn a decent return? Why don't you invest it?"

Within the year, Grizz and his many aliases had a decent stock portfolio. I was earning him a good amount of money. I secretly hoped if I could help him earn money another way, he would cease his criminal activity.

Another naïve assumption on my part.

Chapter Twenty-Nine

One day rolled into another, and before I knew it, I'd been living at the motel for almost three years. Not that those years were uneventful. I remembered one day the previous summer. It was a couple of months after I'd started balancing Grizz's bank statements. Sarah Jo and I had planned a day at the beach. I drove to her house, and we were going to take her car from there. Grizz had business at Eddie's, so he followed me until he got there. I went the rest of the way by myself. It wasn't far at all. But I still considered it a small victory, and that day was the beginning of the end of Grizz's driving rules.

Sarah Jo lived in a really nice neighborhood on the ocean side of Federal Highway. The homes were older, but well maintained. I pulled up about eleven o'clock that morning and parked my car in her driveway next to hers. She had the garage door up. I got out and put my beach things in her unlocked car. I approached the front door and knocked. This particular day was a weekday and her little brothers were at camp. Fess was teaching a summer class at the college. She was home alone.

"You ready?" I asked as soon as she opened the door.

"Yep. I just need to get the beach chairs out of the garage."

I told her I needed to use her bathroom, and she told me she would start loading up her car. It was a little car. A Pinto, I think. It was perfect for her. When I came out she was standing in front of her car with the hood up and two guys I didn't recognize were talking to her.

"What's up?" I asked as I approached them.

"Won't start," she answered, staring at the engine. "Sam thinks he might be able to help me."

"Want me to call and see if maybe just this once we can take my car?"

Before she could answer one of them spoke.

"I think I can fix it," the younger of the two commented. This was Sam, her neighbor. I recognized him now. He was a nice guy. A little older than Jo, and I remembered he'd gotten into some trouble recently. He had graduated high school and fallen in with a bad crowd. I think Jo told me he'd been picked up for vandalism, drugs, the usual. His single mother, Vanessa, had asked Fess for some help getting him out of jail. Jo was certain Vanessa knew about the motorcycle gang and Fess's possible participation, but she was an okay lady. She minded her business, kept to herself, but without being standoffish. She had been very kind to Jo's family when her mother passed away years earlier, and they'd continued a comfortable and amicable relationship since then. It seemed only natural she would go to Fess for some help.

Fess got Sam out of jail and helped him enroll in a trade school. I hadn't heard anything since and thought he was doing well. Still living at home, but hopefully staying out of trouble. I didn't recognize the guy he was with.

"Kit, you remember Sam from across the street."

I smiled and said, "Hi, Sam. How've things been going? Everything good, I hope." He looked up from what he was doing and gave me a wide smile. Whoa. I didn't remember him being that cute. Then again, I didn't remember taking notice of many other men during that time in my life.

"Kit." His smile grew warmer. "Nice to see you. Yeah, things are good. How about you?"

"I'm really good. I'll be even better if you can fix whatever's wrong with Jo's car."

"Aren't you gonna introduce me?"

I hadn't been paying attention to the other guy and now looked over at him. I didn't like what I saw. For starters, he was leaning on my car and drinking a beer. He was probably in his thirties, a little old to be hanging out with Sam, and sleazy-looking. I didn't say hello, just nodded and went back to looking under the hood with Sam and Jo.

"That's Neal," Sam said without looking up.

"So you ladies don't look like you belong to a motorcycle gang," Neal said in an exaggerated, phony southern drawl.

Before we could answer, Sam said, "Shut up, Neal."

"Well, c'mon now, Sam, you was the one bragging in jail that some bikers were getting you out. That you had connections." Neal sneered toward Jo's house and said, "Looks like nothing but an old man and some kids. Your daddy ever ride that thing?" he asked Sarah Jo as he nodded toward Fess's bike in the open garage.

Without waiting for her to answer, Neal started walking toward the garage. Sam by this time was totally mortified and kept apologizing to Sarah Jo while pleading with Neal to shut up and just leave.

This now made sense. Neal must have met Sam during his short stay in jail a couple of months ago. I couldn't figure out the current connection, though. I thought Sam had cleaned up his act and was doing well for himself. I wondered how Neal fit into this picture.

I whispered to Jo, "Call Grizz at Eddie's."

Sam heard me and I saw an expression on his face I couldn't read. Was it fear? Relief? Jo made a beeline for her front door. Neal sat on Fess's bike making motorcycle sounds. In between he was yelling at Jo as she walked up to her front door, "Oh, you gonna call your old man, the big bad gang member? Well, you go ahead and do that, little girl. I bet I can get him to let me take this baby for a ride. You know what? Let's not wait for you to ask him. Get me the key."

Sarah Jo ignored him and went inside her house. I was praying Grizz was still at Eddie's. *Please let him be there. Please let him be there.* This was long before cell phones. In the meantime I was mentally trying to devise a back-up plan in case he wasn't there.

I turned to Sam. "What's with this guy?"

"I haven't been able to shake him, Kit," Sam said quietly. "And I never told him anything about the gang. I swear. He must've heard stuff through the jail. He showed up acting like my best friend five days after I got out. I don't know what he wants with me, and honestly, I don't know how to get rid of him. He hasn't said anything directly, but he's hinted at hurting my mom. I've been giving him money just to get rid of him and then he pops back up unexpectedly and uninvited, like this morning. I don't want no trouble."

"It'll be okay. Don't worry, Sam."

"Kit, I don't want no trouble with the gang."

"I said not to worry."

Just then, Sarah Jo opened her front door and nodded at me. I knew then that help was on the way.

I turned to Sam. "You need to go home now. You need to go inside and not come back out. Okay?"

"I can't leave you and Jo with this maniac," he said. "It wouldn't be right."

We stood there a few more minutes listening to Neal ranting from the garage. I signaled to let Jo know I was okay and she should shut and lock the front door. She knew I would be fine and so she did it without hesitation.

Neal picked this time to start yelling at Sarah Jo. There was a door in the garage that went into the kitchen, and even though it was closed, he knew she could hear him.

"Bring me the key, little bitch, and I'll get out of here and nothing bad will happen," Neal called out in a singsong. "Motorcycle gang, my ass."

I heard a motorcycle. *Finally*. It took less than ten minutes, but felt like an hour.

"Go now, Sam," I told him, my voice low and urgent. "Now. Shut your door and don't come out. Go. Please. We're okay. You know who's coming, right?"

He just nodded and whispered, "I'm sorry, Kit."

Then he walked directly across the street and into his house, shutting the door behind him.

I had been leaning up against the back of Sarah Jo's car.

Grizz rolled up to the curb like he didn't have a care in the world. Neal must have heard him because the garage got quiet all of a sudden. Grizz turned off his bike and got off. He walked up the driveway.

When he got to me, I asked, "Did you bring back-up? Do you want to wait for help?"

He just rolled his eyes and said, "Wait here, sweetheart."

I was confident Grizz could handle Neal, but I was worried maybe Neal had a weapon I hadn't noticed. He could take a gun out at any time and just shoot Grizz.

Then again, Grizz always had a weapon on him. I probably didn't have to worry.

I didn't follow Grizz all the way into the garage. I just stood in front of Jo's car with my arms across my chest. Her hood was still up, and my car was parked next to hers blocking the view of what was going on inside. I was relieved. I didn't want a nosy neighbor calling the police. I still didn't know how Grizz was going to handle Neal. I didn't have to wait long.

During the time it took for Grizz to walk up Jo's driveway, Neal had gotten himself off Fess's bike. I could see him shaking as Grizz made his way into the garage.

"Aw, fuck, man. I'm sorry, man. I didn't know it was you, I swear," Neal said, his voice quavering. "I was just giving the kids a hard time."

He knew who Grizz was. Interesting.

Grizz just stood there with his arms relaxed at his sides and let Neal ramble.

"I heard some punks in jail talking about how the kid had friends in a gang. I didn't know it was your gang, man. I swear. They never said a name. I'll just be on my way like nothing ever happened."

I looked past Neal and saw Jo's face peeking out the door that connected the garage to the house. She had the widest grin I'd ever seen. I smiled back at her.

"Get on your knees."

"What? What ya gonna do to me, man? Man, please don't kill me.'

"Get on your knees now, motherfucker."

Sobbing loudly, Neal lowered himself to his knees. He was shaking more than before. Grizz had his back to me. He walked slowly toward Neal and I heard him undo his zipper.

What? Why was he undoing his zipper?

Neal started whining again, "Aw, man, I ain't no fag. What are you doing, man?"

Yeah, what are you doing?

"Open your mouth," Grizz growled.

"Aw, man, don't make me do this, please."

Sarah Jo and I made eye contact. Her eyes were as big as saucers.

"Open your fucking mouth now!" Grizz yelled.

Neal did as he was told, but Grizz didn't step closer to him. Before I realized what was happening, Neal started gagging. Then I understood what Grizz was doing. He was urinating in Neal's mouth.

Just then, Neal threw up. Grizz stepped back and zipped up. Neal was on all fours and vomiting all over Jo's garage floor. When he'd finished, he'd sat back on his haunches and closed his eyes.

"Sarah Jo, honey, be a sweetheart and get me a spoon, would ya?"

"Sure, Grizz."

Jo returned with a spoon and walked around Neal and

his vomit to hand it to Grizz. Grizz handed Neal the spoon and said, "Eat it. All of it."

While doing my best to ignore what Neal was doing, and not very successfully, I told Grizz about Jo's car not starting and how we came to meet Neal. How he'd met Sam in jail and his threats to Vanessa.

Grizz walked me and Jo to my car. "Go ahead and take your car to the beach. I'll stay and deal with shithead."

"I can't believe you peed in the guy's mouth. I thought you were going to make him perform oral sex."

I could hear Jo giggling as she got our beach stuff out of her car and started putting it into mine.

Another roll of his eyes. "After all this time with me and you can't even bring yourself to say 'blow job.'"

"I said it once. To Jan," I muttered quietly.

He just laughed and took my chin in his hands. "Still my sweet little Kitten. I love you, baby."

"I love you, too," I told him. "Just promise me that after he cleans up, you're done with him. Promise me. No violence or anything. Please?"

"I promise, baby." He kissed me as I tried to block out the gagging sounds coming from the garage.

Sarah Jo and I left in my car and I noticed the garage door went down as we pulled away. I prayed Grizz was going to keep his word and not do any more harm to the guy. My new favorite group was on the radio. Boston was singing "More Than a Feeling." Jo reached over and turned the volume down.

"Gosh, Kit. I thought we were best friends."

I looked over at her, surprised. "We are! Why would you say that?"

"Because, as long as we've been friends, you never once

mentioned your husband's huge dick."

Chapter Thirty

Time continued to pass. I rarely saw Grunt. He was still in college and working on a double master's degree. He was interested in architecture. He still came around the motel, but he had moved the majority of his belongings out. He was living with a girl, Cindy, at her condo on the beach.

I missed his friendship, but I was happy with Grizz. I was getting tired of the motel, though. I told Grizz I was ready for something new. I really wanted to go to college. I think I was envious of Grunt's success and happiness. I wanted to be more than Grizz's woman. Don't get me wrong—Grizz was still very good to me. But there was only so much I could get from a relationship. I needed a purpose.

I remembered when I was first abducted. I was only fifteen then, and had my life planned out. I knew what I wanted. I'd lost track of that in the romantic haze of Grizz's attention. I was starting to feel that stirring of wanting something more.

Grizz detected it before I did and tried to distract me. He had Grunt design a house for us. We spent weekends driving around and looking at open land.

Did this mean he was going to give up the motel for me? Give up the gang? No. He would still continue with his activities and I would become Jan. Live in a beautiful home. Pop out a couple of kids. I was torn.

I didn't have to dwell on it long. Something happened that took my attention away from my growing discontent. Something nobody saw coming. Something Grunt had warned me about years earlier.

It was the summer of 1978. It was a hot Tuesday night in July. Grizz had gone on one of his business trips. He was only going to be gone for two days and had actually asked me to go with him. I didn't feel like it. I was bored and depressed and I wanted to just wallow in it by myself. And that's just what I was doing. Lying on our bed looking at college brochures. I wanted so badly to go to college.

It was after eleven and I couldn't sleep. Damien and Lucifer were in Moe's room with her. I was absently stroking Gwinny's head.

I heard our door open. That was strange. Was it Moe? Did she need something for one of the dogs? Maybe Grizz was home early. I jumped up off the bed.

Suddenly there was a large, hulking presence in front of me. It wasn't Grizz. This man was dressed all in black and was wearing a ski mask. Before I could even register fear, he punched me right in the face and I fell back on to the bed.

He punched me hard enough to knock me out, but it didn't. I wish it had. For two hours, he continued to torture and rape me, repeatedly. He spoke to me tauntingly the whole time in a voice I didn't recognize.

"Grizz's woman, huh? Let's see if he's going to want you after I'm done with you."

That's pretty much how the entire two hours went. Well, at least I can only remember two hours of it. He continued to beat me and bring me to the point of losing consciousness only to make sure I didn't. I was so weakened by the initial punch in the face and the brutality he continued to unleash on me that I didn't stand a chance. I couldn't think clearly enough to come up with a plan to escape him.

Why hadn't I locked the door? I berated myself. But I never locked the door. I never had to.

Who was at the motel? Well, Moe was, and she had my protectors locked in her room with her. Chowder had taken a rare leave from the motel to visit a sister who was dying. With Grizz gone, the pit was empty.

I was alone.

Grunt's words from years earlier haunted me: "Just do me a favor, Kit. Stay sharp. Never let your guard down. You just never know with this kind of lifestyle what can come knocking at your door."

Well, this guy didn't knock. He just walked in. I'd let my guard down. I'd let myself believe that being with Grizz made me untouchable.

I couldn't have been more wrong.

Moe found me the next morning. I wasn't conscious and can only imagine her panic. She couldn't call anyone for help. Instead, she paged everyone who had a pager. She put in her code and 911.

Blue was the first to arrive. He couldn't call an ambulance. Even though I'd been missing for years, a public hospital was still too risky. So he called the doctor on Grizz's payroll. I'd started to come around by the time the doctor got there. I couldn't see anyone. Both my eyes were swollen shut. I still had all my teeth, but I required stitches to my lips and cheek. I was almost unrecognizable. My face was swollen to twice its normal size. I had bite marks all over my breasts, stomach and the inside of my thighs. I had broken ribs and a broken left wrist where I'd held up my hand to try to protect myself.

I was given enough pain medication that I was no longer feeling anything and fighting to stay awake. I don't know how much time passed before I heard him. Grizz. He busted in the room yelling and cursing. I couldn't see him because of my swollen eyes.

As I drifted into a painless sleep I heard him say, "God help the motherfucker who did this. He is going to suffer like no human being has ever suffered."

I almost felt sorry for the guy. It didn't last, though.

I didn't know then that he'd killed my cat.

Chapter Thirty-One

My recovery was slow. I was in an extreme amount of pain and was adamant about reducing the doses of my pain medication. The doctor continued to visit me regularly. After a couple days I was able to open one eye.

During my recovery, Grizz pestered me to death. He was obsessed with finding the guy who did this. He grilled me constantly on anything I could remember, even the slightest detail. Did I remember hearing a bike pull up? What color were the guy's eyes? Was his hair long and did it show beneath the ski mask? What other kinds of things did he say to me?

I wasn't the only one who got grilled. Poor Moe. She took the brunt of Grizz's anger.

"What the fuck were my dogs doing with you in your room while Kit was being attacked? I have those dogs for her protection when I'm not here, not yours'!"

I begged him not to be so hard on her. It was obvious she felt awful and somewhat responsible. He berated her relentlessly. I felt so sorry for her, and when I was finally able to get around, I did what I could to intervene. But, like I said, he was obsessed. And because he didn't know who did this to me, Moe was his whipping post. I honestly don't know if he ever physically hurt her. I hope not. Truth was, there was nothing he could do or say to make her feel any worse than she already did.

Grizz temporarily turned over his business operation to Blue. He was going to expend every effort to find out who did this. Every informant was told there would be a substantial reward for information leading Grizz to the guy who was responsible.

Over the next several months there were a few false leads. I cannot tell you the fear I saw on the faces of the men Grizz paraded in front of me. He would make them talk to see if I recognized their voices. He made them wear a ski mask to see if anything seemed familiar. I was certain I would recognize the voice and physical appearance of my attacker. None of those guys were even close.

I eventually made a complete physical recovery. I didn't do so well with the emotional part, though. I felt like I'd been violated, and I was certain Grizz wouldn't want me after that. But I couldn't have been more wrong. He'd been hesitant after I told him I was healed. I didn't realize it was because he was afraid of hurting me. Once I convinced him he wouldn't hurt me, we resumed our physical relationship.

It was hard for me at first. I couldn't close my eyes. I had to have them open the whole time, and I needed the light on. I had to see it was Grizz. It took me a long time to let him kiss my body. I tensed, waiting for the painful bite. Knowing that I was still struggling with it only fueled his anger. He started picking on Moe again.

I wish I'd noticed the change in her. I was just too wrapped up in what had happened to me; too wrapped up in my own recovery. Looking back, I should've called Grunt and asked him to come back to the motel and spend time with her. I am ashamed to say I didn't notice the depths of her despair and loneliness until it was too late.

It was 1979, and around the fourth anniversary of my abduction. A few months shy of the one-year anniversary of my attack. After my attack, Grizz purposely kept Damien and Lucifer away from Moe. I think this hurt her more than anything, and I felt horrible about it. Horrible enough to defy him and let her see them when I knew Grizz wasn't going to be around.

That's how Chowder found her. Grizz was gone, and I let her take Damien in her room one night. I kept Lucifer with me. Chowder heard Damien crying the next morning, and he let himself into Moe's room.

He found Moe peacefully lying in her bed with an empty bottle of pills next to her.

Dead.

I cannot tell you the extent of my devastation. I felt every emotion possible: grief, anger, despair, depression, guilt. Lots of guilt. I'd always thought of myself as a caring person. How was it I didn't notice how bad Moe's depression had been?

I remembered little things then. I remembered when Grizz would take me for rides to look for land for our future home. Moe was never included. What would have happened to her if we moved out of the motel? Was she expected to stay there indefinitely? I was horrified that I'd not given her future a second thought. I remembered my complaints and gripes about being dissatisfied with my life. What did Moe think about her life? What kind of life had she actually led? Not much of one, really.

Chowder made the necessary calls, and before long Grunt, Blue and Grizz showed up at the motel.

Grizz found me sitting on the edge of the couch staring at the blank TV. I got up and lunged at him. He thought I was coming in for a hug and never expected me to go ballistic on him. I beat on him with every ounce of strength I had in me, and he stood there and took it.

Exhaustion eventually overcame me, and I fell into his arms. He caught me and tried to hug me, but I shoved him away. I sat back down on the couch.

"What are you going to do with her?" My voice was cold. Distant.

"Same as everyone else."

"No." Heat flashed through me and I stood up. "No! Absolutely no way is Moe going to be thrown away and become alligator food. No way, Grizz."

"I suppose we could take her farther out and bury her. If that's what you want, Kit."

I thought a minute. "No. That's not good enough. I know a place. Not until tonight, though. And I need some time alone in her room."

He followed me outside. I walked toward her room. Grunt was sitting on a lawn chair on the motel sidewalk. He had his head in his hands. When he looked up at me, I could see he'd been crying. I went straight to him and threw myself into his arms as he stood up. I don't know how long we stood there crying in each other's arms, but Grizz left us alone.

I asked Grunt to come into her room with me. I wanted to find something personal to bury her with. When we walked in, Moe was still lying in her bed. Nobody had bothered to cover her face. Looking back now, I'm glad I got to see her.

Moe looked more beautiful and peaceful than I'd ever seen her before. She wasn't wearing her heavy makeup. She was lying on top of her motel bedspread wearing a white T-shirt that was several sizes too big for her. It was the only time I ever saw Moe wearing something besides black. I wondered if she'd planned it.

I went through her drawers and found there really wasn't much to Moe's life. Other than her black clothes, makeup, drawing tools and doggie treats, there was nothing there. Grunt and I were getting ready to leave when I thought to look under the bed. There was some sort of metal box. I couldn't get to it. Grunt knelt down next to me and was able to reach it. He pulled it out.

We opened it. There were two items in it. One was a plastic food container. Grunt popped the top off and we noticed what looked like a small piece of old meat wrapped in cellophane. It was Moe's tongue.

The other item I recognized immediately. It was my wallet.

———

Grunt and I looked at each other with the same expression. We both could understand why Moe had saved her tongue. It was personal. If this had a few years earlier, I probably would've thrown up. But I guess living at the motel had hardened me somewhat. I'd seen people murdered, so a shriveled tongue wasn't anything to be upset about.

But my wallet? She'd defied a direct order from Grizz. Why?

We guessed she'd saved it for me. Her life and identity had been taken from her. Maybe she didn't have the heart to destroy my identity like Grizz had commanded her to do that night.

"Thank you, Moe," I whispered.

I took the wallet and put it in my back pocket. I knew without asking that Grunt would never tell.

When I got back to number four I found the bag I was carrying the night Monster abducted me. I no longer used it. It was wadded up in a corner shelf in my closet. I put my wallet inside and forgot about it.

Later that night, Chowder and Blue carefully wrapped Moe in her bedspread and carried her out to the bed of Blue's pickup truck. I rode in front with Blue and Grizz, and Grunt rode in the back with Chowder, Moe and the shovels.

I directed them to the only place that seemed appropriate. It was dark out, but there was a full moon. Enough for me to find the shady ficus tree on a lonely rural road in Davie.

I picked a spot, and Chowder and Grunt meticulously cut and rolled up the grass. Then they started digging. I told them to make sure it was deep. I didn't want any chance of animals getting to her. Grizz gently handed her over the low fence to Blue, who carried her to the edge of the freshly dug grave. Before they lowered her in, I reached in under the bedspread and placed the plastic food container with her.

After they filled in the grave, they put the sod back. It

barely looked like the ground had been disturbed. I was certain nobody would notice.

As we drove away I had to look back. He was there, and he was magnificent—Moe's beautiful, brown horse. He was standing next to her grave.

Years later, as I was being interrogated by the police about my knowledge of the people who'd lived at the motel, I could never bring myself to give up Moe's final resting place. I was able to tell them honestly how she died. Her family would at least have that closure. But I couldn't bring myself to tell them she was actually buried on their property. I couldn't be sure they wouldn't dig her up and move her to a cemetery, give her a proper burial. I knew in my heart this was the only burial Moe would want.

Grunt stopped at Fess's on his way back home and told him what happened. Sarah Jo later told me her father cried like a baby that night. He was upset he didn't get to say goodbye, but he also understood the less fuss, the better for everyone. He asked if he could pay his respects. Grizz wouldn't tell him where she was buried, but I think Grunt may have.

I would drive by that ficus tree many times over the coming years just to say hello to my old friend Moe. The area was still undeveloped and there was never anyone around. But on a few occasions, I saw dried, dead flowers at the foot of the ficus tree. I was pretty sure Fess had been there.

Subconsciously, I blamed Grizz for Moe's death. Heck, I might even have blamed myself. I struggled with my life as it now was. What right did I have to have a happy life when Moe was dead and would never have one?

I started to question my beliefs. Who was I? I reminded

myself that I'd witnessed murders. Then I struggled with why I even had to remind myself. Wasn't a murder tragic? How could I not think about it every single day?

And perhaps worse, I was in love with a hardened criminal. At that point, I think I was starting to wake up from the illusion of my seemingly perfect life with Grizz. How could I convince myself our lifestyle was okay? Who had I let myself become? Did I see a future with him? Was I going to have his children?

I sunk deeper into depression, and it only got worse that summer when Grizz finally found the guy who attacked me.

Chapter Thirty-Two

I can honestly say I never stopped loving Grizz, but after what he did to the man who attacked me, I became afraid of him like never before. Not of what he would do to me—I knew deep down Grizz would never hurt me. But I was very afraid of what Grizz was capable of doing to others.

It turned out it was very much a personal attack. The guy's name was Darryl Hines. He was in love with a blonde hooker in Miami.

A blonde hooker named Willow.

Darryl Hines had heard so much from Willow about how Grizz had cast her out of the gang years earlier because of me. So he decided to do something about it. Darryl was crazy about Willow and wanted to show his love for her.

It was by pure coincidence that he picked a night to come to the motel when I was most vulnerable. He was high on drugs and wasn't even sure if I would be in the room when he burst in. He had to know that if he came in and Grizz was there, he would have met certain death. But that night he was so high he just didn't care. He took a chance and it paid off for him.

Well, it wasn't paying off now.

I believed Darryl Hines needed to pay for what he did to me. But I will never be able to accept how Grizz dealt with him.

The day they brought him to the motel, I identified his voice immediately. It was a voice I'd never forget. I stayed in number four while Grizz marched him out to the pit. Chowder told me how he was kneeling in the pit and crying. He confessed to everything. He was more upset that Willow had dumped him after he told her what he did. She had used him to take vengeance on me, and once he accomplished that, she had no further use for him.

"Seems to me you should be more worried about what I'm going to do to you," Grizz told him.

Darryl was sobbing. "You can't do nothing to me that won't hurt more than what Willow did."

"We'll see about that."

It was July in South Florida. It was unbearably hot. That night, Grizz drove me over to Naples on the west coast. He set me up in an expensive hotel on the beach. He told me he was going to be dealing with Darryl and he didn't want me around. He said I should relax and enjoy myself, not to worry. Like that was going to happen. He left me with a lot of cash and he returned to the motel.

Chicky showed up after two days and spent a day with me. I'd never really let myself get to know Chicky, and it was nice talking to her. We spent the day at an isolated spot on the beach. She told me about herself.

Chicky was forty-six years old. I was shocked. I thought she was much younger. Most of the women looked hardened and old from the drugs and the gang life. Not her. She told me she'd been with the gang for only a couple of years before I came along.

"Yes," she answered without me having to ask. "I was in love with Grizz, too. Who wasn't?"

Then she laughed and waved it off like it was nothing. She told me she had been waiting tables at a local bar popular for its hot wings. Grizz had approached her and asked her to work for him. She said she'd been a stripper in her younger years, so bartending topless wasn't a stretch, and the money was great. Besides, she had a daughter to feed and put through school.

That shocked me. Her daughter was a senior in college. Chicky knew she surprised me.

"Just because I've lived hard and haven't always made the right decisions doesn't mean I don't want better for my girl."

I wiggled my toes in the sand. "How do you handle it, Chicky? How do you handle the awful stuff you've seen at the motel and other places?"

"Just do. As far as I can tell, I ain't done nothing bad to nobody. Unless loving somebody is a bad thing."

I looked over at her. Before I could voice it, she said, "No, not Grizz, honey. I stay around hoping Fess might take notice of me one day. I know he had eyes for Moe, but I think I could be real good with Fess."

I smiled. "Yes, I think you could too, Chicky." We both lay back in our beach chairs and closed our eyes.

After a minute, she said, "He really is in love with you,

you know? Grizz. I've seen him with all kinds of women." She stopped then and said, "Sorry, don't mean it like that. Just that he could pretty much have any woman he wanted and he did, until you came along. I ain't never seen nothing like it. A lot of the men put their women to work, share 'em with other guys. It's a normal thing. But not where you're concerned."

I leaned up on my elbows and looked over at her. "Chicky, I love Grizz with all my heart. I really do. But you know, I don't go to all the biker rallies and different meetings with him. He could be with anyone and I'd never know."

"Yeah, except he isn't." She sat up and looked at me. "I've been to some of those rallies. Those meetings. I've seen women take their clothes off and stick their stuff in his face. He just pushes 'em away."

"Really?" I was surprised. It was something I'd not let myself think too much about.

But now that I let myself think about it, I avoided the pit as often as possible for a few key reasons, one being the dirty looks I got from the other women. They were never mean or disrespectful to me. Grizz wouldn't have allowed it. But I caught the occasional nasty glance. Was that because Grizz was loyal to me? I was a little shocked.

Then I remembered the night I caught him with Willow.

The words tumbled out before I could stop them. "I was pretty sure after I walked in on him and Willow that time that he did as he pleased, regardless of me."

"Oh, I remember that night," Chicky sighed. "You went to Grunt's room to listen to records. Yep. I remember it well. He did it on purpose to make you jealous."

This got my attention. "How could he have done it on

purpose? The timing had to be exactly right for me to catch him."

"He just gave Grunt the signal that he wanted to know a few minutes before you were leaving his room."

"What?" I sat straight up in my beach chair.

"It's a signal system they set up." Chicky sat up, too, waved her hand absently. "I'm surprised you don't know about it. They'd been using it awhile. Now that I think on it, haven't seen him do it since then, but it was a regular thing."

"What kind of system? For what purpose?"

"A while back, when someone would come to the motel that wasn't familiar or known to be trusted, they'd be taken into one of the rooms and shown some hospitality, if you know what I mean. This would give the gang a chance to check them out. Go through their car or saddlebags if they were riding. Whoever was inside knew to flick the outside light twice to signal that the person was going to leave in a minute or two. That's what Grunt did right before you left. Flicked his porch light. You should've seen Grizz drag Willow like a bat out of hell to your room."

"Grunt was in on it?"

"Nah, he just saw Grizz give him the signal that, for whatever reason, meant Grizz wanted to know when you were gonna be leaving Grunt's room. The kid didn't know why."

I laughed. I laughed hard. Grizz had been trying to make me jealous? Well, now that I think about it, it worked. As a matter of fact, if I'd peeked through the crack between the curtain and the window of number four instead of running back to Grunt's room, I bet I would have seen Grizz shove Willow away from him, pull up his pants and tell her to get her ass out of his room.

All with a big, gigantic smile on his face.

I lay back on my beach chair. "Thanks, Chicky. Thanks for telling me."

A day or so after Chicky left, I was visited by Anthony Bear and his woman, Christy. Anthony was a friend of Grizz's. He was the equivalent of Grizz, the leader of his own motorcycle gang, but on the Florida west coast.

I remember the first night I'd met Anthony. It was a year or two earlier, on one of our church trips to the west coast. We'd made a stop before getting on Alligator Alley to go home. I'm sure my mouth hung open as I gaped at one of the most handsome men I'd ever laid eyes on. Grizz was big and definitely handsome, in a rugged way. But where Grizz had light eyes and hair, Anthony was dark. He was a Native American and had chiseled, exotic good looks. He was living proof of that old saying—tall, dark and handsome. Black eyes, black hair and, on at least one occasion that I'd witnessed, black mood. He was bigger than Grizz, at least six foot six, muscular and tattooed. And he wore a single braid down his back that reached his waist.

Christy was a short, tanned, natural blonde with chin-length straight hair and big blue eyes. She wasn't little, but had a traditional hourglass figure, filled out in all the right places. She'd been abducted, like me. I hadn't met her until more recently, and when I did meet her she made it obvious she wasn't happy with her situation. She'd even tried to convince me to help her escape.

The three of us spent a nice day together, relaxing on the beach. It was now the end of the day and we were back in my hotel room. Christy was using the bathroom.

"I'm sorry I haven't let her come see you on her own.

Things are still a little unsettled. I guess I'm still not completely comfortable letting her out of my sight," Anthony said quietly.

"You don't need to apologize. I understand. I remember how it was for me and Grizz in the beginning. I'm just glad I got to see you both today," I answered.

"You're happy with him? You don't ever want to leave him?" he asked.

"I love Grizz. I don't love what he does. I'd be lying if I didn't tell you that I fantasize about a future with him away from this lifestyle."

He looked at the ground. "I'd give it up for her. I've tried to tell her that. I don't know if she believes me."

Wow, I thought to myself. This was an admission I didn't expect, especially from Anthony. If I was going to be honest, I think I may have been a little jealous of his last statement.

"Has she tried to leave recently?"

"No, not for a few months. I don't know if it's because she's finally happy with me or if she's waiting for me to let my guard down."

I reflected back on the last several hours. If Christy was planning to escape from Anthony, it wasn't obvious to me. She came out of the bathroom just then and caught me in a hug that lasted longer than I expected. She didn't say goodbye. She just looked up at Anthony, and he took her by the hand and led her out of the hotel room door. I shut it quietly behind them. I was sad to see them leave.

I walked over to my balcony and looked down at the beach. It wasn't long before I noticed movement to my left and realized Anthony's motorcycle was parked up on the small sidewalk. Before getting on, Anthony turned around to face Christy. He took her face in his hands and bent over to gently kiss her on the lips. It was a tender moment, and I almost felt guilty for witnessing it.

She'll be fine. And I went back inside and closed the balcony door behind me.

Grizz called me every morning and every night, and after a week I started to get a really uncomfortable feeling. I had no doubt he was going to kill Darryl, but wouldn't he have done it by now? And again, why wasn't I calling the police? What was wrong with me?

I couldn't fathom my own heart.

After eight days, Grizz showed up and took me back to the motel. Darryl wasn't there, and everything seemed back to normal. I was certain Darryl was dead, but I didn't know any details. I didn't know if I wanted to know any details.

Eventually, Grunt told me some things. I wish he hadn't. It was my own fault—I asked him. He wasn't there the whole time, but he knew enough.

While Grizz was setting me up in a fancy hotel in Naples, his guys were looking for Willow. They found her and brought her back to the motel. When Grizz got back he immediately ordered his guys to relieve Willow and Darryl of all their clothes. He then had them walked over to the empty cement pool. He told them to walk down the steps into the pool and stay there.

And that's just what they did. They were trapped in the cement pool with no food or water and open to the elements for days. Hot, scorching days in July with no breeze or shelter. Their skin was soon pink and blistered. The nights were cooler, but that's when they were exposed to mosquitos and other bugs.

As if this wasn't bad enough, Grizz had two poisonous coral snakes tossed in there with them. The snakes were always seeking shade during the day so Willow and Darryl could barely keep still if the sun was out. The snakes were always trying to work their way under their wilting bodies looking for relief from the sun.

To make matters worse, Grizz taunted them. Not with words, but with actions. He set Lucifer and Damien up to guard the pool steps where they might try to climb out. He put an umbrella up for his dogs and had Chowder run an extension cord out to a couple of fans so that the dogs would stay cool. He made sure they had big bowls of water that were just out of Willow and Darryl's reach. If Willow or Darryl tried to get out of the pool, Damien and Lucifer were ordered to attack. That was their choice. Be mauled to death by dogs or die from exposure.

Instead of sitting around the pit at night, Grizz used them for entertainment. Whoever came to the motel would sit around the pool instead of the pit and mock the prisoners. Grizz was never there, though. They were allowed to do whatever they wanted to Willow or Darryl as long as they didn't help them or kill them. Needless to say, some of the younger, newer members of Grizz's group really enjoyed this. They tossed heavy rocks, firecrackers and lit cigarettes at them. The one night Grunt was there, some of the guys were spitting at them. They were so thirsty, they were trying to drink the spit. Grunt had seen enough and left.

Willow died first. Then Darryl. They were slow, agonizing deaths that took days and were slightly prolonged by a couple of afternoon rain showers. The little bit of water they got just made their deaths drag out longer. Grizz had his guys toss them in the swamp and there was never any proof that either person had ever existed.

I listened in disbelief as Grunt told me what happened. He was only there one time and couldn't stand it himself. Chowder told him the rest. As much as Chowder hated what Darryl had done, the wizened gang member still thought it was too much retaliation. Even for Grizz.

Froggy couldn't bring himself to be there are at all.

I felt sick. Empty.

Where was I to go from here? I was now nineteen years old. I would be twenty in six months. I still didn't have a plan for my life. I had not witnessed what happened to Darryl and Willow, but it haunted me. I would catch myself staring at Grizz and wondering who is this person that knows such evil? It didn't help that he did what he did in retaliation for what was done to me and Gwinny.

But as much as I wanted to, or told myself I wanted to, I didn't make any attempt at change. I was in love with Grizz. I hated what he did, but I loved him.

Unfortunately, my love for him was causing me to hate myself.

Chapter Thirty-Three

In January 1980 I finally convinced Grizz to let me go to college. I would have graduated high school in 1978 with the rest of my peers, and I was really risking running into a former classmate. But I explained to Grizz that I would just deny it like I had at the vet a few years back when a classmate recognized me. I was already almost two years behind in earning a college degree. Sarah Jo had been at Florida State University in northern Florida since graduating high school. I enrolled at Cole Southeastern University and started working on a degree in business administration with a concentration in accounting. I recognized a person or two from high school, but they never recognized me. I kept my bangs because Grizz loved them, but I'd gotten in the habit of wearing them off my face when leaving the motel. I also had adopted a new wardrobe style.

I liked to wear nice clothes, business attire, to school. If anybody recognized me, they certainly didn't let on. The girl who supposedly ran away in 1975 had long been forgotten.

I was walking out to my car one day and heard someone call my name. Not my real name or alias. My gang name.

"Kit! Kit, wait up."

I turned and saw a really cute guy jogging toward me and smiling. I recognized him immediately. It was Sam, Sarah Jo's neighbor. I hadn't seen him since that summer and the incident with Neal in Jo's garage.

"Sam! How are you? Long time, no see."

He hugged me and asked, "You hungry? Can you grab some lunch?"

I hadn't realized until that moment how nice it would be to have a conversation with someone else. Someone who knew a little bit about my background. I was beginning to realize that secrets could be exhausting. All this time I'd been living in my own little world and had only made two girlfriends outside of Sarah Jo: Carter and Casey. They were my age and went to school with me, and even though we had distinctly different backgrounds and college majors, there was an instant connection. Of course, I couldn't ever bring them to the motel, and our friendship in the beginning was limited to school. But at this point, I hadn't shared my real story with my new friends. With Grunt and Moe gone, it was just me, Grizz and Chowder now living at the motel. Chicky didn't even come around that much anymore. Since Moe died, Fess came less frequently, too. I realized I was lonely.

I immediately took Sam up on his offer and followed him to a diner in Davie.

We chatted for hours. It was strange because I really didn't know Sam that well, and I certainly hadn't heard anything about him from Sarah Jo in the last few years. Sam explained how he'd watched from his living room window that summer day in 1977 as Grizz carried out his punishment of Neal. He saw me drive off and the garage door go down. He told me that less than thirty minutes later a car showed up. Two rough-looking characters went into the house and came out, escorting a crying Neal to the car. They drove off. Grizz got on his bike and left, and Neal never bothered Sam or his mother again.

"You know, I've always felt bad that I couldn't do anything to help you and Jo that day. Felt like a real wimp, Kit. I'm sorry."

"Please don't apologize." I looked at Sam kindly. "For heaven's sake, you were a kid yourself, Sam. He was a bully threatening your mother. You didn't do anything wrong. Please don't feel bad. I never looked at you as a wimp. I didn't think it then and I don't think it now. Now, tell me, what are you doing at Cole?"

He told me how trade school didn't really work out. He'd found he had a knack for social skills and loved working with troubled youth. He was now working full-time at a local YMCA and going to school part-time to get his degree. He wanted to be a social worker.

"So, um, Kit, are you still with Grizz? Are you still like his girlfriend, or something?"

I smiled at him. "Actually, Sam. I'm married to Grizz."

I know this shocked him. "Wow, married." Sam leaned back against the booth. "Didn't expect that one. Would it be rude of me to ask if you're happily married? Just curious, is all."

"No, it's not rude. And yes, I'm happy. I love Grizz. I don't need to tell you I don't love his lifestyle, but yes, I love the man."

He nodded. "I kinda don't get it, though. I mean, I know who he is and what he does, and you just seem like such a sweet, smart girl. I can't imagine you with someone like him. Sorry—I know you love him. It's just difficult to wrap my head around."

"Don't feel bad. Sometimes I can't wrap my head around it, either. I know I shouldn't be talking about this, but I've tried to make up for it, at least in my own mind, by seeing if any good can come out of being with him. To see if there are any negatives I can turn into positives."

"What do you mean?"

Then I told him a story. It had become a source of irritation in my marriage. Grizz had warned me more than once, but I couldn't help myself.

"Fuck, Kit. I can't take you anywhere," he'd said one day in frustration.

I rolled my eyes. "I've asked you not to be such a dirty mouth."

"Well, I've asked you not to get in the middle of every Tom, Dick and Harry fight that you come across."

"I do it because when I've asked you to help, you won't. You don't care! So you leave me no choice but to involve myself. Besides, if we weren't in a crappy part of town to start with, no thanks to your activities, I wouldn't see half the things I've had to see."

"Do you want me to get arrested? Is that your goal?"

"Don't be ridiculous. This is about helping someone, not about you getting in trouble."

"Yeah, but you realize I'm capable of murder where

you're concerned? If I kill someone it'll be on your conscience."

This conversation happened long before the Darryl and Willow story. I knew how Grizz had killed Johnny Tillman, but I'd convinced myself that was somehow different. An isolated circumstance that wouldn't repeat itself. After all, he didn't have Neal killed after the garage incident.

Grizz and I had been arguing about something that had happened earlier that day. Grizz had taken me along with him while he met with one of his associates. We were in his car and had pulled up to a seedy-looking warehouse in a bad section of Pompano Beach. I remembered being there before. There was one car parked in front of it.

Grizz left his car running and told me, "I'll be less than five minutes. People know my car, so nobody will bother you. Besides, I can see the car from that window."

He pointed to a window on the second floor.

I'd gone on many business visits with Grizz and heard this over and over again. I knew he was right. I didn't want to go inside and meet anybody anyway. I pulled out a book and immediately started to read.

I hadn't read two pages when a speeding car pulled in behind me. I looked in the rearview mirror and saw a flash of color. I looked to the left over the driver's seat and saw the source of the color.

It was a brand new yellow Mustang. The driver must have thought he could go around the building, but when he made a right to turn the corner, I heard his brakes squeal. I'd been to this building before. I knew it backed up to a cement retaining wall. There was no back parking lot. He quickly shifted into reverse and was backing up when another car pulled in and blocked him.

I watched in horror as two guys got out of an unremarkable green car. One was carrying a baseball bat and was patting it against his open palm. They looked like serious criminals.

I could see the one guy talking, but I couldn't hear him. I leaned over the driver's seat and put down Grizz's window. In broken English they were telling the guy to get out of the car. If he got out and handed over the keys, nothing bad would happen. This was a car jacking.

I looked up to see if I could find Grizz in the window. I didn't. Surely he heard the tire squeals and would be down in a second. I waited. Nothing.

I got out of the car and went into the same door that Grizz had gone in two minutes earlier. I went up the only set of stairs and walked in on him talking to an old man. I didn't pay any attention and didn't apologize for interrupting.

"Please call the police," I panted, trying to catch my breath. "There's a car jacking going on down there."

The old man started to say something to me, but Grizz put his hand up and stopped him. "Okay, we'll call. Go wait for me downstairs. Don't go back out to the car."

"Okay," I said breathlessly. "Thanks."

I walked downstairs and looked out the glass window of the door I had come through. It was just a kid. He had gotten out of the car like they told him, but he must have done something to make them mad. The one guy had him pushed up against his car while the other guy with the baseball bat was using it to skim through some bushes. Then it dawned on me what had happened. The kid must have turned off the car and got out like they told him to, but he took his keys with him and tossed them in some hedges.

Just then, the guy holding him up against the Mustang grabbed the boy by the scruff of his neck and started marching him toward the bushes. I cracked the door so I could hear what they were saying. He was telling him in broken English that he'd better find the keys or he was going to die.

Die? For a car? He shoved the boy down on all fours and had him scouring the bushes. I could tell the boy was starting to panic. I'm certain he wished he'd just handed the keys over and called the police. He'd tried to outsmart hardened criminals and now he was going to pay. The one guy started kicking him in the ribs as he crawled along the hedge line.

I pulled the door closed. "Grizz?" I screamed. "Are the police coming?" No answer. I knew immediately that he didn't call the police. This was Grizz. Grizz didn't care what happened to other people. I knew what I had to do. I calmly walked out of the warehouse and approached the threesome.

"Excuse me. Excuse me, gentlemen. I just thought you should know that the police are on their way. I think if you leave now, you'll be gone before they get here."

All three of them stopped what they were doing, and the two criminals swung around to look at me. I could see tears streaming down the boy's face. He had found his keys and was holding them up in one hand, still on his knees, while resting all of his weight on the other. I stopped walking. I was now close to them, but not so close that they could take a swing at me.

"Just thought you should know," I added. It came out hoarse.

They didn't move toward me or respond to my

statement. I turned around and started to walk back toward the warehouse door.

I heard one of them muster up a serious phlegm ball and spit. I felt it splatter against the back of my head. I heard laughter.

Just then the warehouse door flew open so hard the glass shattered. Grizz strode toward me. He must have seen me from the second floor walking toward the thugs. He'd seen the guy spit at me through the glass door right before he opened it.

The men behind me started talking quickly in Spanish. I'd had enough Spanish in school to know what they were saying.

"Fuck, Manny! Do you see the size of that motherfucker coming over here? Why'd you have to spit at the girl? You dumb fuck! Leave the kid and the fucking car. Let's go. Now!"

"Get in the car, Kit," Grizz practically growled.

"Don't hurt them. Please, I don't want anyone to get hurt, Grizz."

"They'll be lucky if I let them live."

I didn't go into any more detail with Sam. Grizz didn't kill them. Enough said.

"So basically, you knew if you intervened then he would come to your rescue and, in doing so, rescue the other victim?" Sam's eyes were wide.

"Yes, that's exactly what I was doing. I'd done it before, too, but it never got as bad as the spitting incident. Usually, one look at Grizz and people always stepped away. That was the first time he had to get physical, and I'm sure he wouldn't have if the guy didn't spit at me."

"You realize he was right, though, don't you?"

This surprised me. I had just taken a sip of my iced tea and looked up at Sam. "Right about what?"

"Right about not calling the police. Not getting involved. Maybe you subconsciously want him to get caught."

This shocked me. "No, absolutely not. I don't want him to get arrested. I love him."

"And that's it, Kit. You love him and you feel guilty for loving him so you try to use him to make situations better where you can't. You keep doing it and it's only a matter of time before it won't work out. You're lucky he didn't kill those guys."

Sam was right.

I went home that day and told Grizz I was sorry for involving him in other people's problems. I vowed that day not to ever play rescuer again. Great. Now I was going to have to figure out another way to ease my conscience.

Sam not only became a social worker, but he went on to become a psychologist. Years later, after learning I'd actually been kidnapped by Grizz, he went on to write a book about Stockholm syndrome—the syndrome where the captive starts to care for her captor.

The girl in his book was eerily similar to me. I'd stayed friends with Sam over the years, and that book almost ruined our relationship.

Chapter Thirty-Four

I continued to run into Sam at school and we had an occasional lunch together. I struggled with whether or not to tell Grizz. I didn't feel like I was doing anything wrong, but he was so protective I felt he would scare Sam away.

I wouldn't find out until later that he knew about my lunch dates with Sam. Of course he knew. He knew everything. I never lied, though. If he asked me what I did after school, I told him: I had lunch with a friend. I guess after that first time he had me watched, and whoever watched me must have convinced him it was a strictly platonic lunch. Maybe he didn't bother Sam because he connected my first lunch with him as the same day I came home and apologized. Maybe he was secretly grateful that Sam had talked some sense into me.

Either way, Sam would eventually always be a welcome

guest in our home.

I was on a short break between spring and summer classes when Blue called the motel asking for a favor. I'd continued to remain on good terms with Jan after that first Thanksgiving. We never became super close, but I loved her boys and would babysit whenever I could. They were now school age, and Jan was working at a law firm. She seemed to really enjoy her work, and as far as I could tell, avoided mental breakdowns with a combination of medication and a job she loved.

Blue explained that both boys had come down with chicken pox and couldn't go to summer camp. Jan was having an especially busy time at work. She had gone from part-time receptionist to full-time receptionist and then to legal aide. Was there any way I could stay with the boys for a couple of days? Maybe the whole week?

I didn't have to think about it. They were great little boys, and I welcomed the opportunity to spend time with them. Besides, I could sit by the pool and read while they napped. I wondered to myself if they still took naps. Probably not. But it didn't matter. It would be like a little getaway for me, too. Blue asked if I could stop at the drug store and pick up some lotion. It was supposed to help with their itching.

I told Grizz, and he was okay with it. He'd been busy, anyway. We'd finally picked out some land in a subdivision just southwest of Davie called Shady Ranches. We were having a home built, and it was in the framing stage. Grizz had hired a contractor but had a hard time turning over control of the project. He spent as much time there as he could. I know he didn't mean to intimidate the guy; he was just really enjoying the construction process. Chowder spent a lot of time with him there, too.

I went into our bedroom and looked for something to put my things in. I remembered my old cloth backpack. I found it wadded up in a corner of our closet where I'd carelessly thrown it over a year ago. I stuffed my bathing suit, suntan lotion, two books, and my hairbrush in it. No need to pack for overnight. I wouldn't be spending the night.

I stopped at a drug store and bought the lotion. I threw it in my backpack and drove to Blue's. When I got there, Jan met me at the door with a hug.

"You're really getting us out of a bind, Kit. Blue and I tried splitting up the days to take care of the boys—I'd do mornings and he'd do afternoons—but we're starting to get complaints from work. You're a lifesaver."

"I'm glad to help. I love your boys. You know that. Where are they?" I asked as I tossed my bag onto the bench inside the front door.

"They're in the den."

I made my way to the den and was greeted with a big hug from Kevin. He was the younger of the two. Timmy looked at me shyly. I think he was just old enough now to be embarrassed to have me there babysitting.

Jan yelled from the foyer, "Did you remember to pick up the lotion?"

"Yeah, it's in my bag by the front door."

If I hadn't been so caught up in the boys I might have noticed how long it took Jan to bring the lotion into the den. I might've remembered that day more than a year ago, when I found my wallet in Moe's room. Remembered throwing it in my old backpack.

Because while I was giving my undivided attention to

Kevin and Timmy, their mother was making a mental note of an exceptionally odd name. A name I hadn't heard or even thought about in over five years.

Guinevere Love Lemon.

The house construction was progressing at an extremely quick pace. I'm pretty sure the builder was just scared to death of Grizz and wanted the project over with. Not that Grizz ever did anything on purpose to scare the guy. It was just Grizz.

One Saturday toward the end of that summer, while she was still on break from school, Sarah Jo and I spent the day at the beach. I'd developed a really awful headache and asked her if she could just drive me home. We had my car. I asked her to just drop me at the motel and take my car home. I was certain Grizz would get it back to the motel.

She dropped me off and helped me unload my stuff. Being the best friend in the world, she put my things away, stood in the bathroom while I took a quick shower and tucked me into bed with two aspirin. She closed the bedroom curtains and kissed me on my forehead.

"I'll call later to check on you, Kit. Try to fall asleep. Maybe the headache will be gone by the time you wake up."

My head hurt so bad I don't remember answering her. I did eventually fall asleep and woke up later disoriented. My headache was now just a dull throb. I heard voices. It must've been what woke me up. It was Grizz, and he was arguing with a woman whose voice I didn't recognize.

"I don't understand why I can't see him. Not that I owe you an explanation, but I've cleaned up my act. I have things to settle with him."

"He's not here, Candy."

"Stop calling me that lame-ass gang name, J...."

"Shut up!" Grizz roared. "Don't call me by that name. No one calls me by that name, ever!"

Who was this woman? She'd started to call Grizz by a name that started with a J. Did she know his real name? It was obvious Grizz didn't know I was there. My car was gone, so he would've assumed I was still with Sarah Jo. I was pondering whether to make myself known or not. I could almost sense her eyes rolling as he yelled that last statement at her.

"You and your fucking gang codes. I swear Grizz, you are so over the top. I don't go by Candy anymore."

"I don't give a fuck what you go by, you're not going to see him. He doesn't live here anyway. He's happy and settled. No reason for you to insinuate yourself back into his life because you've had a guilty conscience."

"You are such an arrogant ass. You wouldn't be where you are today if it weren't for me. Don't forget I found your sorry fourteen-year-old ass living behind a gas station. I'm the one that introduced you to the people who put you where you are today. Me!"

"Nobody put me where I am today but me. Besides, when you supposedly found me you were already a washed-up, drug-addicted hooker and you were only seventeen. If anything, you owe me for making sure you weren't living on the street."

So this was a woman who knew Grizz when he was still a teenager. I didn't think I'd run across anybody yet who'd known him that long.

"Well, I certainly don't need your permission to see him.

I can find him on my own and you can't stop me."

"Really, Candy? I can't stop you?"

It got quiet and I knew she was weighing her options. Finally, she spoke in a calmer voice.

"Fine. Will you do me one favor?" Without waiting for him to answer, she continued. "Will you at least tell him I came by here looking for him? Tell him I've cleaned up. Tell him I just want to see him to apologize for all the bad shit that happened. I don't want to upset or interfere in his life. I just want to say I'm sorry."

Grizz said something, but I couldn't hear the words.

I heard the door open and then shut. I got out of bed and went out into the small living room. Grizz wasn't there. He must've walked her out. I noticed it was past dinnertime, so I went into the kitchen and started pulling some things out of the fridge to cook. If I'd had the least bit of curiosity about what Candy looked like I might've thought to go to the window and peek out.

In retrospect, it was a good thing I didn't. I would've witnessed my husband do something awful. I would've seen Grizz walk her to her car, and as she reached for the door handle, grab her from behind and instantly snap her neck. I would've seen him carelessly fling her over his shoulder, signal to three faceless men in the pit to get rid of her car and easily stride to the back of the motel to erase evidence of her existence.

But I saw none of this and wouldn't know about it until many years had passed.

Grizz came back inside less than ten minutes later and stopped short. "When did you get home? I didn't see you pull up."

"Jo brought me home early. I got one of my bad

headaches. Tried to sleep it off.'

"Did you? Is it gone?"

"Mostly. Just a dull ache now really. Nothing like it was. She has my car. Can you get someone to bring it home?" I could tell by his expression he knew I was in the room when he had the argument with Candy. He was trying to figure out if I'd heard anything. I decided to make it easy for him.

"So who is Candy?" I asked while nonchalantly sautéing some mushrooms on the stove.

Before he could answer, I added, "Are you going to tell him? Are you going to tell Blue?"

He gave me a puzzled look.

"That was Blue's crazy ex-girlfriend, wasn't it? The one you told me about? The one he broke up with right before he met Jan?"

"Yeah, that was her."

"You don't look too sure of yourself, Grizz."

"No, it's not that, baby. I just didn't remember telling you about her."

"Well, you did. You never told me her name, but you mentioned her after I met Jan that first time."

He came up behind me and hugged me. He rested his chin on my left shoulder. He must have been really hunched over because I was a lot shorter than him.

"I think you're right, Grizz. Right not to let her see Blue. It might cause Jan to have a breakdown." Before he could say anything, I added, "She started to call you by your real name. Will you ever tell me?"

"Kit, we've been through this a million times," he said and pulled back to look at me. I turned around and faced him. "It's for your own good. As far as you're concerned, my real name is Rick O'Connell."

"Yeah, Grizz, except that it's not." I turned off the stove and hastily brushed him aside. I went into our bedroom and shut the door.

Would he ever let me in? I was married to him and knew virtually nothing about him. Not his name, nothing about his past. Well, except now I knew he'd been living behind a gas station when he was fourteen.

He came in and found me sitting on the bed pretending to look through color palettes from the contractor. I wouldn't look up at him.

"Jason. My real first name is Jason. Okay? I'm not telling you any more of my name. Someday, maybe when we have children, I'll tell you. But it's not because I'm gonna let them use my name. They'll be O'Connells."

Then he told me a little bit about himself. He was born in Florida—West Palm Beach. He never knew his father, and the last name he wouldn't tell me was apparently his mother's last name. Her first name was Ida, and she'd had him when she was just fifteen. That certainly explained why he felt I was "old enough" when he had me abducted.

His mother was a housekeeper for a wealthy family. He said she played the perfect role as housekeeper, but her own home was a wreck. She neglected him. She never beat or abused him; she just ignored him. It sounded familiar. He ran away when he was almost fourteen. He was certain she was relieved and never looked for him. He wasn't living behind a gas station when Candy found him. He was actually selling stolen auto parts.

I asked him why he would run away—he was neglected, not abused. Why put himself out on the street? And how did he make it down to the Fort Lauderdale area from West Palm Beach?

"I ran with an older crowd and dropped out of school because I was making so much money," Grizz said simply. "Eventually, the group made its way south, and I went, too."

He wasn't living on the street, but in a small apartment over the garage of a guy paying him to acquire specialty auto parts. I told him he was really smart for a guy who'd dropped out of school so young.

"I knew how to read and had basic math skills, and that was all I needed," Grizz said, shrugging. "Besides, my education on the street taught me more than any degree I could've earned."

By now Grizz was sitting beside me on the bed. I scooted onto his lap.

"Why do we have to have children before you'll tell me your real name?" I asked as I nuzzled his neck, toying with the earring in his left ear. It was a favorite habit of mine.

I could feel his body shaking. He was laughing. I looked up at him. With a big grin, he said, "I don't know. Figured it might buy some time. Figure we'll have a baby after a couple more years."

"Well, Mr. Won't-Be-Able-To-Avoid-The-Question-Much-Longer, I think I can get you to tell me sooner than you planned."

"Oh, you do now?" He pressed his face into my neck. "What are you going to tempt me with?"

Before I could reply, the phone rang. He moved me back over to the bed and got up to answer it.

"Yeah?" A pause. "Hang on a second, honey. Kit, it's Sarah Jo," he yelled from the kitchen.

I went in and took the phone from him. "Yeah, it's almost gone. Still a little ache." I paused while Jo asked me another question. "No, I haven't told him yet."

"Told me what?" Grizz asked as he took a beer out of the refrigerator.

I turned to look at him. "I think I might be pregnant."

Chapter Thirty-Five

Grizz took me to the doctor the next day, and sure enough, I was pregnant. I was puzzled, though. I'd taken birth control pills religiously, never missed even one time. But I'd had a nasty case of strep throat the month before, and the doctor explained antibiotics can sometimes interfere with the pill. I was just one of those cases.

I told the doctor I was still taking the pill and had only suspected the pregnancy because my last period was very short and light, not my usual full week of heavy bleeding. He told me to stop taking it and not to worry. Some women got pregnant while on the pill. It wasn't unheard of, and we'd detected the pregnancy early on.

I looked over at Grizz, who was smiling. He was happy about this pregnancy. If it was meant to be now instead of a few years down the road, then so be it.

Grizz took me to lunch and immediately started offering up boys' and girls' names. My head was spinning. I was overwhelmed. What about my degree? Could I still go to school and be a mother? I was dizzy with thoughts of the future and how it would all play out. I took some comfort in the fact that the baby would be born after we were in our new home. I would have hated bringing a baby into the world while living at the motel.

Grizz surprised me with something else. He told me that it would take him about six months to wrap up some business and he would be done with the gang. For good. I couldn't have been more thrilled. Jan was going to get her wish after all: Grizz was turning his gang over to Blue.

We decided to keep the pregnancy to ourselves for a little while. It was still early. Sarah Jo was the only one who knew, and I had no doubt about her loyalty and ability to keep a secret.

Morning sickness hit with a vengeance. I couldn't even call it morning sickness; I was sick all day, so much so that I couldn't keep anything down and Grizz wanted to take me back to the doctor to see if they could prescribe something to help. I refused. I'd live with it. I wasn't going to take any medication while I was pregnant. Nothing except for prenatal vitamins, and that was only if I could keep them down.

I was about ten weeks along when Grizz told me he had to talk to me about something. I was sitting on the couch looking through interior design magazines. I'd already picked a neutral color for the baby's room, light green. Now I was considering a theme. Noah's Ark maybe. Or teddy bears.

He took the magazine out of my hands and laid it on the

coffee table. This looked serious.

"Kit, there's something I have to tell you."

"What? What is it?"

"I don't want you to be upset, especially since you're pregnant, but I love you and I'm afraid if I don't tell you and you find out later, you won't like it."

He was starting to scare me. "Tell me now. Whatever it is, don't keep it from me." Had something happened to Sarah Jo or Fess or Grunt? Was Grizz in trouble? Were we in trouble?

"I just heard from Guido," he said, gripping my hands tightly. "He told me your parents were killed in a car accident the day before yesterday. He thought we should know."

I was stunned. I'd never expected this. I hadn't given much thought to Delia or Vince in years. I can't say I missed them; what was there to miss? I had been on my own from an early age. But Grizz was right. I'm glad he told me. Memories washed over me.

"What happened?" I asked quietly.

"Head-on collision. Big semi. Driver fell asleep, crossed the yellow line. It was instant."

I was relieved there had been no suffering on their part and that they weren't the cause of the accident. I didn't hate Delia and Vince. I didn't miss them, either. But I wanted to do what was right.

"Grizz, there's no other family. What are they going to do with them?"

"Probably a box and a state-owned cemetery. I think. Maybe cremation. I honestly don't know." Before I could say anything, he added, "You want me to take care of it, Kit? Would you like that? To give them a proper burial?"

This surprised me, but I guess he remembered how important it was to me that Moe was given a proper burial. At least as proper as it could be.

I nodded. "Yes, I think I would like that. Doesn't have to be fancy, Grizz. Just a decent cemetery and maybe instead of a headstone, one of those plates that are in the ground. Something that shows their name, birthday and the date they died."

"Write it all down for me, baby, and I'll take care of it."

And he did. He was so good at giving me anything I wanted. It never occurred to me that this was another chance at my freedom. Of course, there'd been many times over the years that I could have gained my freedom. Certainly, the death of my parents would've been one of them, but it didn't matter. I wasn't leaving Grizz. At least not on purpose.

A few weeks later I started spotting. I called the doctor in a panic, but he said there was nothing that could be done. It could be nothing. Wait it out and don't do anything strenuous. Grizz made me lay in bed for three days. The spotting continued and he insisted on taking me to the doctor.

I was sitting on the paper covered examining table when I felt something. I didn't move, just looked at Grizz with tears in my eyes.

"I think I just lost the baby."

Chapter Thirty-Six

We were both sad about losing that baby, but we also agreed I should go back on the pill. There would still be children in our future. We would move into our new home. I would get my degree. Life would go on.

And it did. I never went back to the motel after moving into our home, but of course, Grizz had to. Chowder was now living in our old rooms. Monster had moved into one of the rooms, as well.

I decorated our new home. I took care of Damien and Lucifer. They were getting up in years, and it was obvious they'd slowed down. We had friends over for dinner. Grunt and Cindy came regularly. He was now a successful architect with a high-end firm on Las Olas Boulevard. Grunt and I became close a year or so after he moved in with Cindy. Strange as it seems, we spent a lot of time together. I think it was because Grizz wasn't jealous since Grunt had been with Cindy so long. I think it was hard for Grizz, but he knew the key to keeping me happy wasn't going to work if he kept me to himself. My friendship with Grunt was nice, comfortable, safe. I'd also become closer to my college friends, Carter and Casey. I spent a lot of time with them, as well. Sarah Jo was a regular at our dinner table after she graduated college and settled back in Ft. Lauderdale. She was married, too, and had stayed friends with her old boyfriend, Stephen, and his wife, April. They were all regular guests in our home. So were Anthony and Christy, our friends from the west coast of Florida. Even Sam and his girl-of-the-month came over once in awhile.

Chowder only came for Thanksgiving. I finally got to make that turkey, and Jan didn't seem to mind turning over the reins. She was so busy with her job that she actually seemed to be relieved and happy to let someone else do the cooking.

And that is how the next few years rolled by. They were filled with friends, travel, concerts, taking care of our home and animals, long motorcycle rides and as close to domestic bliss as you can get. Our home was on a couple of acres and we had neighbors, but they weren't close by. Still, I didn't want people to be afraid of us. The only rule I had, and Grizz agreed: no gang business at our home.

Of course, our lifestyle was based on an illusion. When you look at it truthfully, I wasn't really even married to Grizz. Ann Marie Morgan was, but let's face it, I wasn't Ann Marie. Our income, which had grown significantly with good and honest investments, was still based on money earned from illegal activity. A lot of it. Grizz had his hands on everything in South Florida at that time: prostitution, drugs, car theft, gambling, blackmail, loan-sharking. He had been sincere about turning the gang over to Blue when I had gotten pregnant, but with the miscarriage soon after, he saw no immediate reason to retire. And so the money rolled in. I never asked, but you can't be with someone for all those years and not have a sense of what they were up to. I picked things up here and there. I wasn't naïve, but I allowed myself to pretend I was.

I knew our lifestyle was built on a foundation of criminal endeavors, but as long as I wasn't involved, I was able to forget it. I'd stopped balancing the checkbooks and monitoring the investments a few years back. It was turned over to an accountant. I pretended when my husband left for work in the morning that his job didn't involve crime. I'd taken a part-time job with a small accounting firm in Miramar. I didn't have to work, and I had a really difficult time convincing Grizz to let me, but he eventually did. I needed to work just to have some purpose in life.

As soon as I got my degree, I'd told Grizz I wanted to get pregnant. If having children was going to influence Grizz to give up the gang life, I wanted to have a baby as soon as I finished school. He agreed, and so I went off the pill. Unfortunately, it didn't happen as quickly as I'd hoped. A year after graduating college, I still hadn't conceived.

What I didn't know during this time was that Blue and Jan's marriage was falling apart. He'd caught her cheating, more than once, with attorneys she'd met on the job. Jan was attractive and always looking to better herself. Being married to the second-in-command of a motorcycle gang didn't hold as much appeal as it once did. She wanted more. I was surprised she'd cheated on Blue. I'd have thought she'd have been scared to cross him, but she wasn't.

Blue came to the house one day and told us the story. I was right to think she should've been afraid. I remembered a hit-and-run incident about four months earlier. Jan was walking to her car in a grocery store parking lot. She drove a nice car and always parked far away from the store entrance to avoid careless dings from someone who might've parked next to her. She was carrying two bags and fumbling with her keys, looking down as she walked, when a car out of nowhere hit her. The driver fled, and she was knocked unconscious and didn't remember anything. It was a miracle she was only banged up and that nothing was broken. Based on the speed the car was going, it was a miracle she was alive.

Blue didn't take her indiscretions lightly. I realized as Blue told us his tale that the hit-and-run was far more than that—he'd ordered an actual hit on her. I also knew he would've needed approval from my husband before doing so. I shivered.

Blue continued with his tale and said he'd finally had enough and kicked her out. Told her he would be seeking custody of the boys. Grizz grilled him about exactly how much Jan knew about the gang. Blue said he never told her anything. She didn't even know about the night he took Grunt.

Grizz nodded. "Okay, so what harm can she do us, if any?"

The unspoken question, of course, was, "Can she tie the hit-and-run and anything else illegal to us?"

"I suppose she could have someone dig into our personal finances, but then she's only implicating herself, I would think," Blue told him. "Other than the fact that I have a motorcycle and a jacket, it's all just speculation on her part. I don't think anyone would touch it. As far as custody, she may be getting free legal advice, but the firm she works for specializes in estate taxes and stuff like that."

I interrupted here. "Blue, Jan knows some things. She told me in detail about Moe's early life and how she came to the motel. How she lost her tongue. She told me who lived at the motel, who didn't live there. She even knew about the night I got Gwinny. If you didn't tell her that, who did?"

"I don't know," Blue looked at both of us, bewildered. "Honest, Grizz. Maybe when Chicky or Willow came over when she was pregnant and off her meds? Remember when we had the girls stay with her once in awhile? I guess she could have heard stuff then. But I didn't tell her where Kit came from or anything like that. Hell, she's never even been to the motel. Doesn't know any real names. Not even mine. I married her under an alias."

Grizz glanced in my direction. I looked down. He knew what I was thinking. He'd married me under an alias. At least Jan got to marry Blue with her real name.

Grizz didn't say anything for a minute. I could tell he was seriously thinking about this. He then asked Blue, "Do you think she talked to Willow, other than when Willow was there to keep an eye on her?"

"I guess it's possible. Fuck, I honestly don't know." Blue gave me a sidelong glance. "Sorry, Kit. Know you don't like the cursing. It's a habit."

More silence from Grizz. I knew Grizz trusted Blue implicitly and was trying to figure out if he had a mole. But with Willow's intense hatred of me, it was very possible that she had been the one who communicated with Jan. Maybe she thought she would find an ally in Jan. There was no way to be sure. Jan would certainly never say, and Willow had been dead for years.

"And you want custody of Timmy and Kevin?" Grizz asked.

"Yeah, I want my boys, Grizz. I can't give up my boys."

"Okay then. I trust you. Go ahead and fight for your boys. If the gang comes up in any way, shape or form, I want to know immediately. Is that understood? You tell her that. You let her know what that means."

"I will. I'll tell her and she'll understand. I'll fight for my boys fair and square. The gang stays out of it. You have my word."

The conversation ended, and it was the last I heard about Blue and Jan's divorce and custody battle for awhile. She'd tried remaining friends with me, but I couldn't bring myself to continue seeing her. I suspected she wanted to be friends with me for other reasons. Maybe she feared more retaliation from Grizz and knew a friendship with me would help her case. Maybe she just wanted to know what I knew, which was nothing. If Blue was telling Grizz things about the divorce and custody hearings, Grizz wasn't telling me. I just figured it was in everyone's best interest for me to stay away from her.

That was how I coped with all of it. Always had. I stayed away physically and emotionally.

It wasn't until the custody hearing that things started to get really nasty. The divorce had been finalized months earlier, and Blue and Jan were sharing joint custody of the boys. Blue told Grizz that it looked like things were going to turn out in his favor. The motorcycle gang was brought up in the custody hearings, but with no proof, Jan was practically laughed out of the courtroom. Blue's attorney attacked with a vengeance, bringing up Jan's battle with mental illness and adultery.

I think that this lulled Blue and Grizz into a false sense of security where the gang was concerned. They figured she wouldn't be able to do any harm now.

But I guess Jan couldn't take it anymore. She finally pulled an ace out of her sleeve like she'd done so many years earlier, when Blue was going to leave her and she suddenly got pregnant.

This time it was different, though. This time, her ace would have a ripple effect that couldn't be measured. It would destroy people. A lot of people.

Jan decided it was time to tell the world about Guinevere Love Lemon.

Chapter Thirty-Seven

I don't know how she managed it. How she was able to investigate my name without bringing it to the attention of Grizz's network of informants, law enforcement and otherwise. I'm pretty sure she didn't know if I was a runaway or had been abducted, but she did somehow find out I'd disappeared in 1975, never to be heard from again.

This was her first step in getting custody of her boys. She was going to bring down Blue by bringing down the gang. By bringing down Grizz.

I had to admit she was one gutsy woman. She was working with authorities to go into the Witness Protection Program. Blue was wrong. Jan knew far, far more than he thought.

I was never certain how she tracked down Froggy without causing notice to herself. Froggy had never gotten over what Grizz had done to Willow. He'd started to slowly withdraw from the group after her exile, and even more so after her death. It was obvious by his testimony on the witness stand that he totally despised Grizz for what he did to her. Froggy was more than willing to tell the authorities everything he knew in exchange for his protection.

The police showed up at our house in Shady Ranches with a warrant and arrested Grizz. He didn't put up a fight as they handcuffed him and read him his rights. He was calm. He was certain his attorney would have him out on bail within hours.

Grizz had been arrested before. It was never a big deal in the past—always minor charges that were an attempt to harass him. He was never arrested for any serious crimes. But this was the first time he was arrested in my presence. He stared at me and listened calmly as they read him his rights and started reciting the list of charges.

"Jason William Talbot, you have the right to remain silent—"

It was the first time I'd heard his whole name.

I'd gotten over my obsession with learning his real name years earlier. I never saw the gang's use of fictitious names as anything but a means for them to cause confusion, anyway. I never saw it as the big deal that they did.

But suddenly, as they listed the charges, Grizz's demeanor changed. He went ballistic, even with his hands behind his back, when they called me by my real name and started asking me questions.

"Are you in fact Guinivere Love Lemon, who disappeared from Ft. Lauderdale, Florida on May 15, 1975?" I couldn't answer. I was in shock.

"Were you a runaway or abducted by this man?"

Grizz knew then that this arrest wasn't for a list of trivial offenses. This would be different. They knew who I was. The big question was had I been abducted or was I a runaway? And how involved had I been in Grizz's criminal activity?

One of the officers said to me, "Answer very cautiously, Guinevere. If you were abducted by this man in 1975 against your will, that's one thing. But if you were a runaway and participated willingly in the Satan's Army gang, it's a whole different ballgame."

"Don't answer a fucking thing until we talk to our attorney," Grizz snapped. "Don't say a word, Kit. Nothing. Get the fuck away from my wife."

He head-butted one of the men and sent him sprawling backwards into our stone fireplace. The man was dazed but didn't appear to be hurt.

I'd started crying, and even though the men were kind to me, I was afraid. Two of them started beating on Grizz. He barely flinched.

"Stop it," I cried. "Please, everyone. Just stop. We'll go with you. Please, no more."

"You can't take her to jail," Grizz snarled. "She can't be in jail. This has nothing to do with her. Leave her alone."

"We're not arresting her, just you, fuckwad." This from the guy Grizz had head-butted. Of course, he said it from a safe distance.

"It'll all be settled at the station," the oldest of the men said.

It was a line right out of an old black-and-white police movie. The detective reminded me of a kindly grandfather. He was probably close to retirement and wanted to be anywhere but here.

He added, "She'll be fine. She won't get hurt. Calm down. This is just procedure. You know how this goes down, Jason." He turned to me and gently took me by the arm. "I'm Detective Banner, and it'll be okay, Guinevere. We just need to ask you some questions. It's all part of the process. Your husband is overreacting."

I looked at him sadly. "He's just worried about me because I'm pregnant."

––––––––

I'd just found out a week earlier I was pregnant again. I wasn't far along at all, but Grizz and I still let ourselves get excited.

"Call Mark. He'll have me out by tonight," Grizz told me as they walked him to our door.

"Not this time, Talbot," one of the officers, a young one, said. "I don't think a judge will give you a bail option. Kidnapping is a federal offense. You'll stay locked up until trial."

"Just call him, Kit."

"No, Grizz," I called after him. "He's not good enough for this. I've got someone else in mind."

I'd been following the career of a very powerful and well-known defense attorney. He was young, but was making a real name for himself in South Florida.

"Who?" Grizz yelled back over his shoulder. I was now following behind him with Detective Banner at my side.

"Matthew," I told him, resolve firm in my voice.

"Matthew who?" he asked as they put him in the back of the police car.

"Matthew Rockman. The kid from my porch."

The car door slammed, and he was gone.

I'd told no one, not even Sarah Jo, that I'd been back in touch with my friend from high school. It just didn't seem necessary.

Matthew had found me back in 1980. It wasn't hard. It was during the time when I was living at the motel and had found out I was pregnant that first time. It was no secret the leader of Satan's Army lived at the Glades Motel.

Matthew pulled in one day pretending to be a lost motorist. Chowder told him he'd passed Flamingo Road miles back. He would have to turn around. He'd casually asked Chowder if the motel was open for business. Chowder had eyed him cautiously and didn't answer, just pointed to the road. But not before Matthew spotted me.

I'd come out, gotten in my car and, without knowing I was doing so, actually followed him onto State Road 84. Armed with information—that I lived there and what I drove—now he could plan a way to see me.

Matthew could have followed me the first day he saw me, but he was worried he'd raised Chowder's suspicions. So he'd parked in Pete's parking lot, facing the highway, for two days before he spotted me driving my Trans Am. He followed me to the grocery store and waited until after I got out of my car to approach me.

I'd recognized him immediately. He told me he didn't want to make trouble, just wanted to talk. And that's all we did. I told him almost everything—everything except my knowledge of Grizz's criminal endeavors.

"You don't need to try and hide what the guy does, Gin. His gang is notorious. I just want to see how you're doing."

"I'm good, Matthew. I know Grizz threatened you that night. I'm sorry for that. But honestly, I'm happy with him.

He's good to me. I'm going to have his baby."

This surprised him. "I just needed to check on you before I did anything. I'm not that kid anymore. I'm not afraid of him."

"Well, you should be afraid of him. Just because you're an adult doesn't mean he can't get to you. That's not a threat, Matthew. I'm just stating a fact. I'm telling a friend, who I care about, to stay away. Please just leave us alone."

"You're certain of that, Gin? I'll keep it to myself if you're telling me the truth."

"I'm certain, Matthew."

I'd given a long explanation then, about how I didn't approve of or participate in Grizz's gang activity, but had found myself falling in love with him anyway. Matthew couldn't equate the straight-A, mild-mannered girl with the grown woman who was married to the brutal leader of a motorcycle gang. But he also remembered my neglected home life, and how much I loved the attention his family lavished on me.

Our conversation went from me convincing him to leave us alone to two old friends catching up on each other's lives. I had been sitting in his car talking to him when he got very quiet and stared out over his steering wheel. I guess he just couldn't let it go.

"You know, your abduction influenced my decision to go to law school." He looked at me now. "I didn't like being threatened, feeling helpless. I knew the guy who took you was a criminal. I'm going to law school to bring down scumbags like him."

I noticed that the knuckles on his left hand had whitened. He was clenching the steering wheel hard.

Tears sprang to my eyes. "Please don't call him that." He

started to interrupt but I held up my hand. "He has treated me better than anyone ever has. I love him, Matthew. I'm doing everything I can to get him away from this lifestyle. Please leave us alone. He promised me he would quit when the baby comes. I believe him."

He sighed and looked back out over the steering wheel. The conversation turned lighthearted again. He told me how he loved law school. I joked that I was glad the end of my tutoring him didn't interfere with him going off to college. It was a nice talk.

I hadn't seen or spoken to Matthew since that day, but I read the newspapers and watched the news. He was young, but blazing a trail through the justice system by winning impossible cases. Don't think the irony wasn't lost on me that he told me years ago he was going to law school to put the bad guys away, and now he was the best in the business at setting them free.

I reflected on all of this as I waited in Detective Banner's office, sipping watered-down coffee and waiting for Matthew to show up. When he finally did, Matthew brought a man with him I didn't know.

"Gin, this is Cary Lewis. He's not with my firm. I can't represent Jason because of our history. But I'm putting you in the hands of someone who is better at this job than anyone I know. You trust me on this, I hope?"

I looked up at him from where I was sitting. "If you tell me you have no hard feelings toward him, if you can look me in the eye and tell me that, then yes." I took a breath. "I trust you."

Chapter Thirty-Eight

It's not necessary to go into the details of the following years. Besides, I found the legal proceedings and jargon too much to retain. I'll stick with the facts as I remember them.

I never saw Grizz again as a free man. He was denied bail and stayed incarcerated in the county jail for almost two years while Cary Lewis negotiated with the prosecutors. I stayed very close to Matthew during this time. Even though it was in an unofficial capacity, I needed him to explain everything that was happening.

Cary did his best with me, but between the pregnancy and the press, I needed Matthew and Sam. They were instrumental in getting my high school and college degrees transferred over to my real name. They protected me from the media. They were with me from the very beginning of this nightmare. They even arranged for me to live with

Stephen and April.

Stephen, who was Sarah Jo's high school boyfriend, had remained a close friend, and most importantly, he and April had no association with the gang at all. They welcomed me into their home until the media frenzy died down. My college girlfriends, Carter and Casey, took turns staying at my house to care for Damien. We'd lost Lucifer a year earlier to bone cancer. When I was finally able to move home, Carter moved in with me.

One thing Grizz insisted on from the beginning was leaving me out of everything. He told them he abducted me. He told them about the threats early on to prevent my escape, and how he tricked me into the marriage.

The story made headlines: "Missing Girl Found Married to Leader of Notorious Motorcycle Gang." People started to come out of the woodwork.

"Yes, I thought I recognized her, but she seemed so happy, I was certain she hadn't been abducted."

"That bastard threatened my life if I didn't get her guitar back." This from the pawnshop owner where I hocked my guitar that first Christmas.

"You say he threatened your life?" Cary asked him on the stand. "You weren't monetarily compensated to retrieve the guitar?"

"Well, yeah, but money or not, I still didn't have a choice. My life was at stake."

Even Diane Berger, the girl from the vet's office, probably thought she was helping, but in reality, it didn't make me look good. "I asked her right out if she was Ginny Lemon and she said no. She even had some weird accent. She was probably brainwashed."

"Don't worry about it," Cary and Matthew told me.

"Can't prove she really saw you. Maybe it was a look-alike with an accent."

Except that it wasn't. The prosecution was able to pull the vet's records and show Rick O'Connell did have a dog there during that time that was being treated for a snake bite.

Every time we thought something might go our way, someone else would come forward. And with Jan and Froggy's statements, we knew it was going to be an uphill battle. Froggy, whose real name was Larry Most, stated under oath that he witnessed Grizz murder more than one person. Even with the details, there were never any bodies to substantiate his claims. They would have to get more witnesses. And they did.

One thing that surprised me early on was there was never a mention of Grunt or Fess. Jan and Froggy never once brought them up. I believe it was because Jan really did care for Grunt, and I think they both felt sorry for Fess. He was just a regular guy trying to make a living and raise three kids by himself. The authorities did eventually get to them through other witnesses, but by then, Grizz had cut a deal.

In the two years it took to prepare for trial, I'd also gotten married and had our daughter. We named her Miriam. We called her Mimi.

This may be hard to believe, but Grizz practically forced me to get remarried. I remember the day well. I was only about two months into my pregnancy and was visiting him in jail.

"Kit, you love me, don't you?" he asked.

"You know I love you, Grizz. We'll get through this. You'll get out. We'll get our lives back."

"Kitten, I'm never getting out of here. You need to know and understand that now."

"Stop it! Don't talk like that."

"You're a smart girl. You need to face reality so we can make a plan. You said you love me. I need you to prove it."

I looked at him with vision blurred by tears. "Tell me. Tell me how to prove it."

"I want you to get married."

I was so stunned I couldn't even object. We were speaking on telephones through a glass partition. "I want you to promise me our child will have a father when he or she is born. Promise me that, Kit."

"Our baby will have a father, Grizz. You. I can give it your last name. Talbot." Then something else occurred to me. "Married to who? Who would I marry? Besides, we're already married."

I knew deep down our marriage wasn't legal. Maybe Rick O'Connell and Ann Marie Morgan were married, but Jason Talbot and Ginny Lemon weren't. Yet in our hearts, we were.

"Kit, I can name five guys who care enough about you to marry you tomorrow. I know probably two of them are already in love with you. Hell, even Fess would marry you if we asked him."

"You can't be serious. And as much as I love Sarah Jo, I don't want to be her stepmother. Who else could you possibly be talking about? Besides, I find it hard to believe you suspect not one, but two men of being in love with me and they're still alive." I picked up a tissue to blow my nose while resting the phone on my shoulder.

"You once told me I was a smart guy. Do you remember? The night you told me you were pregnant that first time. I told you how I dropped out of school, and you were surprised by how I survived. How I made something out of nothing. You remember that?"

"Yes, I remember. So what?"

"You were right, baby. I am smart. Smart enough to let those guys fall in love with you because I knew this day might come."

I couldn't believe what I was hearing, but after talking to Cary and his explanation of the seriousness of Grizz's predicament, I gave in.

I was married within weeks of having that conversation with Grizz. A divorce wasn't necessary since our marriage was never legal. Just as Grizz had asked of me, I was legally wed to another man when our daughter was born.

She was a big baby. No surprise there, given the size of her father. I was in labor for twenty-four hours before they finally performed an emergency C-section. As I was wheeled into surgery, I remember my new husband and friends telling me, "We'll be here when you wake up."

Grizz insisted she be given my husband's last name and that she was never to know Grizz was her biological father. He made me swear I would never tell.

"I believe you when you tell me you love me, Kit. If you really do, you'll never tell her."

"If she tries to, someday she can look back and figure out the timing, Grizz. I don't see how I could keep it from her."

"Then lie. Tell her you cheated on me. I don't care if you tell her that. I don't want her to know I'm her father."

Mimi would grow into a beautiful girl. She would never ask, and I was able to keep my promise to Grizz.

Cary told me Grizz wanted to plead guilty in order to

protect everyone else. The problem was he would have received life in prison without parole. There was no way Grizz would agree to stay in prison for life.

So he would plead guilty in exchange for a death sentence.

"No!" I cried when they told me.

"Don't worry," Cary explained. "I don't think the State of Florida is in the assisted-suicide business. They wouldn't be able to agree to that. He'll have to go to trial. Having him live the remainder of his life in prison would make them happy, but they chance him getting out on a technicality somewhere down the road. I have no doubt the prosecutors will push for the death penalty. It's still too early to know if he'll get it and you need to prepare yourself in case he does."

"I don't care if he wants the death penalty. I'm counting on you, Cary, to make sure he gets life in prison. And if he does get it, he can maybe get out on a technicality somewhere down the road?"

"Ginny, of course I'm going to do my best to protect him from the death penalty. But, you need to know that if he does get life, there's no guarantee a technicality might come up."

"But Matthew told me you were the best, Cary. I'm expecting you to get him out of this!"

"You don't understand, Ginny. There is no getting out. And Jason knows it. He's having me negotiate with the prosecution so certain people aren't touched. Especially you. They'll dig. They'll find a way to bring you down to get to him. He's trying to avoid that."

"But we've got Sam!" I blurted out, tears swimming. "Sam will testify for us. He'll talk about the Stockholm syndrome. How it was normal for me to stay with Grizz."

"You're the main reason, Ginny, but do I need to tell you how many people are involved in this? How many names have come across the prosecution's desk? All of them: Grunt, Fess, Blue, Chowder, Chicky. Even Eddie, the tattoo guy. Even he'll be left alone. Of course, he'll have to go back to just doing ink and nothing extracurricular. But the list is endless."

Then he answered an unspoken question. "He's only giving up his informants who took bribes. Nobody he blackmailed."

I was secretly relieved to hear Grizz's inside network of law enforcement informants weren't all bad. I was glad to know the law in South Florida wasn't as corrupt as I'd originally thought.

That's pretty much how it went during the two years leading up to the trial. Two years of negotiations. Who would they go after? Who would they leave alone? Grizz insisted Chowder, whose real name was John Lawrence, be allowed to remain at the motel as long as he wanted. It didn't matter. Chowder died of a heart attack before Grizz went to trial.

Our home was also off the table. I was able to keep the house and everything on the property at the time of Grizz's arrest. It included everything in our home, our cars and his motorcycles. I also didn't have to worry about money. There was enough to pay for the attorneys and live comfortably for a very long time.

Years ago, and without my knowledge, Grizz had Fess

and Grunt open up investment accounts in my real name—
so much for the gang's code of not using real names. It
wasn't an issue, anyway. Early on, Grunt, Fess and their
finances were left alone in exchange for Grizz's cooperation
on other matters. Grizz gave up two men who headed up
his drug empire in exchange for their immunity. They were
off the table and it was early in the negotiations, so their
names never got released to the public. I was grateful. It
would have affected their careers. And besides, there were
bigger fish to fry.

The negotiations continued. Another man, I actually
think it was the old man from the warehouse in Pompano
Beach, was given up for Chicky's immunity. And that's how
it went until the day of Grizz's trial. Just like a chess game,
Grizz meticulously calculated each move. He gave up the
goods on some people in order to protect others. He even
insisted some of the people he protected bear witness
against him at trial.

He was doing his best to convince a jury that he should
get the death penalty.

And he did.

Chapter Thirty-Nine

Grizz waited on death row in a prison in North Florida. It was about a five-hour ride by car. I tried to visit him. But after the first year he told me no more. I had to move on with my life. I had to raise our daughter. Be a good mother. Be a good wife.

"Do you love him?" he asked me one day. "It's okay to tell me, Kit. It's okay if you love him. He loves you and has taken care of you and Mimi. My time has passed."

"Yes," I answered, as I looked at my hands in my lap. "I love him."

It was the last time I saw Grizz until the day of his execution.

The year after that conversation was the worst. I think I mourned Grizz the hardest then. There was so much emotion. There was so much guilt. Why had I saved that stupid wallet? Why hadn't I gotten up on that stand and told the jury how good he was to me?

Because Grizz wouldn't let me. The prosecution didn't come near me because of the information Grizz gave them. It was like Christmas for them. One present after the other. Other than to ask me to corroborate things Grizz had told them, they kept their word. I was left alone.

I called him years later to tell him I'd had another baby. It might come as a surprise that a prisoner on death row could receive a phone call. But this was Grizz. Being on death row never changed his status as leader of Satan's Army. He still managed to possess a great amount of influence over his present circumstances.

He'd known I was pregnant. Even in prison, Grizz had found a way to keep tabs on my husband and me. But that day I told him something he didn't know.

"We named him Jason." The phone went silent for a long time. I wasn't sure if he was still there.

"I love you, Ginny. I'll always love you."

It was the first and last time he called me by my real name. I started to answer that I still loved him, too, but he'd already hung up.

It was true. I still loved Grizz. I wasn't in love with him like I had been, but I cared deeply for him. My husband understood. There was no jealousy or insecurity from him. Besides, if it weren't for Grizz, I wouldn't be married to the man I was completely and totally in love with today.

Chapter Forty

The day after Grizz's execution, back home, my husband and I decided to use the day to do something special.

"Hey, you two. Long time no see," Eddie said as he hugged us both.

We hadn't been in to see Eddie since he'd added our son's name to the tattoo on my husband's left arm. He'd surprised me on our third wedding anniversary. The tattoo was a beautiful eagle holding up a heart between its wings. Inside the heart was my name: Ginny. I thanked him for not using Guinevere. He'd joked at the time that he didn't think Eddie had enough ink. There was a ribbon that wrapped around the heart and dangled on one side of the tattoo. It said "Mimi." When our son was born, he went back and had Eddie add another ribbon with the name "Jason." It was a beautiful work of art and a testament to our happy family.

Eddie looked at my stomach and teased, "Time to add another ribbon?"

"No," I answered. I held up my left hand. "I need you to work your creative magic with this," I said as I practically shoved my ring finger under his nose.

This time, I didn't faint.

————————

It was Sunday morning. Two days after Grizz's execution. My husband and I sat in our den waiting for the phone to ring. We had gone to a sunrise Mass to be home in time for this phone call. In retrospect, I wish we'd missed the call. Just like climbing on the back of Monster's motorcycle twenty-five years ago would change my life, the damage resulting from this phone call was irrevocable.

When the phone rang, he hit the speakerphone button and said, "We're here, Leslie. You're on."

Leslie stammered a little. She must have sensed we were weary of the interview process and was hesitant about her first question. I knew what was coming.

"I guess I really wanted to ask Ginny what that little communication was about right before Jason's execution," Leslie said, her voice growing steadier. "I mean, it's obvious there was something going on between you two, and I think it's probably important and would be a good way to wrap up the interview. You know, the end to this epic love story."

"That was nothing," I said firmly. "Grizz was just trying to be in charge again. An old joke. He was messing with me. Not important and totally not relevant to this story. You're not missing anything."

She didn't say anything for a minute. Then she blurted,

"But the love story. That's what I really want to play up. The love between the hardened criminal and the sweet, innocent girl. That's what the readers want, a love story, and I need something to make the conclusion pop." She cleared her throat. "That signal he gave you. It must have meant something. Can't you give me something here, Ginny?"

I sighed and leaned back in my chair. I hadn't realized I'd been sitting at attention.

"The only thing I can tell you, Leslie, is I've spent three months letting you interview me, and the real love story was right under your nose the whole time and you didn't see it. A story about a man who has loved me from the very beginning, from the first glance. The man who always was and still is my soul mate. That's the only love story now. Yes, I loved Grizz, that's true. That story is over. Don't romanticize it. I've built a new life with—"

She cut me off. "She doesn't know, does she? You haven't told her yet. I suggest you do before she reads it in my article."

Who was she talking to? I looked over at my husband. He didn't answer her. He pressed the disconnect button on the phone.

"Well, that's one way to end an interview," I said to him.

My husband, Tommy—I never used the gang name Grunt anymore, just as he never called me Kit—just smiled and winked at me.

But then he turned serious. "Gin, I need to tell you some things. Some bad things."

I practically scoffed. What bad things could Tommy possibly have to tell me? I seriously doubted he could surprise me with anything.

"Okay, I'm listening. It can't be that bad."

But it was.

There, listening to Tommy tell me the story of Leslie's accident three weeks ago, I was stunned. I felt like I was hearing the story in an out-of-body experience, like it was being told to someone else and I was just there, watching from above.

I don't know how to explain it. I knew the major players. I'd spent enough time in Leslie's company to understand her personality, to actually know how it played out with her and Grizz.

As Tommy told me the details, I felt like I was watching a movie unfold. And I wanted to throw up.

Chapter Forty-One

Leslie Cowan sat confidently at the metal table. She'd interviewed hundreds of people and had a bit of a smug attitude about the upcoming interview.

She'd caught wind of this story through a friend of a friend and thought it would go great with *Rolling Stone's* expose on celebrity bikers. She'd spent most of the last couple of months interviewing the other main character in this story, and she had exactly one hour to wrap it up with the sole person who would not be around to answer any questions in the coming weeks.

Jason Talbot was to be executed in a matter of weeks. She wasn't going to put much credence in what he had to say. She felt she'd gotten the meat of her story already. She was really here out of sheer curiosity.

She'd heard of his brutality, but she was not the type to

be intimidated by anyone. She'd interviewed street gang members, drug dealers, rapists, murderers. The worst society had to offer. This would be a piece of cake.

She wanted to ask him about his relationship with Ginny Lemon, now Ginny Dillon. It would be interesting to ask the man, who was so cruel to others, why he'd had such tender feelings for a fifteen-year-old girl? Why didn't he kill her? Why did he keep her with him as long as possible? Why would he go to the lethal injection table for her?

She was pretty sure Ginny had exaggerated his feelings toward her. Leslie wanted to find out what he really thought. She would be able to get the truth out of him. She was a top-of-the-line investigative reporter. She could wrap the worst interviewee around her little finger. She'd done it before, and she'd do it again.

A man who was facing death in a couple of weeks would be so vulnerable. He would be putty in her hands and spilling his guts in a matter of minutes.

She looked up when she heard the door open. A guard came in, followed by a man of incredible size. She'd seen pictures and knew he was big. But she didn't expect him to be this big.

Behind him was another guard. The prisoner, wearing an orange prison-issue jumpsuit, was handcuffed and shackled around the waist. He took small steps, and she could hear the shackles around his ankles clanking. Her gaze wandered up until she met his eyes.

The mesmerizing, green eyes Ginny had mentioned more than once. She had only seen pictures that didn't do them justice. She thought that, too, had been exaggerated. She was wrong.

Without taking his eyes from hers, he slid into the seat

across from her as the guard unshackled his handcuffs from the chain around his waist and re-shackled them to a steel bar on the table.

She looked away then and said to the guard, "Thanks, I can take it from here."

The guard refused, told her under no circumstances was anyone ever to be left alone in a room with Jason Talbot.

"But he's shackled," she replied with dismay.

"Doesn't matter. You got a problem with that, you leave. We're staying here with you."

The taller guard locked the door behind them, and they both leaned up against opposite walls.

She started to argue, but it was no use; the guards calmly and firmly expressed the rule one more time.

"This is for your own safety regardless of the shackles," the shorter guard said.

She huffed like he was being ridiculous, and the guard said, "Then consider this interview over."

He started to unshackle the prisoner but she stopped him. "Fine. Stay. Whatever."

She looked back at Jason then, and a chill ran down her spine. She had never been the focus of such a penetrating look. His eyes were cold, and she was trying not to tremble.

"Thank you for agreeing to see me, Jason," she began. "You know I've been interviewing Ginny the last few months. Seems you two have an interesting past. I was hoping you could tell me more about your relationship with her."

"I'm sure Kit told you everything. I don't have anything to add."

She was starting to feel something she had never felt before in an interview. She was getting a little giddy. There was something about his power and intensity that was extremely attractive, and she was losing her focus. She felt silly that he could make her feel this way. He exuded raw sexuality like no one she'd ever met.

She tried to imagine being only fifteen and having to deal with him. It's a miracle Ginny survived.

"Well, why don't you tell me something then that Ginny didn't know. Surprise me."

"Oh, I'd like to surprise you, darling."

A shiver ran down her spine. Could she actually be enjoying herself flirting with this murderer?

She pasted on her coyest smile and kept asking questions. He replied with one-syllable answers. These were questions she already knew the answers to, thanks to Ginny. So Ginny had been telling her the truth. Well, well.

"Jason, this is all pretty standard stuff that I already know. Can't you give me something else here? Something to shock my readers?"

He stared at her for a minute. "I've answered every question. What exactly do you want to know?"

She swallowed back her aggravation. "For one thing, I cannot believe that in all that time you spent with Ginny, there isn't one secret that you kept to yourself. Something she never knew. Doesn't know, to this day. I know the real-name secret already. That obviously had to come out." She leaned in provocatively. "What else is there?"

"There's nothing. Why would I keep a secret from Kit?"

"Um, because she kept a secret from you?" This was the moment she'd been waiting for. She'd been baiting him along this whole time to lead up to this." *God, I'm good.*

This got the rise out of him she was hoping for. He was such an egomaniac. There was no way he could fathom

Ginny keeping something hidden from him.

In a split second, the doubt in his eyes was gone, replaced by his natural arrogance.

He gestured with his hands, motioned for her to bring it on. They were shackled to the table, but he still had some leeway.

"Let's hear it, then, reporter lady. What's this supposed secret that Kit kept from me?"

"If I tell you, then you'll tell me something? Something you never told Ginny. You promise?"

"Yeah, sure. Let's hear it first."

"Okay. How about that Ginny lost her virginity to Grunt?"

He laughed out loud then. "Stupid bitch. I knew that. I'm the one who told him to do it!"

"You're not listening to me, Jason. Ginny lost her virginity to *Grunt*. Not that disgusting billy-club you told him to use."

She knew she was wrong to tell him. But, as she quickly reminded herself, she'd promised Ginny it wouldn't be in the article. She'd never promised Ginny she wouldn't tell Jason.

Leslie knew she'd surprised him. She knew instantly this was one thing he definitely never found out. Well, screw him. Stupid idiot. Let him chew on that for a minute.

With the look of someone who'd just devoured her victim, she leaned toward him and, in her haughtiest tone of voice, purred, "So, now, you owe me—"

Faster than lightning and before the guards could intervene, Grizz used both feet to kick Leslie's chair out from under her. This quick action and the fact that she was already leaning toward him caused her to fall face forward and within his reach. He was able to grab her head and smash her face into the metal post that was keeping his hands fastened to the table. There was the sickening sound of teeth breaking as blood spurted everywhere.

The guards got to them as quickly as they could. One pulled Leslie out of his grasp as the other started beating him down with a stick. He never flinched. He just laughed.

"You motherfucker!" she screamed.

She was bleeding profusely from cuts on her forehead, nose and mouth. It was hard for her to talk. She was definitely hurt, but she hadn't started to cry. She was in shock.

The guard got her on her feet and started half-walking, half-carrying her toward the door.

As she was leaving, she heard Grizz call out, "You wanna know something? I'll tell you something. Come back and see me."

Chapter Forty-Two

I stared at Tommy. "That's why she looked like she was recovering from an accident at the execution? Grizz did that to her?"

"Yeah, he did it."

"Oh, Tommy. He knew. He knew before he died what happened between us." I put my head in my hands. "He must have been so hurt. Felt so betrayed by us."

"He was, Gin. That's why he gave her one more phone interview before he died. He told her something. Something she's going to put in her article. Something you don't know. Something that will hurt."

Before I could ask him what it was, he added, "Grizz was sorry, you know. I talked to him after he talked to Leslie. He said after the anger wore off, he was sorry he told her. Hell, he was going to order a hit on her from prison so it didn't get printed. I talked him out of it. I didn't want her to die because of a secret coming out. The time for killing is over. I hope you agree."

"My heart hurts knowing he died feeling betrayed."

"He didn't die feeling betrayed. I spoke with him, and you saw him nod at me. He understood."

Then something occurred to me. "Oh no, don't tell me he told her about Miriam being his daughter. Please don't tell me that's it."

I didn't think this would have been a hard one to figure out if someone took the time to calculate Miriam's birth date and my marriage to Tommy. Nobody really seemed interested and, surprisingly, I was never asked. I just wouldn't have wanted it printed for Mimi to read.

"No, it's—"

I cut him off. "Is it the real story about the first time he saw me? Not in Guido's driveway when I was thirteen like we told everybody? I was only six. You know that story, don't you? Grizz told me he went ballistic when Delia and Vince took me to Woodstock. That's when he put Guido next door. That's not too big a deal. I don't see how that could hurt anybody." I was rambling.

"Yeah, I know that story. It's not that."

Tommy took a deep breath and started to tell me about Grizz's childhood. Grizz's real childhood. Yes, Grizz had told me the truth about his mother, but he didn't go into specifics. I'm not surprised. The details Tommy was providing were too horrific for me to even imagine. It ended in his parents' death by his own hand. Both of his parents. It shed some serious light on why he was the way he was. I don't know how anybody could have made it through a childhood like his and come out unscathed.

I interrupted Tommy. "Well, it's an awful story, but I don't see how it could hurt me."

"No, Kit, it's not that either," Tommy snapped. "Let me finish."

I was stunned. Not only did Tommy never raise his voice to me, but he hadn't called me Kit in almost fifteen years.

"He just wanted you to know everything. From the beginning. It obviously started with his childhood, but that's not what he told Leslie."

And then Tommy told me.

Not just the secret that Grizz told Leslie out of anger, but another one, as well. He was right. It hurt.

I wished it was the story of Grizz being Mimi's biological father. I wished it was the story about Grizz first seeing me when I was just six years old in front of the convenience store. Grizz told me that story the day he married me.

No, it was much, much worse.

Like a deer caught in the headlights, I listened in stunned silence as my husband told me of Grizz's betrayal. Secrets Tommy knew from the beginning. Secrets he'd kept from me. Secrets that made me feel my heart had been removed from my chest and placed on my lap.

The first one didn't surprise me too much. It concerned Delia. It stung, but it actually made some sense.

But the other secret I was certain I would never fully recover from. It would be in Leslie's article.

And I would look like a fool.

For the second time in my life that I could remember, I used profanity.

"Grunt, you son of a bitch." I stared icily at him. "You

shouldn't have stopped him from ordering a hit on Leslie."

Epilogue

The two men sat and gazed at each other over the unremarkable but rather large wooden desk. They were in an office, though the owner of this particular office, located in a maximum-security prison in northern Florida, was apparently a minimalist. No trinkets or knickknacks adorned the only bookshelf. No awards or degrees were displayed on the walls. The desk was sparsely furnished with the necessities. A telephone. A blotter, which also served as a desk calendar. A container with pens and pencils. No plants, no family photos.

The only indication that this office was used regularly was sitting on a small knee-high table that was up against a wall. A chess set made of ivory. The pieces were elaborate and detailed in their design. It was obvious there was a game in progress. The small table that it sat on was flanked by two cushioned chairs with wooden armrests. A warm light glowed over the table and its contents from a wall sconce. This small setting was in such sharp contrast to the rest of the office décor that one might have to blink to see if it was indeed reality.

The chair behind the large desk, which the bigger of the two men occupied, was oversized and comfortable. The chair of the person facing the desk was hard and uninviting, probably on purpose. If someone was to look down on this scene, they would never have known that one of the men, the larger man behind the desk, was to be executed by lethal injection in less than a week. He didn't look like a prisoner. He didn't look like someone who was scheduled for execution. He wasn't wearing prison-issue clothing. He was in jeans and a T-shirt. He exuded power and confidence. He seemed to be in a position of authority.

"Okay, what have you got?" Grizz asked.

Blue looked at him without answering. The expression on his face caught Grizz off guard. It was an expression Grizz didn't recognize. Blue looked uncertain, hesitant maybe. They locked eyes. Neither would look away.

Blue finally said, "You're not going to like it."

"I'm not going to like what?" Before Blue could reply, he snapped, "You know what, it doesn't matter. First things first. Has Leslie been handled?"

"Yes. She'll need more convincing, but I've got it handled."

"The other thing?"

"Done. Flawless. Just like you said."

"Okay, now what is it I'm not gonna like?"

"I found her."

"You found who?"

"Jan. I found my boys."

Grizz leaned back in the chair. He'd been leaning forward, his elbows on the desk. He cocked his head to one side, considering. "I knew you were still looking for your boys. What is it I'm not going to like?"

"I talked to her. I scared the shit out of her. She never thought she'd be found. She said she would tell me everything and let me work my way back into the boys' lives if I just left her alone." Then he sneered, mostly to himself, "As if she has a choice."

Grizz raised an eyebrow. "Tell you everything? What's left to tell?"

Blue tossed an oversized envelope on the desk.

"These photos of Jan and the boys were taken by the P.I. I hired to find them."

Grizz opened the envelope and flipped through the photos, scanning each one quickly without paying much attention. He stopped when he got to a certain one and asked without looking up, "Why is there an old picture of Grunt in here?"

Blue didn't answer. Grizz looked up and asked again, "Why is Grunt in this picture?"

"It's not Grunt." Blue's voice was toneless, but his eyes were hard. "It's my youngest, Kevin. Apparently, you aren't the only one whose woman Grunt fucked."

Grizz recovered quickly from the surprise. He leaned forward again, tossed the pictures on the desk and rested the weight of his massive arms on his elbows. He motioned for Blue to continue.

"Jan said—she said it was Grunt who orchestrated your arrest, Grizz."

There. It was out.

Grizz sat there a moment, let it sink in. Did he believe what Jan had told Blue? Possibly. Maybe. He already knew Grunt had manipulated him the night he took Kit's virginity. The billy-club had been Grunt's idea. Yes, looking back with perfect clarity he could see it all. The muscle in his jaw clenched.

Blue's voice had a dangerous edge. "That piss-ant little brother of yours has been the enemy all along. Not that Jan was an angel. That slut must have slept with him when he was just a kid. The whole time that bitch thought he was my little brother and she still did it!"

Grizz looked at Blue and sighed. He remembered how he'd insisted, on Grunt's very first night at the motel, that Blue pretend to be his older brother. It was an order, and Blue took on the role willingly. Blue had always assumed Grizz was Grunt's brother. He never questioned it.

"Fuck, Blue. There's something I never told you. I guess you believed something and I let it ride. I didn't think it really mattered, and I thought I was protecting the kid. It would've come out in that bitch's article. Thanks to you, it won't, but you should still know."

Grizz steeled himself. "Grunt is not my little brother." A pause.

"He's my son."

November, 1966

The young biker had just pulled into the Mindy's Market on Davie Boulevard. It was a privately owned convenience store similar to a 7-Eleven, but with more of a homey atmosphere. The kind of place you wouldn't associate with a franchise, but with a family-owned business.

He had just turned off his Harley and put the kickstand down. He was studying the knuckles on his right hand, which was still on the handlebar. His knuckles were scraped raw, and large chunks of skin were missing. There was a lot of blood. After a few seconds he took the last Lucky Strike from its crumpled packet, tossed the empty packet to the ground and wondered whether it was too early for a beer. He lit the cigarette, which dangled from his mouth as he closely examined his hand again. It was possible that he broke it. He had just come from what would eventually be a long list of fights too numerous to count. He would use the convenience store bathroom to clean up and make a better assessment. But first, he would finish his cigarette.

That's when he saw her. She had just come around the side of the store. There was no parking on the side because it was right up next to a sidewalk that paralleled the road. He didn't see an adult. She must have walked there by herself. He thought she looked small to be walking around alone, and he wondered how close by she lived. She was a cute little thing. Long brown hair held up in a sloppy ponytail. Bangs almost covering her oversized brown eyes. She wore a wrinkled pink T-shirt and cut-off blue jean-shorts. Her knees were scraped but not bleeding, and their whiteness was in stark contrast to her tanned, bony legs.

She had on white sneakers with purple pom-poms tied to them.

Just then, a boy who looked to be a little older than her came barreling around the store. *Good. She's not alone. She has a big brother.*

Before the biker could ponder why he would even care, the boy spoke. "Hey Gwinny, your mom is a hippie-whore-pothead."

No, this wasn't her brother. He was a bully. The biker wondered if he'd deliberately followed her.

Without turning around to the boy she replied, "And you, Curtith Armthrong, will be begging her to thell you her pot when you're a teenager." The reply was delivered in a very calm and even voice with a whopping lisp. The biker noticed then that she was missing her two front teeth.

Curtis Armstrong didn't know what to say to that, so he just waved her off and turned and ran back around the side of the store. She went inside.

The biker caught himself smiling, something he rarely did. *Spunky little thing*. He was almost finished with his cigarette. He lifted his sunglasses and wiped his face with his arm. He was sweaty and grimy from the fight.

He'd just put his sunglasses back down when she came out. She walked straight toward him. She was carrying a small brown bag. He threw the last of his cigarette on the ground and stepped on it. He was still straddling his bike and crushing what was left of the cigarette with his heavy boot when she appeared at his side.

She reached into her brown bag and pulled out a box of bandages. She handed it to him and said, "Here, thethe are for you. Your hand lookths hurt real bad."

He didn't know what to say or do, so he found himself taking the box from her tiny hand. He was shocked by her observation. He'd been watching her when she first showed up and couldn't remember her looking back at him. How had she noticed his hand?

Before he could reply, she bent down and picked up the discarded and crinkly cigarette packet he had so carelessly thrown down earlier. She turned around and walked toward the corner of the store where she'd first appeared. She tossed the litter into a garbage can. Then she stopped and looked back at him.

"You thouldn't thmoke. You could get lung canther." Then after a brief pause, "And nobody likeths litterbugths."

And with that she was gone.

He couldn't help himself. He smiled again. He got off the bike and walked around the corner of the convenience store. He saw her walking, ponytail swaying with each step. He didn't see any sign of Curtis Armstrong so he turned around and went into the store. He walked up to the clerk at the cash register. He wanted to ask about the little girl, but he didn't want the guy behind the counter to think he was a pervert.

"Just saw some bigger kid picking on that little girl that walked out of here. Looks like she handled herself pretty good for such a small thing." He waited to see if the guy would say something. He did.

"Yeah, that was Gwinny. She walks here every day by herself to buy her mom cigarettes. She's a sweet little girl. Smart, too. It was probably Curtis, and I'm sure she gave him a piece of her mind. He's always picking on her."

"I hope she lives close by." And then after thinking about how that sounded, he quickly added, "If she has a long walk it's more opportunity for the kid to bully her."

"She lives down the street right here," he said pointing to the side of the store where Gwinny had first appeared. "But I'm not sure how far. Did you want something?"

"Yeah, pack of Lucky's."

The clerk rang up his purchase without taking notice of the biker's hand. At least if he did notice, he didn't show it. The biker paid for his smokes and walked out the door. He tossed his newly purchased cigarettes into the garbage can. He'd been smoking since he was twelve. Maybe it was time to quit.

He'd forgotten all about the pain in his hand. He got on his bike and started it up. He rounded the store on the side where Gwinny went. He looked up at the street sign. S.W. 23rd Avenue. He idled as he looked down the street and noted it was a nice block with small houses on each side. He could see her far off in the distance. She obviously hadn't arrived at her house yet or turned off any side streets.

When she turned a slight curve and was no longer in his

line of sight, he slowly drove the distance to the curve. He cautiously rounded it. He didn't want to scare her if she heard the bike and thought she was being followed, which she was. But it didn't matter. She was no longer there. She must have gone into one of the houses.

He wasn't real familiar with this neighborhood and figured that instead of turning around he would just follow the street and see where it came out.

Unfortunately, he came upon a dead end. The houses at the end of Gwinny's block were fancier. A little more upscale. He could see through some of the backyards that these homes were on the water—hence, the reason for the dead end. He turned the bike around in the small cul-de-sac and headed back the way he came.

That's when he saw her. He caught a flash of color on his right. She was on the side of a house trying to lift an oversized watering can to water some hanging plants. She was struggling under the weight of it. If she noticed him, she didn't show it.

He found he wanted to watch her, but couldn't. It wouldn't look right and might scare her, or alert someone in the neighborhood to his presence.

He didn't gun the bike until he was past the curve and out of view from anyone who may have seen him pass Gwinny's house. He couldn't help but wonder if her hippie-whore-pothead mother took care of her. He couldn't fathom why he cared. Then it occurred to him.

The bandage offering was the first time in his life that someone actually did something for him. Never once had there ever been even a suggestion of someone who gave a damn about him. No one. This little moppet was the first.

He knew then what he was feeling was a brotherly

protectiveness toward her.

He vowed then and there to keep an eye on the little girl. He could go unnoticed in the background and just keep tabs on her. Make sure she was okay. And that's what he did. For the next nine years.

He had no way of knowing then that the brotherly care and concern for a child would turn into love. That she would become his obsession and the one true love of his life. That she would eventually be the reason for his death.

Even if he did know it then, he wouldn't have changed a thing.

An Excerpt from Book Two in this Series
Out of Time
1976

Grunt leaned his head against the wall and sighed. He was sitting on his bed trying to concentrate on his homework, but he couldn't. He closed his eyes and immediately saw her. Kit. She was laughing at something he'd said during one of their chess lessons. Well, they used to be lessons, but she was smart and could almost beat him. He'd thought more than once about letting her win, but that wasn't Kit's way. She would have to beat him fair and square. Maybe one day she would.

Kit was the girl who lived a few units down from him. Now that he thought about it, he couldn't really call her a girl. She had been living with the gang since she was fifteen and was married to their leader. She was now sixteen and had experienced more in the last year than some grown women would in a lifetime. No, Kit was definitely no longer a girl. She was a woman. And she was the woman he had been in love with for a very long time. Even before she came to the motel.

He had accompanied Grizz many times over the years to keep an eye on the young girl, who was then called Gwinny. He didn't know why Grizz took him along. Maybe people were less suspicious of a man who had a kid with him. He was sure they assumed he was Grizz's younger brother or son. It didn't matter. He always looked forward to the times he would be able to watch her. He didn't remember the exact moment it became love. There had been too many times to count how often he'd observed her do something over the years that melted his heart.

He remembered her first night at the motel. It was last May. He didn't know Grizz was going to bring her here. He had secretly hoped maybe Grizz would step aside and let her find her own destiny. If that was the case, Grunt was certain he could insert himself into her life. He'd imagined it a thousand times—casually running into her somewhere. Making small talk. Making her laugh. Hell, he'd even thought about enrolling in her school, but that charade would be too difficult to maintain. Especially since he was already in college, and he had no doubt that Grizz wouldn't have allowed it.

He laughed to himself at the memory. People in love are willing to do desperate things, he thought. He'd never imagined Grizz was falling for her, too. He knew about the obsession, but couldn't remember when it became more than that for Grizz. He was too busy wrapping himself in his own fantasies of a life with her. A future. Unfortunately, as long as Grizz was around, no other man would ever have a chance with Kit, let alone a future.

Her first night at the motel was seared in his memory. He had been leaning back in a lawn chair staring into the fire. Willow and Chicky were arguing about something.

Monster pulled up on his motorcycle. He could tell there was a female on the back. He's certain he gasped when he noticed it was her, and Monster was walking her toward the pit. What the fuck?

He half listened as Willow argued with Monster about the girl being a "thank you gift." Bullshit. He knew better. She was only fifteen and probably scared to death. But if she was scared, she certainly wasn't showing it. He watched her as she calmly observed the exchange between Willow and Monster. He knew she hadn't seen Grizz when he walked up next to her. What would her reaction be to him? He watched as she noticed Grizz for the first time, her eyes slowly moving up his body until they reached his face. She showed no emotion that he could detect. When Willow lunged for her and Grizz intervened, she never even flinched. He couldn't believe how brave she was that night. The dying campfire cast an almost angelic glow on her face. The face he had loved for a long time. And now she was here, and she belonged to Grizz.

He'd watched that first night as Moe led her to number four, listened as Grizz told the gang they were never to discuss her. They weren't to look at her, speak to her or address her presence at the motel. Ever. He then watched Grizz turn around and go inside.

It was only a few minutes before Moe came out. She was walking toward the pit with her head down. Grunt jumped up and walked quickly toward her. He gently took her arm and led her to his unit. He heard some laughter from the pit. Let them think what they wanted. Once inside, he asked her, "Is she okay? Was she crying or anything?"

Moe looked up at him with an odd expression on her face. She nodded. Shit. Which question was she answering?

He grabbed a piece of notebook paper and a pencil and handed it to Moe.

"Let's start over. Is she okay?"

Moe nodded yes.

"Please don't make me ask you, Moe. Just tell me what's going on inside number four."

Moe wrote, "Seems okay. Not crying. Not afraid of him."

He was relieved. "Good. What else?"

Moe retrieved something from her pocket. It was a wallet. She laid it on his bed and wrote something else on the paper. "Have to burn it."

He looked at her without saying anything. Seconds ticked by.

"Will you keep it? Will you hide it? Will you do that for me, Moe?"

She nodded yes.

He took the paper she had been writing on and crumpled it up. He would take it out to the pit and toss it in the fire. He left Moe standing in his room. He ignored the whistles and lewd catcalls concerning his and Moe's time together. *Assholes.*

If he had taken even a moment to stop and look back at Moe before he left the room, he would have seen an expression on her face he hadn't seen before. The look of a woman who loved someone who could never be hers. It wasn't just the age difference that would have stopped it. Moe had the look of a woman who just realized the man she loves is in love with somebody else.

It was the look of despair.

Grunt was jolted back to the present by a loud commotion outside. He got up and went to his window. He shook his head as he watched the scene. Typical—some guys had lured a young couple back to the motel and were tormenting them. Grizz commanded the dogs to be quiet, but he ignored what was going on just a few feet away from him. He was talking to Chico, who was probably setting up some of kind delivery. It didn't matter. Whatever it was, it was certainly illegal.

Just then, Grunt noticed movement to the left. Kit. She was walking purposefully toward Grizz. She said something to him that Grunt couldn't hear. Grizz replied to her, but apparently it didn't satisfy her because she didn't go away. He saw Grizz nod to Chico, and Chico said something to one of the other guys. Grunt saw her flinch when the couple was executed.

She turned around and started back toward number four. He could see her face clearly. She was upset, but trying to control it. Good. This would work out for him. He wouldn't have to come up with a plan to lure Kit away from Grizz. Grizz's ruthlessness would push her away. He would wait. He needed some time anyway. He would graduate college, make something of himself and be able to offer her a life away from this band of criminals. It would just take some time. He would let Grizz continue to show her what a bastard he truly was. Chess was Grunt's game, and he was the best. This wasn't chess, but it would be the most serious and important game he'd ever played in his life. Each move would have to be painstakingly calculated.

He smiled as he watched Grizz striding toward number four. The game was on and Grunt hadn't lost one yet.

Acknowledgements

I was raised in South Florida, primarily Ft. Lauderdale, and did my best to remember it as it was in the 1970s. I'm not certain I got it right every time, but I tried. I also gave some fictional names to some real places. This particular motorcycle gang—their names, their motel, their rituals, all of it—exists only in my imagination. The idea for Grizz sprang from a very old memory of somebody I briefly knew when I was fifteen.

There are so many people to thank and acknowledge for their help with this novel. It's impossible for me to list them in order of importance because every person contributed in an important way. Some served as beta readers. Others offered their advice, which I didn't always follow, but was happy to hear. If there are errors, they are strictly my own. My apologies if I accidentally left someone out.

My deep thanks go to the following:

Jim Flynn, who never once doubted my ability to bring this story to life. Grizz's love and protection of Ginny is based on how Jim has treated me every day during our thirty year marriage.

Kelli Flynn, who called me from New York City on a very cold day as she made her way down First Avenue and told me I should write a book. It was the actual moment Nine Minutes was conceived. She consistently challenged me when I would send her excerpts. She posed as Ginny for the front cover. She also decided that Ginny needed a friend her own age. Chowder was my original choice to be Kit's friend and confidant. Grunt was Kelli's idea. I think she was right.

Katie Flynn, who spent exhaustive hours researching everything from popular song titles in the 1970s to rattlesnake bites and everything in between. She did everything she could, without complaint, including running our household when I needed to just "write one more chapter."

Jessica Connor, editor extraordinaire and cherished friend. Her guidance and encouragement throughout the entire process kept me focused and gave me confidence.

Cheryl Desmidt, who edited one of my first drafts and did her best to keep me true to the 1970s.

Mary Dry, one of my early beta readers who listened patiently and offered advice when I would run ideas past her. It was Mary who insisted Kit could not cheat on Grizz.

Kelli Blasi, another early beta reader, who gave me the idea for Matthew Rockman.

Michael Blasi, who told me, "Throw two coral snakes in the empty pool with Willow and Darryl. You know, if you really want Grizz to be as rotten as you say he is."

Christy Waymouth, an early beta reader, who provided valuable feedback that actually made me re-write some aspects of this novel so they would flow easily into Book Two.

Tommy Cooley, who very early on gave me some insight to help with the Grunt character. It only seemed natural that Grunt should be named after him.

Sarah Jo Morgan, who gave me her likeness and name for Sarah Jo. She researched popular names in the 1960s and told me that Grizz couldn't smoke Marlboros. He had to smoke Lucky Strikes.

Matt Brodie, photographer and book cover designer, for creating my dream cover.

Allison M. Simon, who kindly and patiently answered my never-ending questions about self-publishing. She guided me in the final steps of this book's release.

Chase McKeown, who posed as Grizz for the cover.

Tyson Keanum, whose hair and make-up expertise gave Kelli (Ginny) the perfect look for the cover.

Thank you also to Pat Blasi, Mary McGrath Connor, Carolyn Franz, Kaye Heller, Jennifer Hewitt, Joanie Kelly, Gail Milne, Susan Paine, Glenna Petryszak, Deanna Klingel, as well as to Harley Haven in Columbia, S.C.

And finally last, and in no way least, to Susan Anton who didn't laugh at me when I told her the real reason I wanted to write this book. Her reaction gave me the courage to write the first word.

My heartfelt thanks to everyone involved in the process of making Nine Minutes a reality and to everyone who has actually read it. Thank you. I'd love to hear from you!

Beth Flynn
P.O. Box 2833
Cashiers, NC   28717
beth@authorbethflynn.com
www.AuthorBethFlynn.com

Made in the USA
Lexington, KY
21 January 2015